Terrabyte Security

by

Tena Stetler

*Mountain Town Mysteries Series,
Book Two*

Cover Art by *Kristian Norris*

The Wild Rose Press, Inc.
PO Box 708
Adams Basin, NY 14410-0708
Visit us at www.thewildrosepress.com

Publishing History
First Edition, 2024
Trade Paperback ISBN 978-1-5092-5701-0
Digital ISBN 978-1-5092-5702-7

Mountain Town Mysteries Series, Book Two
Published in the United States of America

Dedication

To my husband of many moons whose support is unwavering. To my friends and family who are always there for me. To my readers, for whom I spin the stories. Thank you so much for your continued support.

Chapter One

A New Beginning and Reason for Concern.

After her whirlwind romance, wedding to the love of her life, and reception with all the townspeople in attendance, Candle couldn't help but smile widely. Sitting in her comfy high-back chair behind her solid oak desk and hutch she'd found at Raven's Hollow's antique store, a new chapter of her life began. The hutch held lots of interesting cubbies and drawers with little wooden knobs for her to explore. She wondered what delicious secrets this antique desk once held, or may still hold. But that was an adventure for another day.

The door to her new office of Terrabyte Security opened with a bang. Papers scattered across the floor in the autumn breeze as Miacoh, her husband and the new Chief of Police in Aspen Ridge, rushed in with a lunch bag from Sunrise Cafe held high. "Wanta share lunch with me?" He leaned over the desk and planted a smacking kiss on her lips, stooping to scratch Terra behind the ears as the pup got to her feet, all wiggles, beside Candle's chair.

"Crime take a break for lunch today?" she asked with a Cheshire cat grin and got up from her desk to gather the documents then went to pile them on her desk, pausing for a moment. *I should probably put those away now.* Her stomach growled. *After lunch would be soon enough.*

"You betcha. The two full-time and one part-time officer, plus Reka our new receptionist/dispatcher in the police station, gives me a chance to disappear occasionally. A luxury your father never had during his thirty-five years as Chief of Police of Aspen Ridge."

"Town wasn't nearly so big back then either." She snickered. "Now you get to deal with the growing pains of our sleepy little town."

He handed her a grilled cheese sandwich, a small bag of chips, and a bottle of cola. Easing down in the chair opposite her, he took out a burger, fries, and pop. "You're welcome to snatch fries if you want." His head swiveled around and he jerked a thumb toward the empty desk across the room. "Where's Gabby? You give her the day off?"

Before she could answer, the phone rang and Candle picked it up. "Terrabyte Security."

"Hey, Candle, can we schedule a new security system install for next Monday, after hours?" Joe, the owner of the town lumber store wanted to know.

"Let me check with Cayson and see what his schedule looks like. You know he is now working part-time for Miacoh as an officer."

"I heard. Things they are a changing. How's your dad?"

"Doing great. He and Mom jetted off to Hawaii for a couple of weeks enjoying themselves."

"Well-deserved. Gotta get back to work. Let me know." He disconnected the call.

Taking a bite of her sandwich, stringing cheese from plate to mouth, she closed her eyes as she chewed.

"Kelly makes the best grilled cheese sandwiches." Opening them again, she peered up at Miacoh. "I don't know what's keeping Gabby. She was supposed to drop off the twins at school and come to work. I haven't heard a thing from her. I'll give her a call." Candle picked up her cell phone, finger poised to touch the screen.

Miacoh nodded in agreement as he took a bite of his hamburger, then swirled a french fry in the ketchup and popped it in his mouth.

The door banged open and Gabby rushed inside, wind scattering the papers again. Terra jumped up and barked, circling Gabby. This time Miacoh scooped up the papers, put them on Candle's desk, and plopped a procedural manual on top, winking at his wife.

Gabby paced the floor between Candle's desk and her own flinging her arms in the air as she talked.

Gabby couldn't talk if you tied her hands down. Candle's smile faded as she became aware something was terribly wrong.

"Ben is missing. There's no one to run his office since he and his ex-partner, Ken, parted ways over a major disagreement. I dropped Natalya and Nash off at school and checked the office to see if he returned early, but no. He's missing," she wailed. "What am I going to do?"

"Whoa, slow down, Gabby. How do you know Ben's missing?" Candle jumped up from her chair to catch her best friend mid-stride.

Tears rolled down Gabby's cheeks. "He caught a red-eye last night to Las Vegas to tie up loose ends from Ken's unauthorized dealings. Ben never arrived in Las Vegas. Airport security showed him boarding the plane, but he didn't get off the plane in Vegas. If he'd had a change in plans, he'd have called me. I haven't heard a thing from him."

Miacoh stood and offered his chair to Gabby. She plopped down in the seat and began to sob.

"Gabby, we are going to need your husband's calendar, itinerary, flight number, and hotel reservation. I'll have Cayson start tracking down his movements."

"Did I hear my name?" Cayson, a tall Aussie with the high cheekbones of a Norse god and shaggy blond hair of a Swede swaggered into the office. His cocky smile faded as he surveyed the faces in the room. "What's wrong?"

Miacoh filled him in as Candle got her friend a cup of hot chocolate and offered one-half of her grilled cheese sandwich. Gabby waved off the sandwich and sipped the hot chocolate. The liquid surface rippled from her shaking hands.

"The only thing I could think of was coming here and then to the police station, though he left from the Aspen/Pitkin County airport. His car is still in the parking lot." Gabby sniffled and took the tissue Candle handed her and dabbed at her damp cheeks.

Miacoh hiked his hip on the corner of Candle's desk and rubbed his chin. "It's going to be in Pitkin County's jurisdiction. But if you hire Terrabyte to investigate the disappearance we can help the possibly overworked, understaffed Pitkin County Sheriff's office. First thing you need to do is to report Ben as a missing person to Pitkin County Sheriff."

"But we live here." At Miacoh's stern look and raised eyebrow she said, "I'll go there right away. But the twins will get out of school in a couple hours. What am I going to tell them?"

"The truth. I'll pick them up from school, if you're not back from Aspen," Candle insisted. She returned to her desk and pulled out a document. "I'll need you to sign this contract for service so I can authorize Cayson to start on the case, pro bono of course."

"Of course not." Gabby fisted her hands on her hips and popped up from the chair. "Money is no object. I'll not be a charity case. I'm aware of what your typical retainer is and will make a check out to you today." She opened her bag and took out her checkbook. "Then I'll zip up to Aspen. Thanks for picking up the kids."

"If you'll leave me the keys to Ben's office, I'll go post a note on the door indicating he's out of the office for a few days. Also I'll record a message to the same effect on his answering machine," Candle offered.

"The answering machine won't be necessary. He has a service that takes his calls when he's out. I'll contact the service. Tell them he's out of the office for a few days and have them take messages keeping the appearance of business as usual. After the partnership upheaval, we don't want his clients to get nervous. More than that, I don't want his family to swoop in here and try to take over, as they are prone to do."

"You didn't tell his family he's missing?" Candle's brow creased. "What if he went there for some reason?"

"Not possible. He would never do that without telling me. His marriage to me caused a rift between him and his family which widened when we had the twins. Then we took the kids out of the family's privileged private schools."

"I understand. But at some point, the Pitkin Sheriff

5

will want to contact his family. Your failure to do so could put you in a difficult position." Miacoh ran his fingers through his hair and rubbed the back of his neck.

"Don't worry, Gabby. We'll stand behind you. Run interference between you and his family if necessary." Candle put her arm around her best friend.

With the tissue, Gabby wiped her eyes, blew her nose, and straightened. "I'm all right. Thanks." She signed the contract and handed it along with the retainer check to Candle. "I'm off to Aspen to talk to the Pitkin County Sheriff's Office. I'll be back as soon as I can."

"Do you want Cayson to accompany you?" Candle asked.

"No. I know the officers there. They've had a couple run-ins with Ben's family when he moved his main office to Raven's Hollow and made Aspen's office the satellite office in the hands of his partner, uh ex-partner."

"When you return, you'll need to fill us in on the business and partner split. I imagine Pitkin County is going to ask the same questions." Miacoh eased off the corner of the desk and rocked back on his heels with thumbs in his pockets. "They'll want to know if the split had anything to do with Ben's disappearance."

"Do you and Ben have an attorney?" Candle asked.
"Yes."

"You might want to contact him. See if he has time to accompany you to the sheriff's office." Candle glanced from her friend to Miacoh.

"Not a bad idea." Miacoh nodded.

"Why would I need an attorney? My husband is missing," Gabby insisted vehemently.

"Calm down." Candle put a hand on her best friend's shoulder. "We're only looking out for your best interests."

"These types of cases can get sticky. Say the wrong thing. Boom, you'll be a person of interest. Especially taking into consideration your relationship with his family." Miacoh stared at Gabby. "Not trying to scare you but prepare you. Understand?"

"I appreciate your concern. I'll call Mr. Goodwell. Have him meet me there." Gabby picked up her bag and walked to the door.

"You sure you're all right?" Candle peered at her friend, trying to keep the concern out of her voice and off her face. "We can figure out something else and I can accompany you."

"No, I'm fine. We pay a huge retainer to Mr. Goodwell to be at our beck and call. Unless he's out of town, he'll accompany me." Gabby straightened her shoulders again. "Sorry for being such a…"

"Nonsense. I'd have the same reaction if Miacoh came up missing. Maybe worse. Of course without the additional worry of children."

Gabby touched her phone's screen and held it to her ear. "Mr. Goodwell please." She sniffed, paused for only a moment. "Dan, something has come up. I need you to meet me at the Pitkin County Sheriff's Office immediately. I'm on my way. I'll explain when I see you. If you get there before me, please wait outside." She tapped the screen again, shoved the phone in her bag, turned and waved to Miacoh, Candle, and Cayson. "I'll be back soon and fill you in."

Candle watched her best friend march toward the door, open it, and close it confidently. "She's back and under control. Wish I could have gone with her."

"Probably better you didn't. The twins are going to want an explanation when you pick them up from school. Had you sent your mom or Gabby's mom, emotions could cloud their judgment."

Candle fisted her hands on her hips. "What am I supposed to tell them? Gabby didn't authorize an explanation for them."

"Tell them the truth. Gabby had an appointment and she asked you to pick them up. Take Natalya and Nash home and wait for their mom. Take Terra along with you. She'll keep the kids busy. If things get more complicated, she'll call you, and we'll decide what to do at that time. Meanwhile, I'm going to file a missing person report on Gabby's behalf at the station." Miacoh brushed the fry crumbs from his pants.

"Okay, I came in in the middle of this situation. I understand Gabby's husband, Ben is missing. Where's he missing from? Why does she need our firm to search for him, and which agency am I working the case for?" Cayson directed his gaze to Candle first and shifted to Miacoh second.

Miacoh filled him in from beginning to end. "I believe Candle will want you on the case for Terrabyte. My hands are tied until Pitkin County asks for our assistance. Even then jurisdiction can get sticky."

Candle rummaged around in her bag for the SUV keys and held them up triumphantly, then noticed a dark-haired woman, with high cheekbones and bronze skin pacing outside the office. She cleared her throat to get the men's attention then jerked her chin toward the window. All eyes shifted to the front window of Terrabyte's office.

Chapter Two

Am I Crazy? Is Someone Stalking Me? I've Got to Have Help. Will They Believe Me?

A Native American woman paced in front of Terrabyte Security wringing her hands. The phone calls, strange faces in her windows, and stolen work products had to stop. It was bad enough her professor plagiarized her work, claimed it as his own, stole her identity and emptied her bank accounts, then disappeared off the face of the earth, not to mention blew up the college chemistry lab. *Okay, I'm not the only one he victimized. But I'm one of the few that didn't have a trust fund to fall back on. Oh, this is such a mess.* She covered her face with her hands for a moment and took a long cleansing breath, then continued pacing.

Pausing mid-stride, she sensed eyes on her. She whirled around to find three sets of eyes staring at her through the window. The woman she knew as Candle, who'd blown the professor's scandal wide open, curled an index finger beckoning her into Terrabyte's office. Her pulse quickened. Her heart nearly beat out of her chest as she wiped her sweaty palms on her jeans. *Should I stay, explain myself, and ask for help, or take flight as I have these many months?*

Candle circumvented the woman's choice by

stepping out of the door into her path with a reassuring smile. "Can we help you?"

She tugged on her denim jacket, straightened her shoulders, and swallowed hard. "I sure hope so. I'm Molly Malone Reacher."

Candle extended her hand. "Happy to know you, Molly. I'm Candle Bearclaw. Terrabyte Security is my company. Why don't we step into the office and talk?" Candle pulled open the door. Miacoh grabbed the edge of the door and held it open.

Molly's gaze darted around the office as she trudged in behind Candle. She kept her bag held tight against her as her fingers twisted in the strap.

"Have a seat." Candle motioned to the wooden chair in front of her desk, then glanced at Miacoh and Cayson. She jerked her chin at the tall, black-haired man in uniform. "Miacoh, is the Chief of Police in our little town." She waved a hand toward the tall, blond Aussie. "Cayson is my investigator, part-time security alarm installer for Terrabyte, and on occasion part-time officer for the Police Department." Miacoh dragged another chair across the floor and straddled it. Cayson stood behind Miacoh. Terra, the pup, thumped her tail on the floor and attempted to get to her feet as Candle signaled her to stay with a hand gesture. "This is our company mascot soon to be security specialist, Terrabyte."

She eased down onto the edge of the chair. Her gaze darted from one to the other. "I...I... don't know where to begin. I was an undergraduate student for Professor Raymond D. James and worked as his TA part-time, until I discovered he was plagiarizing my work. I confronted him. He denied it and dismissed me as his TA. Then he replaced me with a girl named Erin. You, Miacoh, Cayson, and the feds blew the scheme wide open. Students scattered, the guilty as well as the scared. Me being one of the latter. It was quiet for a while, then random charges I didn't make started appearing on my credit cards. I got bills for credit cards and debts I never applied for." Molly wrapped her arms around herself and rocked back and forth on the chair.

Candle put a hand on Molly's shoulder. "So after the professor left the country, charges you didn't make began appearing on your credit cards? Were they in the United States or abroad?"

"Mostly stateside, but a few foreign. My bank is handing those. I reported the identity theft to the police. They are investigating and suspect another student in the professor's entourage is responsible." Molly twisted the strap on her bag tighter.

"The illegal activity appears to be wider spread than we or the authorities were made aware. Any paper trail that you know of?" Miacoh shifted in the chair.

"A lot of the paperwork, IDs, etcetera, were destroyed in the fire, I'm told. The reason I'm here is, now, I'm being stalked. Threatening notes left on my windshield. Someone broke into my apartment and trashed it. A few rarely used credit cards I left in a file came up missing. More surfaced that I didn't know anything about. Several pages of my new thesis were stolen. Thank God they were not the last draft of my dissertation. After Professor James stole my original work, I had to start all over, then it came to light what he'd done. The college said I could continue with my original, but I wanted to put the whole thing behind me. I guess I'm not the only one he plagiarized, but now someone has stolen my identity and is threatening to shut me up permanently if I continue to make waves." She raised her arms up over her head then let them drop. "Over a few stolen credit cards and a college paper? Really?"

"Identity theft is serious business. It carries hefty prison time in federal prison. Not to mention plagiarism on top of that." Miacoh shook his head. "This situation is serious. The threats should not be taken lightly."

"That's why I'm here." She opened her bag, took out several pieces of paper, and placed them on Candle's desk. "These are just an example of what I've received. I destroyed the rest."

Miacoh picked up a couple of notes and shook his head. "Sounds like you're being watched. They seem to be familiar with your routine. Do you do the same thing every day?"

"Mostly. Until the identity theft is sorted out, I've no money to do much else. I tried to get into another apartment, but my credit is trashed. I'm scared to stay there now but have nowhere else to go."

"What about family? Friends?" Candle inquired.

She fiddled with the strap of her bag. "My family history is sketchy."

"If we are going to help you, we need to know everything about you. We don't need surprises popping up when least expected." Candle met her gaze and gave her a pointed but understanding smile.

She sighed. "My parents, Scottish nationals, befriended a Native American girl barely out of her teens. Not sure the circumstances concerning the pregnancy, but the woman was adamant, and made my parents promise, that her child never be returned to the tribe. You know back then adoption by non-Native American families, like my parents, was frowned upon to say the least. The tribal courts cited the 1978 Indian Child Welfare Act which according to my parents required Native American children to be adopted by other indigenous families."

"I would have to do research into that situation, but the more urgent matter is does your history have anything to do with your being stalked, your intellectual property being stolen or plagiarized? Has your past caught up with your life now?"

"I don't know. You wanted to know everything."

"Yes, yes, continue." Candle discreetly glanced at her watch.

"My family moved around a lot. I believe my parents were always looking over their shoulders." She squirmed in her chair.

"Were you legally adopted?" Miacoh stared down at the young woman before him.

"Yes, but not by the tribal courts. That part of the story is a bit fuzzy. I do have a legal birth certificate that has stood the test of time. Got into college and a driver's license without any hassles. Unfortunately, when I turned eighteen, my parents were killed overseas while working for a humanitarian effort. The family history that I didn't know died with them. Or so I thought. Then amongst my parents' belongs that were returned was a sealed letter addressed to me."

"More secrets?" Candle inquired.

She glanced down at the floor. "More sordid and heartbreaking family history. I placed the letter in a safe deposit box." She pulled a chain with a key dangling from it out from beneath her shirt. "But I did locate my biological maternal grandmother. She is Hopi and had a tale to tell that shattered my world. Grams welcomed me into her home, shared my heritage, my native language, traditions, and—" Molly hesitated for a beat and drew in a long breath. "—shared the atrocities she'd endured that befell her daughter, my mother."

"And those were?" Candle gently put a hand on the woman's shoulder.

"My mother was stolen as a child and placed in an Arizona boarding school. The school's stated goal was to 'civilize' Native Americans, Alaska Natives, and Native Hawaiians, which was often carried out through abusive practices. She escaped and returned to the rez. But she became involved with unsavory characters and became pregnant not once but twice. Apparently, I have an older brother. No one knows what happened to him." She sadly shook her head. "None of this relates to why I'm here."

"I've been in the investigation business a long time. You'd be surprised at what may be related. I can't help you if I don't know your entire story."

She stood and took a couple steps toward the door. "Maybe this was a bad idea. Forgive me for bothering you."

Miacoh blocked her exit while staring at Candle.

Candle slid a glance at the clock, then put a hand on the woman's arm. "Okay, you don't need to tell us everything today. However, be aware, if your background comes into play in this investigation, you'll have to trust us enough to confide in us. Now let's sit down and you continue."

She paused for a moment, surveying the individuals in the room, then returned to her chair clutching her bag even tighter. "I learned a lot during my research for my current thesis on missing and murdered indigenous women and girls. They are faced with unbelievably high rates of violence throughout the country today." She straightened her shoulders. "Did you know that murder rates on certain reservations can be tenfold higher than the national average? Which takes us back to at least one reason my birth mother required that promise from my parents."

"Was the stolen dissertation on this topic? The professor tried to pass it off as his?" Miacoh's eyebrow winged up.

"No. I changed my topic after learning what the professor was doing. Figured it might be a bit difficult for him to pass the indigenous woman and girls thesis as his own. However, it is the rough draft of that one that several pages are missing from the break-in."

Cayson leaned against the desk and crossed his ankles. "Is there any chance you've ruffled any feathers researching your project? Could the stalking be related to your research, rather than to the professor's illegal activities? Or maybe something else entirely?" He shrugged one shoulder. "Sorry, gotta ask."

She turned her dark eyes on him and hesitated. "I don't think so. There are still several of the professor's minions, like Greg Corner, Roy, and others working to re-establish the lab and its projects. One in particular, Murdock Welsh, I had a bit of a run-in with. He's running the show of getting the lab up and operational again under the supervision of the current professor. When I questioned his efforts, he told me to mind my own business or I could wind up as collateral damage. He poked his finger in my chest and shoved me backward then turned on his heel and strode off."

"What did you do?" Candle wanted to know.

She shrugged. "Nothing. I've applied to an institution that offers an online doctoral program. No dissertation. Student has only to complete a capstone project to demonstrate knowledge and provide new contributions to the field. I'm still enrolled at the school while I look into another matter. The threatening notes appeared on my car when it was parked in the lab's temporary parking and shortly after my altercation."

"Let me get this straight. You changed your whole field of study?"

"Not exactly. Once I started researching indigenous women, violence, and deaths never reported, I felt it was my calling. Still, I need to support myself, so chemical engineering seemed like a viable choice. But now...I want out of this situation without becoming collateral damage."

"I must point out that you may be jumping out of the proverbial frying pan into the flames. Violence against indigenous women and girls is a hot topic. Even hotter is the fact that, as you've uncovered, only a small percentage gets reported and an even smaller number of cases are ever solved." Miacoh stared steadily into her eyes. "Are you prepared for such pushback?"

She hung her head and stared at her hands folded in her lap. "Yes—Well, I don't know. Guess it depends on who is after me and why?"

"Which is the reason you're here." Candle leaned back against her chair and tented her fingers. "First order of business. Find you a safe place to live. Second, a source of income. I may have an idea on that one. Third, get your education back on track. The online alternative may be your best bet at this time while we unravel this mess."

"You'll take my case?"

Miacoh and Cayson gave a slight nod of their heads, as Candle unfolded her fingers, placed her hands flat on the desk, and stood. "More investigation is needed to sort out the threads of this mess. But yes, we'll take your case." Candle opened the top desk drawer and took out a piece of paper, scribbled on the document, and handed it Molly. "My contract. This way we are able to investigate on your behalf legally. Can you afford a $250.00 retainer?"

She swallowed hard. "Barely." She pulled out her wallet.

Candle put a hand over her hand. "We'll work out the money when I get back. I'll leave you in the capable hands of Miacoh and Cayson. I have a pressing matter to take care of. Miacoh, get ahold of Dad. We used to have a designated safe house in town, more like a little cabin on the edge of town on Bear Paw Lane, never used except as my playhouse. I don't think the town ever sold it, but Dad would know if that's an option."

"I can do that." Miacoh nodded.

"Cayson, take her there. Otherwise, put her up in a hotel under an assumed name, and don't let anyone see her coming or going. Gotta hide her car too. No one can know where she is." Candle grabbed her backpack and slung it over her shoulder. "I'll be back as soon as I can. If you need me, you know how to reach me."

****

Miacoh reached for Candle's arm. "May I have a word?"

"Make it a quick one." Candle sprinted toward the

door. "Come on, Terrabyte. Car ride." The dog jumped up from the floor and raced to the door, tail wagging furiously.

Outside he closed the door, took Candle by the shoulders, and turned her to face him. "Aren't you taking on a little more than you can handle? You don't even have a receptionist to answer the phones with Gabby gone. Security system installations are scheduled. Not to mention your best friend's husband is missing. Unless I miss my guess, her strained relationship with her in-laws will make her the first person of interest. Then you have the Molly mess."

"That's what Gabby's lawyer is for. I have an answering service. You saw Molly's face. And you of all people should understand. I couldn't turn her down. Gabby will have my full attention, but at the moment, you are better suited to assist her than me for the reasons you just stated. Cayson can handle…" Her phone alarm went off. "Shit. Kids will be out of school shortly."

He rolled his eyes. "Don't tell me your sixth sense or whatever is telling you to take Molly's case."

"Something like that." Candle smiled beguilingly. "Gotta go." She opened the SUV door. "Up, Terra." The dog jumped into the vehicle and settled down in the back seat glancing from one of her persons to the other as Candle buckled her in.

Cayson stepped out of the office. "I hate to interrupt, but I have installs today, plus a repair. I don't want to sound unkind, but babysitting a client is not on my calendar or in my job description. Besides, how do I keep her out of sight?"

"You don't have a job description," Candle shot

back, glancing at her watch.

"What do you expect me to do? Take her with me?" Cayson shoved his hand in his pockets.

"Not a bad idea. I was considering offering her the reception position after I talk with Gabby and run a background check. But Molly is smart. She might be able to assist you at least for today."

He put his hand up, palm facing her. "No. No. I don't need a PhD student..." He glanced through the front window to the woman sitting in the chair staring at the floor.

"It would be the last place anyone would look for her." Candle followed his gaze.

"Okay, just until Miacoh finds out about the safe house. If I get finished and still haven't heard from either of you, I'll set her up in the Lazy R B&B. Probably safer there than a hotel."

"It's settled." She yanked open the driver-side door, gave Miacoh a kiss, and climbed into the vehicle. "Gotta go. Don't forget to call Dad. Kinda fill him in on what's going on. But don't let him cut his vacation short. Mom'll kill me."

Miacoh scrubbed his hand over his face. "Yeah, right, kinda fill in the retired Chief of Police, on the job for thirty-five years, on what's happening. Not going to happen. He'll grill me within an inch of my life, and you know it. Especially where his daughter is involved."

She rolled down her window, leaned out, and gave Miacoh another kiss. "You can handle him. Oh, and run a background check on Molly. I'd like to put her to work right away."

"Appears you already have. What if she's a wanted

murderer?" Miacoh's lips twitched.

"She's not." Candle grinned up at him. "She'll pass with flying colors. I can feel it."

Cayson clapped his friend on the shoulder. "She's got your number."

"Quit whining and get to work," Miacoh growled and strode toward to the police station next door. He paused to glance back at his friend. "You got it handled. Right?"

"Do I have a choice?" Cayson yanked open the glass door to the office.

Candle waved, pulled away from the curb, and turned down the street.

Chapter Three

Gabby's Dilemma.

Candle spent the next hour giving the school the information they needed, collecting the twins from school, and answering their many questions without telling them a thing. *CIA training comes in handy sometimes.* She bit back a smile. Heading toward Gabby's house, she took the back route and back tracked a couple of times to make sure she wasn't followed.

"We're here," she announced hesitantly surveying the area, then pushing the unlock button on the vehicle's door.

Twins Natalya and Nash released their seat belts and tumbled out of the SUV. They paused as Terrabyte barked and tugged at her harness still hooked to the seatbelt restraint.

"Don't either of you release Terra from her seatbelt. Stand right beside the SUV." Candle stepped out of the vehicle, opened the back door, snapped on the dog's leash, and put her on the ground.

"Why didn't Mom pick us up?" Natalya stared at Candle with those huge blue eyes.

"Candle already told us. Mom's at Dad's office fielding calls. You know he went on a business trip." Nash fisted his hands on his hips, glared at his sister, then raced to the porch.

"Hey, wait for me," Natalya squealed.

Candle shook her head and sprinted after them. She had no idea how Gabby handled these two bundles of energy. "Both of you have to wait for me to open the door. Before I do that, Terrabyte has to do her business. Do you have homework?" She proceeded to guide everyone into the back yard. After Terra did her business, Candle peered through the back window. Making sure there was a key panel at the back door, she proceeded to unlock the door and punch in the code to silence the alarm then relocked the door.

"Some." Nash shoved his hand in his pockets then pulled them out in an exasperated gesture. "Can't we play with Terra first and wait for Mom to get home?"

"Yeah, Mom always helps us with our homework. Then Dad checks it." Natalya snickered. "Mom hates when he does that."

"Since I don't know when your mom will return, homework is the first item on your agenda. Terra will still be here." The sad-faced kids trailed in. "I can help you with your homework."

The twins shrugged out of their backpacks and made a beeline to the dining room table where a tray of veggies, a bowl of what looked like dip, and a plate of chocolate chip cookies rested in the center of the table. Napkins and paper plates were set next to the veggie tray.

"Wow, looks like your mom made a snack for you two." She stood in front of the snacks, effectively blocking the twins. "Wash your hands first. Mind if I have a carrot?"

"Help yourself." Nash grinned mischievously.

"After you wash your hands."

"Of course." She followed the twins to the sink.

After they ran water over their hands with a squirt of soap, the twins and Candle returned to the table.

"She always has a snack prepared for us." Natalya grabbed a carrot, dipped it in the bowl of white creamy stuff, then scooped up a couple of cookies.

Candle put a restraining hand against the girl. "I don't believe cookies come first." Dipping a couple more carrots in the bowl, she popped them in her mouth one at a time. "A few veggies on your plates first, please, then cookies."

"Mom lets us eat what we want." Nash dipped a stick of celery into the creamy stuff, put it on his plate along with a couple of veggies, then added three cookies.

"I doubt that. But I'm here and it's my rules." Candle ruffled the boy's reddish hair. "Finish your snack and get on your homework." She glanced at the corner of the family room where one big desk and two smaller ones were arranged around a large corner picture window. "Is that where you do your homework?"

"Yeah, Mom set up our study office in that corner. She can help us while handling her business."

The twins reluctantly picked up their backpacks from the floor by the table and carried them to the desks.

Terrabyte, nose stuck in the air sniffing around the table, plopped down. "No, girl, no human food." She took a tiny treat from her pocket and tossed it to the dog. Terra snarfed up the treat and trotted over to where the twins were sitting with their plates and books at the desks.

"No begging from Natalya or Nash either." Candle's voice held a hint of amusement.

An hour later, snacks gobbled up, homework finished and checked by Candle, the twins rushed to the back yard. Holding Terra's toys in their hands, they scrambled out the door and the pup scampered after them.

****

Gabby's sedan rolled to a stop in front of the home. She trudged up the steps, unlocked, and pushed open the front door.

"You look like someone pulled you through a knothole backward. Was it that bad?" Candle greeted her best friend and swung an arm around her friend's shoulder.

Gabby hung up her coat and tossed her purse and briefcase on the sofa. "Yeah, it was bad. So glad you suggested I take our lawyer with me. Especially when I insisted Ben's family not be contacted right away."

"We told you that. I bet your attorney told you that too. Hardhead." Candle shook her friend's shoulder a bit.

"I know. But you have no idea the problems they can cause. Even to the point of suggesting that they take the twins. I'm not emotionally prepared to take care of them until Ben is found. If he is found."

"They didn't really say that."

"Oh, the minute they were contacted, they were at the sheriff's office within minutes spouting off, slinging implications, and yes, they did say exactly that. Dan finally shut them down and told the sheriff's deputy to charge me or let me go."

"I bet the sheriff's office didn't appreciate the circus Ben's family caused."

"Oh, no. I think that's why they finally let me go. Then they insisted Ben's family leave telling them the office would be in touch, if necessary. Thank goodness, I could fill the sheriff's office in on the partnership problems out of earshot of the family. Ben deliberately didn't tell his family yet."

"I'm sure they'll find out shortly."

"I'm going to have guards posted around the office here in Aspen Ridge. I wouldn't put it past one of his family members to try and break into the office to see what they can find."

"What about the other office in Aspen?"

"Ben moved everything of value or importance out of there when he discovered his partner's transgressions. In fact, I believe he may have relocated most of the important paperwork not necessary for day-to-day operations to a safe deposit box at our bank. The key should be upstairs in our bedroom safe."

"You have a safe in your bedroom?" Candle stared incredulously at her best friend since childhood.

"Yes, Ben insisted. It's a long-convoluted story of his distrust of 'my in-laws' as he likes to refer to them."

"Wow, talk about a dysfunctional family. Anyway, obviously they let you go. Does that mean you are not a person of interest?"

"They told me not to leave town. But I believe they are going to look at his business partner and his dealings." Gabby collapsed onto the sofa. "Where're the kids?"

"Outside in the back yard playing with Terra. They didn't hear you drive up."

"That's why I didn't put the car in the garage. The garage door goes up and it's a signal to the kids to come running. I wanted to talk with you first. Until this situation is sorted out and Ben located, I'm going to have to run his office. Or at least field the calls until…" A big teardrop rolled down Gabby's cheek, followed by several others as she covered her face in her hands. "What am I going to do?"

"Let's not get ahead of ourselves. We'll find Ben. Miacoh is feeling out the sheriff's office this afternoon. As far as my office, don't worry, we got it covered."

Gabby lifted her head out of her hands. "You sure?"

"Yep. You're not going to believe the kind of day I've had since you left." Candle proceeded to tell her about Molly, her ties to the chem lab, the adoption, everything, since officially Gabby was still part of Terrabyte Security.

"Wow, are you sure—"

"Don't even go there. You're our first priority. But we must keep from stepping on the sheriff's office's toes. What better way to do that, than to be in the middle of a complicated case like Molly's. Besides, you helped me narrow down the applicants for more techs last week. Guess I'll be adding to the staff. Cayson is only one person with his hands full."

Gabby wiped her face with the back of her hand hearing the back door open and thundering paws enter along with noisy kids' chatter and footsteps.

"I've told them nothing. So, it's all your show. I'll go move your car into the garage, in case your in-laws show up sooner rather than later."

Gabby rummaged around in her purse and tossed

the keys to Candle. "I made them pretty mad and threatened them with a restraining order. My lawyer is going to request one be issued. He wasn't sure we have enough grounds, but…It'll take a while for them to digest the threat and get their lawyers on it." Gabby smirked. "Hey, you hooligans. Homework done?" She hugged the twins to her and grabbed Terra's leash as Candle shut the front door.

Candle returned, tossed the keys to Gabby, and ruffled Terra's fur as the pup bounced around her feet. "How about dinner? I have a frozen meal in the fridge at home along with peanut butter cookies. I'll let Miacoh and Cayson know to grab a salad and rolls on their way home."

"I don't know. The kids have school tomorrow and your meals turn into movie marathons."

"True. We'll keep it low-key. Come on, load into the SUV, and off we go in search of sustenance." She grinned at the kids, who in turn stared at her like she'd grown another head.

"Popcorn?" the twins cried in unison.

"After supper." She peered out the window to make sure no one was lurking about before handing Nash Terra's leash. "You two get Terra settled in the SUV, hook her seatbelt through the harness, then belt yourselves in."

The twins rushed out the door. She glanced at Gabby. "Do you want to stay at my house tonight? We've got plenty of room. Your in-laws will probably be watching you as soon as they regroup. Your current security system needs serious upgrades outside. Perimeter cameras, motion detectors, and panic alarm. We can get those installed tomorrow. Your current computer system should handle the new load with a few software tweaks."

"I can't ask you do that on top of everything else," Gabby balked.

Candle fisted her hands on her hips. "Want to deal with a surprise ambush by your in-laws?"

"Definitely not." Her friend grimaced.

"To that end, you may want to contact the children's school. I gave them the bare bones of the situation, said you'd be in touch. So you should fill them in on what they need to know, and add a no-contact order for your in-laws."

"You're right. I don't want them picking up the kids and whisking them off somewhere. One battle at a time. I'll grab a few things. Stay at your house tonight. Fill in the school when I take the twins tomorrow."

Gabby's phone rang. She glanced at the screen and turned the phone off. "So it begins." Tossing the phone in her bag, she pulled out another holding it up. "Company phone. My in-laws don't have the number. I've got to call Dan, give him this number to contact me." She touched in a series of numbers and put the phone to her ear as she rushed upstairs.

Once all the family's items were in the SUV, Candle took the back roads and doubled back on the way home, not wanting to give Gabby's in-laws an easy time of detection if they were following.

Chapter Four

Business As Usual—Or Is It?

Cayson's irritation melted away as he gazed at the woman sitting in the chair, her fingers twisting in the bottom of her sweater and eyes staring at the floor. Upon his opening the door, her shoulders straightened in a jerky motion. She lifted her eyes to meet his. "Cayson, is it?"

"That's right." He extended his hand and grasped the cool sweaty one she offered.

"Sorry to interrupt your day. I'll try to stay out of the way."

"You'll do no such thing. Boss lady has plans, and you're part of them. What do you know about computers, programming, or installation?"

She offered a shy smile. "I installed my own home security system when I suspected someone was entering my apartment without authorization. It wasn't the best, but certainly better than nothing. Computers, I know enough to get myself into trouble. I encrypted files on my laptop so others couldn't access them. A lot of good that did me. Prof simply took my work and called it his own. In the end, his treachery was discovered, wasn't it? Someday he'll pay—" She lifted her warm chocolate brown eyes to his. "—won't he?"

"At the moment, we can't touch him. He fled to a

country with no extradition. It's usually only a matter of time before those types of individuals try to sneak back into the United States. Several government agencies will be waiting for him." Cayson grinned.

"That's something. I took basic programming in college. Wasn't bad at it." She shrugged.

He handed her a clipboard with several pages on it. "Our work orders for today." He picked up a small tool belt and added wire cutters, crimps, a handful of connectors, screwdrivers, and a couple of miscellaneous items from his own. He gently slung the belt in her direction. "This should be enough to get you started."

She grabbed the belt and affixed it to her waist. "Not a bad fit."

Snapping his fingers, he walked to the back room and emerged with a pink chambray shirt emblazoned with the Terrabyte logo and embroidered with Gabby on the pocket. "You look about Gabby's size. She won't mind if you borrow one until Candle makes other arrangements."

She held it in front of her. "Yep, it will fit. Pink isn't my color, but it will do. Is there somewhere I can change?"

"Sure thing. Down the hall, hang a left, and you'll see the ladies' room. Put a hustle on it; we're running late already."

Yeah, the pink clashed with her beautiful bronze skin, but if she worked out Candle would get her her own shirts. The sway of her hips as she made her way to the ladies' room caught his attention. *Down, boy. She is a client and possible co-worker.* He took a deep breath and glanced away only to see Miacoh push through the open office door.

The chief's gaze did a quick sweep of the room then he flashed a grin. "Explained the situation to Hunter. There is a safe house on the outskirts of town, not too far from Candle's cabin. Hasn't been used in years, if ever according to him. I'll run by the house and check it out. If necessary, get a detail on it to make it livable." He clapped his friend on the shoulder. "Cheer up. She might surprise you."

"Didn't sign up for babysitting duty," he growled and frowned, then reiterated his conversation with her. "So might work out okay."

"That's the attitude. Candle called. We need to pick up a few things for supper. Gabby and the twins are staying with us for the night at least, maybe longer. You and Molly will be joining us for supper." Miacoh shrugged one shoulder. "Gabby's in-laws raised a real stink at the sheriff's office. She's concerned they'll show up at the house before she can arrange security."

"Wow, that's not what she needs right now. Husband missing, covering at his company, kids. Poor woman has her hands full without interfering in-laws." Cayson ran his fingers through his unruly surfer blond hair. "Do you think her in-laws would try to take the twins?"

"I really don't know. But in Candle's opinion, better safe than sorry. You'll be installing cameras and beefing up Gabby's security system first thing tomorrow morning. Candle suggested you may need to tweak your schedule."

"Not necessary. I'll go over there at dawn. It won't take long to make the additions and programming and I'm on my way."

"What's this about dawn?" Molly stepped into the

room.

"Work schedule tomorrow."

"Am I still with you tomorrow, safe house, or B&B?" Molly twisted the handle of her bag. "I appreciate all you've done for me. I don't want to be a pain, but I'd like to get settled somewhere. Not had much sleep in the last week or so."

"Understood." Cayson connected the answering service, picked up his tools, and jerked his head toward the door. "Time to go."

"We'll get the safe house checked out and hopefully we'll have you settled there after dinner tonight." Miacoh frowned at his phone and punched in a number, then walked out the door toward the police station.

Molly scooted out the door and waited on the sidewalk for Cayson to set the alarm and lock the door.

He pointed toward the silver and black crew-cab pickup truck with Terrabyte Security's name and phone number emblazoned on the magnetic sign stuck to the driver-side door.

"How long has Candle owned Terrabyte Security? Everything looks fairly new." She reached for the passenger door handle. Cayson beat her to the handle and opened the door. "Wow, and they say chivalry is dead." She let out a nervous giggle.

"Nope, just don't want you to scratch my truck with your tools." He glanced at her tool-belt where a screwdriver hung out blade first. "She started Terrabyte the company, not her dog, when she arrived here after leaving her former employer. Didn't have a store front or anything set up, then things blew up here, the college and all. Terrabyte had to take a back seat for a few months. Now she's back on track with more business than we can handle." He ran his fingers through his disheveled hair. "I guess it's a good problem to have."

"I guess so." She followed his gaze, tucked the offending tool inside the bag, and climbed into the truck. "Sorry about that."

He guffawed loudly. "Only kidding. Can't have you ruining my reputation."

"So—are you a playboy?"

"Nope, just a confirmed bachelor. Left the military a few months ago, hooked up with Miacoh and Candle as they were in the middle of the murder investigation and Homeland Security mess, then decided to stick around to help them get Terrabyte off the ground."

"Oh. Has Candle lived here all her life?"

He chuckled. "You got a lot of questions for a client and security risk." He walked around the truck.

"Probably because I want to get my life back and I'd like to know who's helping me."

He paused in front of the truck. "You saw or heard us in action during the chemistry lab explosion and tying up loose ends afterward. That should be enough of a recommendation." He jerked open the door, jumped inside the truck, and waited for her to fasten her seatbelt.

"Obviously, you and Miacoh must have been black ops. There's a defiant, unshakable air about both of you. Funny, Candle has the same no-nonsense, don't mess with me vibe going too. But with her it's more subtle, not less dangerous, just kinda like still waters run deep. If you know what I mean."

"Not really, but I'll take your word for it." Passing several houses dotting the landscape, he turned onto a gravel road, pulled into a circular driveway, and cut the engine. "First stop, Jansen's place." The two-story lavender and white house had a story book appearance with purple shutters and an oval door. "Their security system isn't working right so we're troubleshooting."

"I don't know anything about troubleshooting systems."

"I guess you'll learn." At the stricken look on her face, he snickered. "Don't worry. I'll introduce you as my trainee. Everyone in town knows our business is booming." He knocked on the door.

A petite woman with one pointed ear sticking out of her long silver hair blinked at them with huge green eyes. She carried an infant, with the same ears, eyes, and what looked like a tiny pink wing escaping the blanket while the child sucked its fist. "Hi there, Cayson." The woman quickly arranged the blanket to cover what appeared to be a wing.

Molly's mouth fell open and her eyes rounded. She took two steps back, her heel slipping off the top step of the porch. Cayson turned and caught her by the tool-belt yanking her back beside him.

Another small child circled around the woman, his feet several inches off the ground as his blue wings beat furiously. "Mom, I'm starving." The blue-winged child whined.

"This is Molly, my new trainee. Molly, this is Calliope Jansen. Her son, Coaster, is the whiny one, and—" he gently touched the baby's tiny pink cheek, "—this is January. They recently moved here from Raven's Hollow. Her husband applied for the town attorney's position and his qualifications were too good to pass up just because his family is a little different."

The woman shifted the baby from one shoulder to the other bouncing the girl on her hip as she fussed. "Come on in." She opened the door wider and motioned them to follow her.

"Is Jason home?" Cayson asked.

"Nope. He's at the town hall today prepping for some kind of court case this afternoon." She thrust a sheet of paper into his hands. "Left you a list of what's happening and when. The system works part of the time and doesn't other times." She pointed to a panel with the door wide open. The little boy had grabbed the door and was swinging back and forth.

Calliope grabbed the boy by his pointed ear and grounded him. "That's enough. You know better than to show your wings when strangers are here. Where are your manners? We have company."

The boy shifted from one foot to the other uncomfortably, tucked his wings in his back, and said nothing for a moment. "We know Cayson."

"That's it. Time out in your chair. Right now." His mother pointed to a chair facing the corner. Then turned her attention back to Cayson. "I'm afraid we'll have to use magic to tame this one." She jerked her thumb in the direction of her son. "At least until we are accepted in Aspen Ridge." Her expression turned dubious. "Pekabo indicated there wouldn't be a problem when she told us about the position. Now, I'm not so sure. Blending into a nonmagical community with two small children may be tougher than we thought. Though Jason is mortal—" she shrugged "—turned out our children are not." She sighed.

"Aspen Ridge is a great little town that will embrace your family. Give them a chance." Cayson moved to the panel, tugging Molly behind him. "Besides, not all things are as they seem." He turned and grinned at Calliope.

As the initial shock wore off, Molly stared into the panel and clicked her tongue as Cayson shone his flashlight beam inside. She pointed at two loose wires and one that looked like it had been gnawed through. "Could that be the source of the problem?"

"Good eye." Cayson switched off the power to the panel, tightened the wires, and replaced the others. He narrowed his eyes at the little boy, who sat transfixed while taking little peeks at him then turning around to face the wall. "Coaster, have you been checking out the panel since you moved in?"

Coaster bounded out of the chair, raced to his mom in the kitchen. He grabbed a bowl of cereal she prepared and began spooning it into his mouth. Calliope blew out a breath and placed a hand on her son's shoulder. "We'll discuss the time out later. Mr. Erickson asked you a question."

"Mama, I didn't mean to. I was looking at the panel when we were moving in. One of my wings hit the door and it popped open. I only wanted to see…"

"Oh dear." Calliope circled her hand over her son's head. A light shower of gold shimmered around him and disappeared. "You could have been seriously hurt. When we tell you to stay away from things, that doesn't mean do it while we are busy. Now your powers of flight and magic are disabled for the time being until I talk with your dad." She put the baby in a bouncy swing and walked into the living room. "The boy is forever taking things apart to see how they work and surprisingly enough, he can usually put them back together."

"Well, this panel is placed out of the reach of most children's curious hands. However, I don't believe the house was built for flying children. We can put a lock on it…"

"I'll do one better. I'll put a magical lock on it. That will take care of the problem." She wiped her hands determinedly on the towel tucked into her waistband.

He powered up the panel. Green, red, and blue lights blinked on. "Calliope, check your monitors and see if everything is working. Toggle through all the rooms in the house and outside." Turning from the panel, he watched over the woman's shoulder.

"Seems all is working except that one outside camera in the back left. I'm not getting anything there."

"We'll go outside and check it out." He pointed to the back door. "May we use that exit?"

"Sure." She hurried to unlock the door.

Cayson motioned for Molly to follow him. Once outside the door, Molly screeched to a halt in front of him hands fisted at her hips. "You could have warned me. Magic folk, mortals, clearly Calliope and her children are faeries. Correct? What or where is this Raven's Hollow?"

"Still full of questions." He ambled to the defective camera. A squirrel in the tree chittered loudly at him. "I'm going to get the ladder out of my truck. Be right back." He sprinted around the house, returning with the ladder and a black box in record time. He shimmied up the ladder and popped open the plastic covering over the arm that held the camera. "Just as I thought. Squirrel chewed through the plastic covering in the back and these wires. Molly, open the black box and hand me the metal covering for this arm."

Molly did as instructed. "Did the noisy squirrel tell you what it did?" She giggled.

"Something like that. Smart alec." He sheathed the wiring with the metal, then clambered down the ladder. "We'll check with Calliope, but our work is done here."

"So what can I expect on the next job?"

"Nothing out of the ordinary. Jansens are one of only two magical families in Aspen Ridge. Pekabo met Calliope in a ceramic class in Raven's Hollow, a town of magical creatures. It's only an hour's drive from here. Calliope mentioned her husband was looking for a job in the 'outside world.' I guess it's tough to compete alongside lawyers with magical powers if you're mortal. Pekabo told Hunter about Jason since the old Town Attorney for Aspen Ridge wanted to retire. Jason's credentials were impeccable according to Miacoh and Hunter. The town couldn't pass him up. Pekabo was sure the Aspen Ridge community would embrace the little family. Guess we'll see." He shrugged. "Pekabo is rarely wrong. The woman has a sixth sense about people."

"Wow, this town is more diverse than most. And the other family?"

"Town's close-knit, but it's got secrets." After putting his tools in the truck, he sauntered to the house and opened the back door. "Calliope, is the camera online?"

"Sure is. You do good work, Cayson." She glanced at Molly. "You too. Could I interest you two in a warm peanut butter cookie and lemonade?"

Cayson licked his lips then checked his watch.

"You betcha. We only have one more service call today."

Chapter Five

Meanwhile Candle has Her Hands Full with Twins, Gabby, and Now…

Candle pulled into the driveway and cut the engine. The twins shoved open the vehicle doors and ran toward the house, Terrabyte right behind them barking. "I didn't see anyone following us, so it's probably safe to assume that your in-laws are probably still fuming or plotting."

"Oh, you have no idea," Gabby whispered as she jumped out of the SUV in pursuit of her two offspring.

"Terrabyte. You halt right there," Candle commanded. The pup hesitated only a minute while looking after the twins, then her butt hit the ground with a low grumble. Candle caught up with the dog and clicked the leash on her harness. "You know better than that."

"So do the twins." Gabby chased after the twins, who sped up when they saw her coming, grabbed both by the collar, and gave each a shake. "Guess you two will be considering your actions in the kitchen's chairs for fifteen minutes."

"Aw, Mom. Just 'cause you had a bad day—" Nash began.

"Thirty minutes." Lips thinned, Gabby shot him a warning look that would peel paint. "Keep up the smart mouth and you'll be eating dinner in one of Candle's guest rooms."

Natalya trudged into the house and plopped down on one of the kitchen chairs giving Candle a puppy dog eye look.

"Don't expect me to countermand your mom. She scares me too." She gave a slight shiver. Opening the fridge, she perused the contents, then did the same to the freezer. "Looks like we are in pretty good shape food wise. I'll just text Miacoh with a short list of items to pick up before he heads home."

"I'm happy to reimburse you for our portion of food." Gabby grimaced. "I'm really sorry about this."

"Don't worry about it. You've got enough on your plate. Speaking of that plate, we need to talk." She wandered into the living room out of earshot of the children, crumpled up newspaper, carefully placed kindling and aspen logs on top, then she lit the edges of the papers with a match and turned to her best friend.

Gabby gave the twins sitting on the chairs a stern look before following her friend. "About what exactly?"

She lowered her voice since after the remodel the cabin was open-concept and very little privacy on the lower level. "Oh, let's see. Ben's recent travels. His partner problems. Who would benefit from his disappearance? What happened at the police station? Why expect your in-laws to make a grab for your kids? Pretty good for starters."

"After the twins are in bed. Those two have extraordinary hearing when you don't want them to hear, but if you do, they are deaf." She let out a little giggle.

"You're going to have to tell Nash and Natalya what's going on soon for their own safety."

"I know, I know. They are somewhat aware of the discord between us and Ben's parents. Especially after we moved back to Aspen Ridge and the school switch." Gabby let out a long sigh. "I'm going to need to contact my parents too." Her phone played a merry tune. She glanced at the screen. "Speak of the devil. It's Mom."

"Better take it and explain. You can go upstairs into the first bedroom on the right to talk to her."

"Thanks."

Candle returned to the kitchen. The kids remained seated on the chairs. Terrabyte sat in the middle of the room glancing from one child to the other wagging her tail uncertainly. The pup rushed to Candle when she entered the room all wiggles. "The kids are in time out, so they can't play right now," she explained to Terra. She filled the pup's food bowl and freshened the water. "Okay, I can't let you kids go, but I can offer milk and chocolate chip cookies." She grinned.

"Mom doesn't let us have cookies this close to dinner time," Natalya whimpered.

"It's not that close to dinner." Nash glanced around. "We may never get to eat again. Cookies would be good."

Candle couldn't help but stifle a laugh. "Oh, I think dinner will be sooner rather than later. We're waiting for Miacoh to bring a few things from the store." She poured two glasses of milk and took the cookies out of the cookie jar, handing one to each child. "That'll keep you two from starving."

Miacoh burst through the front door, grocery bags in hand.

"Oh good, he's here." Candle rushed into the living room then glanced back at the children to make sure they were still seated.

"What's the deal—" He glanced around then lowered his voice. "—with the limousine parked at the end of our street? I didn't want to interrogate them before knowing what was going on. Cayson and Molly are on their way here. Should I delay them?" He took his phone out of his pocket.

Candle whipped around and stared at Miacoh. "We just arrived a little while ago. There wasn't a limo parked anywhere around our street." She rushed to the door. As she reached for the knob, Miacoh blocked her way. "Let's figure out what's going on and if it involves us. Could be one of our neighbors."

"Highly unlikely." Gabby frowned making her way downstairs. "I saw the limo out the window before I came down." She glanced toward the kitchen where the kids were. "Didn't take them long to locate me."

"Maybe not. I'll have Cayson drive by Gabby's house on his way here. See if someone has set up surveillance there too. Which would mean, they aren't sure where Gabby and the kids are residing. A good thing."

"Hmm…Mom didn't mention anyone hanging around the neighborhood that didn't belong." Gabby pursed her lips and grimaced. "But she was too busy telling me what I should do that I didn't get much of a word in edgewise. Like go to their house." She tucked the phone in her pants pocket. "Maybe I should call her back and…"

"No. Let's let Cayson handle it."

"I'm not sure I want Molly mixed up in whatever is

going to go down with Gabby. I'd forgotten about the in-law-problem."

"If you are planning to have her work for Terrabyte Security, you don't really have a choice." He raised an eyebrow. "The safe house is clean, stocked with food and essentials." Silent for a moment, he rubbed his chin. "Maybe best to drop her off at the safe house before Cayson comes here or goes by Gabby's place. Don't want someone following him or them and complicating things with Molly."

"Good idea. I have casseroles in the freezer I could add to her supplies."

"Well, actually, I stopped by here on my way to check on the safe house, borrowed a couple casseroles out of the freezer before I realized we were having guests." He flashed a chagrined smile and touched a button on his phone screen. "I'd better call Cayson or he'll be here."

Candle grinned. "Way to think on your feet, Chief. We have plenty of food stocked in the freezer."

Miacoh strode to the back door, clipped a leash on the bouncing Terra, and stepped outside, phone to his ear.

Gabby stood in the middle of the living room floor, her expression vacillating from fury to nearly tears as she shifted from foot to foot.

"Gabby, don't do anything rash." Candle moved quickly to the front door as if reading her best friend's mind. "Don't want a confrontation if we can help it."

"What do you suggest?" her friend retorted hotly.

"Let Miacoh handle it. Your in-laws may only guess you're here. We don't want to confirm anything. After all, your car is still in the garage at your house and we left a few lights on but pulled the curtains."

"You're right." Gabby plopped down on the couch, head in hands. "Where is Ben? I need him. How could he disappear like this?" A tear rolled down her cheek. She wiped it viciously away with the back of her hand and sucked in a breath. "Better check on the kids."

"Yeah, we need to get dinner started." Candle hurried into the kitchen, flipped on the oven, and took out a beans and ham dinner she prepared a while back from the freezer. Zapping them in the microwave on defrost for a few minutes, she transferred them to the oven to finish warming. She didn't like mushy beans, which was what they'd be if she left them in the microwave.

"Gabby, grab the cornbread mix from the cupboard to the right of the sink and mix it up. You know where the pans are."

"Sure thing. Kids, go wash your hands and play quietly in front of the fireplace. Stay away from the windows."

"I got new coloring books and crayons just for you. They're in the wooden toy box at the end of the couch." Gabby tousled Nash's hair and tugged on Natalya's braid before the kids rushed to the bathroom.

"Why do you still have that purple recliner and sofa?" Gabby blurted.

"It's a reminder of how far I've come. Besides, I happen to like purple, and they are really comfortable and well-built. They annoy the heck out of Miacoh, which makes it all the better." She laughed. "Did you fill your mom in?"

"Yes, they are worried and not pleased that I didn't run to their house with the twins. I tried to explain, but…you know Mom."

"Afraid I do. Once they think about it, they'll understand."

"Understand what?" Nash appeared in the kitchen, his sneakers squeaking on the hardwood floor as he skidded to a stop.

"Why you are always sticking your nose where it doesn't belong." Gabby laughed and ruffled his hair again.

"Aww, Mom, that's not true. Natalya does that more than me. It's what girls do." Nash turned and ran smack dab into his sister's fist to his gut.

"That'll teach you to say bad things." Natalya's grin faded as her mom grabbed her arm.

"You two want to spend the rest of the night in separate rooms or back on the kitchen chairs?"

"No, Mom," the twins chorused. "We're starved."

"Then sit down. Supper is almost ready." Gabby glanced at Candle to confirm the statement.

"Yep." She put the ladle in the bowl of beans and pulled the cornbread out of the oven. "You guys sit down and eat. I'm going to see what's keeping Miacoh and Terrabyte." Candle slipped out the back door into the cool evening air before Gabby could protest.

She found her husband in the middle of the yard, facing the street, throwing the squeaky toy for Terra.

"The limo hasn't moved, and no one has gotten out. Can't tell if they have binoculars or what. But figured if I played out here with Terra, it would appear normal for us." He slid his arm around Candle and pulled her to him kissing her soundly on the mouth then whispered, "I don't think they know anything, but we'll keep them guessing. If I go out there and demand to know who and what they are doing parked there, in an official capacity, it may tip our hand."

"If they storm the house, or become difficult?"

"The restraining order paperwork is all filled out and I've a judge ready to sign off on it in a matter of minutes. One phone call, and I'll pick it up. Then the battle will begin for Gabby. Rather it not come to that. Our focus has to be on finding Ben. Not sure how much more emotional trauma Gabby can stand."

"You're right. Come on in the house. We are ready to eat." She brushed her lips over his. "Thanks for being so understanding."

"A person goes missing in my jurisdiction, I'm damn well going to find out what happened."

"Actually, you did say it was Pitkin County's jurisdiction."

"That's where he left from, but he resides in Aspen Ridge which makes it my business. Or at least that's what I'm going to claim when talking with Pitkin County."

She shrugged. "You know what you're doing." Fingers entwined with his, they walked back to the cabin. He opened the door for her as her cell phone rang. She yanked it out of her pocket and stared at the screen in puzzlement, and tapped the green icon on her phone. "Hi, Mom."

"What's going on over there? Is Gabby with you? Do you know where Ben is? He's in trouble on a plane somewhere. Or was. Something about papers, contracts, software, oh, I'm not sure. But he's not a willing participant— I don't think."

"Slow down, Mom. Start at the beginning. Let me put you on speakerphone so Miacoh and Gabby can hear." She stepped into the kitchen flooded with delicious aromas. Gabby and the twins sat at the table spooning up soup and munching on warm cornbread.

"No, don't do that. I don't want to upset Gabby," Pekabo said in hushed tones.

"Don't worry about that. She's already upset. She discovered Ben was missing this morning when he didn't get off the plane in Las Vegas as planned. A missing person's report has been filed with Pitkin County Sheriff."

"Why on earth Pitkin County? He lives in Aspen Ridge. Anyway...I had this vision. You've got to do something right away. I also saw an older couple, no faces, taking or rather trying to stuff the twins in a black limo. I didn't see Gabby anywhere. Your dad and I should catch the first plane back home."

"That's not necessary. Miacoh and I have the situation in hand right now. You know what they say about too many cooks spoil the soup. Dad's retired, remember?"

"This is a matter of life or death, not soup, for heaven's sake." Pekabo's voice rose. "You don't think we could relax and enjoy ourselves when Gabby's family is in dire peril. Do you?"

"Mom—take a breath. Is Dad there?"

"Of course. But he didn't see what I saw. We gotta help Ben. Tell Gabby to keep those kids close."

"Believe it or not, we are already on that too. Send me an email with every bit of the info from your vision. We'll sort it out here." The knot in Candle's stomach pulled tighter. "Don't worry. I'll call you when we know anything."

Her father got on the phone. "Let me talk to

Miacoh."

"Sure, Dad, but we got this handled." She handed the phone to Miacoh, mouthing I tried.

He nodded in understanding, disappeared out the back door, closing it behind him.

Gabby grabbed hold of Candle's arm like a vise-grip. "Pekabo had a premonition, didn't she?"

"Yes." Candle debated with herself about how much to tell her friend, but in the end felt her best friend in the world deserved to know. She flashed a bright smile at the twins. "Good food?"

With mouths full, the twins chorused, "Yes." Then turned their gazes to their mom. "What's a premonition?"

"A dream about someone." Candle ruffled the young boy's unruly hair just like his dad's. "Nothing to worry about. Now eat up before Miacoh gets in here and eats everything. Including dessert."

Terra skidded to a stop in front of her food bowl inhaling the small piece of cornbread Candle left for her, then eying the twins.

"Don't even think about it, pup." She leaned down, scratched Terra's ears, and pointed to the dog's blanket. "Go to your place and stay." Terra's tail wagged uncertainly, but she slunk over to her blanket, circled twice, and lay down. She returned her attention to the twins. "Now don't you two feed her from the table or Miacoh will get your dessert. Understand?"

Nash and Natalya nodded solemnly. The back door opened and Miacoh breezed in tucking the phone in his pocket. "Did I hear right? I get both of your desserts?"

The twins giggled. "No way."

While Miacoh teased the twins, Candle tugged

Gabby toward the living room, out of earshot of the kids, and repeated Pekabo's conversation.

Gabby's face turned white as a ghost, she sucked in a breath, and her knees buckled. Candle nudged her onto the sofa and sat down beside her.

"We've got to find Ben before it's too late," Gabby insisted. "And that no-good scoundrel of an ex-partner of his. He's got a hand in this. I just know it."

"All good options, but let me bring Miacoh up to speed and see where his gut leads him."

"By that time it may be too late." Gabby threw up her hands. "By that time he could be halfway around the world or worse." A tear trickled down her cheek followed by another. She wiped them away with the back of her hand as she glanced toward the kitchen.

"So you suggest we go off all halfcocked and…"

"No, of course not. But we don't know how much time Ben has."

"Nor do we know how accurate my mom's vision is. There was a time when we both poo-pooed her abilities entirely."

"Then we grew up and she made us believers along with most of the town. After she found the mother of that little girl, whom the father had attempted to ship off in a cargo trunk while he absconded with the daughter…"

"One of many." Candle put her finger to her lips as foot falls sounded toward them, then stopped, paused, and began to pound upstairs.

"Okay, kiddos. You have three treats each. Now run upstairs and hide the treats anywhere. Don't make it too easy. She's really good at this game. As soon as you tell me, I'll let Terra upstairs to find them." Miacoh edged toward the living room with a wiggling, barking Terrabyte held by the harness. "Now what's this I hear about your mom's vision and my gut?"

"Oh no. Did the kids hear too?" Gabby wrung her hands, eyes big as saucers while she blinked up at him.

"Nope. Part of being a paranormal creature with extraordinary hearing and sight among other things." He winked at Candle with a Cheshire cat grin, then sobered at her stormy expression.

She filled him in. Gabby added her thoughts as to the ex-partner. Miacoh rubbed his chin thoughtfully. "Or he could be right in our own back yard." He stepped to the window and peered out the curtain. "Limo is still there." He glanced to the top of the stairs. "Ready, kids? Can't hold her much longer."

"Ready," came excited voices from the second floor.

He let the pup go. She raced up the stairs, tail wagging and barking all the way. "That'll keep 'em busy for a while."

"We're wasting time," Gabby squeaked.

"No. We're not." He turned his phone's screen so the women could see recent texts he'd received and sent.

Chapter Six

Reconnaissance Mission.

Cayson glanced at his watch as Miacoh's message sped across its face. "Mmm...looks like we'll have to take the cookies and lemonade to go if that's all right. Been a change of plans."

"Sure. No problem." Calliope took two go mugs from the cupboard, filled them with lemonade, and slid several cookies into a plastic container, then snapped the lid shut. "There you are." She handed the items to Molly with a grin. "You do have to share."

"Of course." Molly handed a go cup to Cayson with a mischievous giggle, holding tight to the container of cookies.

Calliope smiled while walking them to the door. "I guess possession is nine-tenths."

In one quick motion, Cayson snatched the container of cookies and held it out of Molly's reach while they walked down the sidewalk to his truck. "Now I have possession."

Inside the truck, he opened the container and offered her a cookie. He checked his phone and gave a low whistle. "Gotta make this last stop quick. The safe house is ready. Complete with a casserole, cold beer, and sodas. Bet you're hungry."

"You'd be right. Care to join me?" she asked shyly.

"You betcha."

He stopped the truck in front of a small blue and yellow house. The yard was neatly trimmed, with flower beds put to rest for the fall and winter. "This is the Granger house." He grabbed his tools, walked up to the door, and knocked. Molly scurried along behind him. "Mr. Granger is a do-it-yourselfer. Which gets him in more trouble than not. A little knowledge in the wrong hands is a dangerous thing." He chuckled.

"Kinda like me?" She smirked.

"No. You follow instructions quite well."

Mr. Granger answered the door with fried wires in his hand and a wire crimper in the other. "Thought I had it but…"

Mrs. Granger stood staring over her husband's shoulder hands on hips. "But he didn't. Blew a couple of breakers he did."

"Let's take a look." Cayson opened the electrical panel and noted the breaker to the alarm panel nearly melted in place. "Gotta shut down your electrical while we get to the source of the problem and repair it. Will that be all right?"

"Sure. Gotta be fixed, don't it?" Mrs. Granger smiled at Cayson then shifted to glare at her husband. "Can we put a lock on the panel when you are through?"

"Sure, but it could be inconvenient at times. Especially if you lose the key."

"Nope, got a little combo lock right here. Should fit just fine." She held up a small but sturdy lock.

He clicked his tongue and glanced from Mr. to Mrs. Granger. "Should work."

An hour and one-half later, Cayson packed up his

tools and waved goodbye. "Now, Mr. Granger, call me if you have problems with the system. Repair will be faster that way and less expensive."

Mr. Granger nodded and shoved his thumbs in his belt loops.

"Think he'll listen to you?" Molly glanced back at the couple and smiled. Mrs. Granger wagged her finger at Mr. Granger.

"Doubt it. This isn't the first time something like this has happened." He grinned. "Keeps Terrabyte in business. Now off to the safe house. Food and cold ones await." He started the engine and pulled away from the curb. Glancing in his rear-view mirror he made sure no one was following. Driving the side streets, he backtracked then circled the block before pulling in front of the safe house. The building wasn't as he had imagined. It was a pretty little cottage with terracotta-colored shutters against a buff exterior, a well-maintained yard, a fenced back yard, and large picture window facing the street. "Here we are."

She frowned. "Oh, then you won't be needing my help anymore?"

"Nope, didn't say that. Only that it's your residence, for now, and is prepared. We have a full schedule tomorrow of repairs and new installs. Not to mention research into your case. There'll probably be other cases that need our attention. You're a full-time employee."

"What about Gabby? I don't want to step on any toes especially since I'm not from around here."

"Don't worry about it. Appears Gabby has her hands full at the present time. Her position wasn't ever meant to be permanent or full-time. She has a set of lively twins that keep her busy, not to mention part-timing it at her husband's office."

He stepped out of the vehicle, stretched his legs, and tucked his weapon in his waistband holster. "Molly, I want you to stay in the truck while I go in and check the house out. Miacoh went through the house earlier, but this is my watch." He rolled the windows up and locked the vehicle. After searching the perimeter, entering through the back door, and exiting out the front, he returned to the truck. "All clear."

"Let's grab your gear and get it in the house." Handing her a couple of small bags from the bed of the truck, he hoisted the large suitcase on wheels onto the street. "Is that all you have?"

She cast her gaze downward at her one sad suitcase and shifted the two other bags on her shoulders. "Yeah, I left my house in a hurry taking only what I'd need short term. Didn't realize I may not be returning." Trudging along behind him, she sighed.

"Hey, don't let the situation get you down. We'll get it straightened. Then you'll get on with your life." He lifted the suitcase onto the porch and opened the door. The interior was cozy, painted in a golden buff, with light pastel accents. A few landscape paintings hung on the walls. It was obvious that Pekabo had decorated the cottage. After Molly entered the house, he closed and locked the door. "Feel free to make yourself at home. There are two bedrooms and a master down the hall to your right. The bathroom is to your left, and a fully stocked kitchen is straight ahead."

"It's nice. I like the open concept of the living and family rooms connecting to the large country kitchen. Reminds me of one of my parents' kitchens. It was where everyone gathered as I was growing up." A wistful smile spread across her face lighting her eyes. "And where my shortcomings were addressed, around our kitchen table."

"Your parents are deceased. Correct? Where'd you go after they died? Siblings?"

"That is a long story for another time. I have one older brother. I'm not sure where he resides."

"I didn't mean to pry. Like Candle said, if there is anything in your background that is relevant to the situation you're in now, we need to know. Otherwise, your personal life is just that, personal and private. Although I'll warn you, Candle is extremely good at wheedling info out of people." He chuckled. "Tomorrow, we'll need your next of kin for emergency contact. You'll need to fill out other employment papers, since it appears Candle has taken you under her wing."

She hesitated. "Don't exactly have an emergency contact—my Grams. But she's very old. Any bad news about me would kill her. I can't have that on my conscience."

"But if—" He glanced at his phone as the text message alert sounded. "Miacoh wants me to call him. Go ahead and get settled. I'll be back." Crossing to the back door, he gave her one last look and closed it.

"Miacoh, what's up?"

"How're things going with Molly?" Miacoh asked.

"Good. We are at the safe cottage." Cayson hiked a hip on the porch railing.

"After you get her settled, I need you to meander by Gabby's parents' house. See if there is any surveillance by the in-laws there. Stop by the office and see if there is any surveillance there. You can grab one of the undercover vehicles, then head over to our house."

"Are there more developments since this morning? I was kinda considering spending a little time with Molly. She seems pretty down, and I'm starved."

"We'll bring you up to speed when you get here. Do what you feel necessary, but don't spend all evening at it," Miacoh snapped.

"Yes, sir," he shot back and disconnected the call. Turning on his heel, he yanked open the back door. The aroma of chicken enchilada casserole made his mouth water, and his stomach growled loudly.

"Guess you are hungry. I won't have to ask." Molly smiled as she set out the silverware on napkins beside plates.

"Wow, something smells great." He inhaled deeply.

"The label on the dish said Candle's chicken enchilada casserole, please return the dish." Molly chuckled. "Candle is quite a cook, among her other talents."

"So I've heard. Actually, both Candle and Miacoh are fantastic cooks. Why do you think I stick around?" He laughed. "Only kidding."

He grabbed a couple of cold ones from the fridge, set one in front of Molly, and took a swig from his bottle. Glancing at his watch, he plopped down in the chair and picked up a fork. Sliding a bite of the casserole into his mouth, he nearly moaned. "Good stuff." He pointed to his plate.

Molly licked her lips and the back of her fork. "It sure is. So nice of them to provide food for me."

"Oh, I'm sure Pekabo prepared most of it. You just happened to pull out Candle's meal." He took another bite.

"Pekabo? What kind of name is that?"

"Candle's mom. She's a topic for another day." He snickered. "Great lady, but hippie through and through, not to mention a talented artist and… A few of her paintings are hanging in Candle's office."

"Oh. I look forward to meeting her. I saw you looking at your watch. If you need to be somewhere, don't let me keep you. I'll get settled and go to bed." She yawned wide. "Been quite a day."

"Yep, Miacoh was on the phone. I've another assignment this evening before I head home. Part of Gabby's investigation."

"Do you all put in long hours?"

"Sometimes. But it's feast or famine, so we roll with it. New company and all." He wiped his mouth with the napkin, pushed to his feet, and carried the dishes over to the sink. "Sure you'll be all right here tonight?"

"Of course." She followed him to the sink chewing her last bite and added her dishes to the sink.

He took out his business card, scribbled something on the back, then handed her the card. "My personal cell is on the back. Call if you have any problems. I'll be back early morning to pick you up. We have to work on Gabby's security system tomorrow, unless Candle needs you in the office. Either way, I'll be by to get you." He walked through the entire house again, checking windows and the security system. "Make sure you set the alarm once I close the door."

"Will do." She walked him to the front door.

"Thank you for everything. I hope you get to go home soon."

"Me too. Bed will feel good tonight." He strode out to his truck, paused to wave, then watched her go back into the house and waited for the alarm beep. Driving slowly around her block, satisfied all was well, he turned the truck onto the main road and drove toward Terrabyte Security. At one point, it appeared he'd picked up a tail. But the vehicle turned off five streets before he arrived at the office. Still, he circled a couple blocks to make sure.

The well-lit, gravel parking lot behind the office showed no signs of suspicious activity as he drove in and parked. He took the magnetic sign off the door of his truck and tossed it in the back seat, switched vehicles, then started off to check Gabby's home.

Parked across the street, down half a block from Gabby's house, a vehicle with two occupants inside caught his attention. He circled the block and drove by the car slowly on his second pass, indiscreetly getting a picture of its license plate. The driver started the engine and drove off in a hurry spraying dirt and gravel everywhere. S*trange, you'd think if they were trying to be inconspicuous, they would have tried not to draw attention. He shrugged. Amateurs.*

At the stop light before turning back on Main Street, he paused then decided to drive by Ben's office on the off chance the surveillance team relocated there. Cayson called Miacoh, brought him up to speed, then gave him the estimated time of arrival to Ben's office.

Even before he turned the corner onto the street where Ben's office was located, flashing lights reflected off the low-hanging clouds and the sound of a security alarm blaring pierced the night. He pulled over to the side of the road in view of the chaos, turned off his headlights, and called Miacoh.

Chapter Seven

Break-In. It Will Be a Long Night.

Miacoh pulled his phone out of his pocket and stared at the screen for a moment. "Cayson, what's happening? Can you hold on, I've another call coming in."

"Make it quick, boss. I believe someone broke into Ben's office."

No sooner than he'd put Cayson on hold and answered the other call, Gabby's phone rang.

"It's the alarm company from Ben's office." She put the phone to her ear. "Hello." There was a short pause. "This is Gabby." Another short pause. "When? How bad?" She listened a moment more. "I'll be right down."

"Miacoh here."

"Sir, I answered a burglary call. It's Ben's office. Gabby isn't at her home." The deputy paused for a moment.

"We'll be right there." He hung up and returned to Cayson's call. "Cayson, go ahead and contact the officer on scene. We'll be there shortly."

Gabby stood stock still for a moment before grabbing her coat and starting upstairs.

"What are you doing?" Candle stared after her friend.

"Gotta get the kids up so we can go check on Ben's office. You know it's been burglarized."

"I do." Miacoh said calmly. "But waking the children and taking them to the scene is only going to traumatize them more."

"I'll stay here with the kids in case they wake up. Gabby, you go ahead with Miacoh. Check on the damage and catalog anything missing. My bet, someone is looking for—"

"Let's not make assumptions." He helped Gabby into her coat. "We'll be back as soon as we can. Meanwhile, I'm going to station a patrol here at the house on the off chance this is a ploy to get at Gabby and the twins." He pointed to the door leading to the garage. "We'll go out this way. My patrol unit is inside. No use confirming to whoever is watching the house who left and who stayed."

Candle moved the curtain at the front window and peeked outside. "The vehicle is still parked in the same place. I can confirm two people inside, but there may be more."

"Let me know what the car does after we leave?"

"Will do." She followed them to the door and closed it behind them, then set the alarm.

He waited until the alarm beeped inside the house, then held the car door open for Gabby. When the garage door rolled up, he pulled out lights flashing.

Arriving on the scene, he spotted his officer, the unmarked car Cayson was probably driving, and a county sheriff's vehicle. "Looks like it's a party."

Gabby said nothing but stared through the windshield at the flashing lights and officers milling around. "You could pull around back. It's a covered entrance way. I have a key to the back door—less chance of anyone except law enforcement seeing me."

"Great idea." His vehicle rolled to a stop, and he jumped out. "I'll be right back as soon as I check in and tell them our plans. You stay put." Outside the vehicle, he paused for a couple of beats to let his eyes grow accustomed to the flashing lights and darkness beyond. *Huh. No sign of Cayson. He must be inside.*

A few minutes later, he returned to the vehicle and drove around back.

Cayson greeted him at the back door and opened Gabby's passenger door as his boss exited the driver's side. Ascending the few steps to the office, Cayson led the way. "The building has been cleared. It's a mess in there. Someone was looking for something. They went through desk drawers and ripped open couch and chair cushions. Pulled out books from the bookcase. I didn't see a safe." He turned to Gabby. "Was there one here?"

She sucked in a breath as she entered the small reception area. "No—well—yes there was, but Ben emptied it after the partner split and stored the contents in a safe deposit box. I have a key and he secreted his key away in our house somewhere." She ran her fingers over the reception desk. "The computer is missing."

Her shoes squeaked on the hardwood floor as she made her way down the hallway to Ben's office with Cayson and Miacoh close behind. She stepped through the open office door to a scene much the same as the rest of the office. Papers and files scattered all over the floor, the desk chair toppled, and bookshelves emptied, the contents spilled onto the floor. She opened the cubby where his computer usually set. "It's gone, but they left the printer. Picking up the paper tray, she slid it into place, her lips set in a thin line. "The people who did this—do they have Ben?" Her eyes shimmered with unshed tears. She sniffed and blinked the tears away.

"It's a good guess. Apparently, they didn't find what they were after. What about his computers?"

"Day-to-day business records, contracts, that sort of thing. The software and proprietary info are going to be on his laptop at home. We do have a safe there and he stored that laptop in it."

"Any thumb or flash drives?"

"If there are, they would be in the safe too. Unless he needed the info at the office, then he would have taken one with him. Since he was going on a business trip, it's hard to say what he took. But it would not have been an original. Especially after the fiasco with his ex-partner."

"Excuse me for a moment. Your house will be the next target if the intruder didn't find what he was looking for here." Miacoh turned, retraced his steps to the back door. Once outside, he flagged down his officer and the sheriff's deputies. "Would the three of you mind checking out this address?" He handed his business card with Gabby's home address on the back to his officer. "If the perps didn't find what they were looking for here, the home address will be next. Report back to me as soon as you get there. Mrs. Alrich and I will be along shortly."

A drizzling rain began as he stood outside pondering his next move. *Could things get any more complicated?* He moved under the overhang at the back door. The fog rolled in making the landscape look like something out of TV murder mystery. His phone pinged indicating an incoming text.

CB —*All's quiet here. No movement. How about on your end?*—

—*Good to hear. Whoever broke in ransacked Ben's office, computer and a few files are missing. Will be a late night.*—

CB —*I won't wait up. Got a busy day at the office tomorrow. Don't keep Cayson too late, he's got early morning service calls and is booked all day.*—

—*Copy that. Night.*—

He tipped back his hat and heaved a relieved sigh. Two sets of footsteps descended the stairs.

Cayson emerged first followed by Gabby. "Not much more we can do here tonight."

"I called the 24-hour insurance line and reported the break in. They'll have someone out here tomorrow." Gabby held tight to her shoulder bag. "I'll meet them here. After I drop the kids off at school."

"I'll station one of my officers at the school to avoid any in-law problems. You do know you're going to have to meet with them soon. Straighten this out or get a restraining order."

"I was going to do it tomorrow while the twins are in school. Now, I have to meet with the insurance company. Hopefully, I can have a sit-down with my in-laws tomorrow afternoon before the kids get out of school."

"Sounds like a plan. Keep me in the loop. Give Cayson your house keys. He'll go over to your house and check it out. Where is your safe located?"

"It's in a panel under the floor on the left side of our bedroom closet."

Cayson caught the tossed keys mid-air. "I'll let you know if anything has been tampered with. If not, I'm going to head home after picking up my truck, then get some shuteye. Got a long day tomorrow that starts before dawn." He pulled his collar around his neck and dashed out into the rain to the car.

Miacoh and Gabby dashed for the squad car. Once inside, he turned on the wipers to clear the window as the rain continued to splatter. His cell buzzed. He looked at the screen. "Its my officer." He tapped the screen and put the phone to his ear.

Chapter Eight

Long Day Starting Before Dawn Nets a Few Surprises.

The buzzing of Cayson's alarm sounded a long way off as he rolled over and squinted at the time display. The urge to smash the damn thing was strong, but he avoided temptation and tapped the off button. The glorious aroma of freshly brewed coffee floated into the bedroom. Thank goodness for timed coffee makers. He got to his feet, stretched his arms toward the ceiling, then bent from side to side. After gathering his clothes, he padded over to the window he'd left open just a crack. The pre-dawn hours were his favorite time of day even after only a couple hours of sleep. Inhaling deeply of the crisp morning air, every fiber of his being slugged off the night's sleepiness and embraced the morning. Wisps of lacy clouds floated across the moon and trees swayed in the light morning breeze casting shadows on the surrounding area. Soon the sky would burst into bright yellows, oranges, and red as Mother Nature welcomed a new day. Sauntering to the bathroom, he turned the shower on full cold, then adjusted it to cool, shivering as the water hit his warm skin.

In the chair next to his bed, he pulled on blue jeans, his company logo shirt, shoved his socked feet into boots, and strolled into the kitchen. A bag of bagels sat in front of the toaster. He popped two down, poured the steaming hot coffee into a go cup, and the rest into a large thermos. The bagels popped up. He smeared cream cheese on them and dropped the goodies into a thermal bag.

I'll offer to take Molly to breakfast after Gabby's upgrade is done. Providing nothing goes wrong. On his way home the night before, he'd stopped by Gabby's, as instructed, and made sure nothing was amiss. No one had tampered with the doors or the hidden safe, no suspicious vehicles in the vicinity; so he'd reported to Miacoh, picked up his truck, and arrived home close to one o'clock in the morning. Running on two and a half hours of sleep would catch up with him quickly, thus the big thermos of coffee.

With Molly's help, he hoped to knock out the rest of his service calls, drop her at Terrabyte, and go home early. He scrubbed his hand over his face, then gulped down half the go cup of coffee. *This will never work. I'll have the mug of coffee gone before I leave the driveway.* After adding two scoops of coffee to the machine, he washed the glass pot and slid it under the fill spout. The pot sputtered and hissed as the water on the bottom evaporated on the warmer. He gathered his equipment bag, slung it over his shoulder, and bounded out to the truck. The rain-washed spring mountain air had a bite to it as he rushed back to the house. He downed the rest of his mug and refilled it. Then he poured more of the steaming liquid into another thermos, gathered the bagels bag and original thermos, and grabbed a jacket. The lacy clouds were building storm clouds to the west over the mountains.

A thin orange line gave the first hint of dawn as he pulled in front of Molly's safe house. Before he could make his way up the path, she came bounding out of the door and shut and locked it.

"Good morning, Cayson! Such a glorious day looks to be on hand." She danced down the steps across the path, then whirled around in front of him grinning. Her long black braid bounced down her back, and her brown eyes sparkled as her feet skidded to a stop before him. Surveying him from head to toe in the porch light, she blinked. "Someone pulled you through a knot hole backward?" She paused. "Rough night?"

"Yeah, break-in at Ben's—Gabby's husband's office last night. Really tore up the place. Didn't get home until about one this morning."

"Anything missing? Any word on Gabby's Ben?"

"Files and his computer. Doesn't appear they found what they were looking for, according to Gabby."

"That poor woman, missing husband, problem in-laws, twins, and now she'll have to deal with the insurance company to put things right at the office."

He nodded while walking to the truck. "Wait, how'd you know about the in-laws?"

"Your voice carries something awful. I have excellent hearing. The phone call last night." She tugged at the shirt she had on. "I washed Gabby's shirt last night, so I'd be in uniform today. I'll get with Candle sometime later this afternoon. See what she wants me to wear in the office." She tilted her head up to peer at him. "Or will I be working with you most of the time?"

"I have no idea. Today, we have the security upgrade at Gabby's house in addition to what was already scheduled. So, I'm calling dibs on you for the day. If we get done early, I'll drop you at the office and I'm going home to get more shuteye." He yawned, took another swig of coffee from his mug, and handed her the small thermos.

She turned to ensure her bag was still in the back seat where she'd left it last night. "Looks like you have enough coffee for a small army. If that's what's in that huge thermos."

"Are you always this chipper in the morning?" He tried to keep the irritation out of his voice.

"No. I'm usually a night owl. Allergic to morning—really. But this is the first time I've gotten a good night's sleep in months and am not so worried about the day ahead. Besides, I like a challenge and learning something new." She glanced at him. "I'll shut up now."

He smiled. "There's a bagel in the bag for you to go with the coffee. Depending on how long we're at Gabby's house, we should have time for breakfast afterward. My treat."

"Sounds great." She took the bagels out of the bag, handed one to him, and took a bite out of hers. "Yum."

The thin orange line burst into fiery fingers of red, yellow, and orange as the sun rose over the eastern horizon. When they neared Gabby's house, he slowed the truck, circled her block, then another making sure there was nothing suspicious in the area. He backed into her driveway and unloaded the additional security cameras, motion detectors, spools of wiring, and miscellaneous upgrades. He handed Molly several sheets of paper.

"Listed on the first page are the serial and model

numbers of the additional equipment we'll be adding to her system. Her system's username and password are at the top of the page. The directions are on the other pages. If you have any problems, let me know." He unlocked the door and pointed to a closet across the room. "All the equipment is in there and she has another computer and monitor in their master bedroom upstairs. Once everything is connected, we'll need to make sure the devices are all communicating with each other before we leave."

"Got ya." Molly strode to the closet and tried to turn the knob. "It's locked."

"Oh, yeah, the twins." He examined the key ring he'd been given, walked across the room, and tossed the ring to her. "Bet one of these keys fits the closet. I need to get outside, so nothing grows legs and walks off."

"It's way too early in the morning for people to be up to mischief." She tried the first key, then the second which turned in the lock. "Success."

"Great. Holler if you need anything." He spent the next three hours installing the cameras so they wouldn't be detected. He installed outdoor, wireless motion detectors around the perimeter, and he made sure their range went from the ground to above the house with no gaps in coverage. Only once did he have to assist Molly. Otherwise, she got the new installations up and operating on the system without a glitch. *She is impressive.*

Gathering up the boxes and miscellaneous items, he tossed them in the garbage bin or spare parts drawer in his truck. He slid into the seat of his truck, prepared the invoice on his tablet, and sent it to Candle at the office, then sprinted to the front door. "Hey, Molly, you about ready to leave?"

"Yep. I made sure the computer upstairs talked with the unit downstairs, then called the police department to make sure they were connected and the license was updated. There is a small filing cabinet, the key is on the key ring, in the closet with the previous alarm information in it. I took an empty file folder and put all the paperwork in it." She waved around a green folder. "What should we do with it? I don't feel comfortable just tucking it back in the file cabinet."

"No." He took the folder from her. "We'll give it to Candle. She can attach the invoice to it and give it to Gabby." He wrapped his arm around her shoulder and squeezed her to him. "Look at you, Ms. Efficient alarm programmer. You've earned yourself a big breakfast at the best place in town, Sunrise Cafe, which happens to be across the street and down a block from Terrabyte Security. We'll drop the paperwork off, eat, then drive to the next job."

A closed sign still hung in the office window and only the undercover car sat in the parking lot. "Candle must have had a late night too. She's usually here shortly after the crack of dawn."

He unlocked the door and held it open for Molly as Candle charged out of the police station next door. "Hey, boss, how are things? Any word from Ben?"

Candle rushed through the door to the office. "No, unfortunately. But his phone just came online. I want to see if I can triangulate its whereabouts with one of my own programs. Molly can catch the phones while I work on this."

Cayson grabbed Molly's arm. "Oh, no. Leave the

answering service on. She's coming with me the rest of the day. I'll return her later this afternoon."

"Hey, I'm not some piece of equipment you can squabble over." Molly grinned but didn't pull away from him.

"Oh, is that how it is, big man? You call the shots now?" Candle stared at him.

"No. I'm running on two hours of sleep and don't want to make any mistakes by trying to finish everything by myself and on time."

Candle snorted and waved her hand dismissively. "Don't worry about it. You can have Molly for now. Except her shirts won't get ordered until she gets back here. I moved two of your installations from this afternoon until tomorrow and Friday. New schedules are on your desk. Figured you'd be beat today. However, if I locate Ben's phone and it's not just tossed, I'll need all hands on deck. It's a long shot, but it's all we've got. Cases come first." She booted up the computer and searched the screen. "Molly, we may have a lead on your stalker too. One of Miacoh's officers is working on it."

"That's wonderful." Molly clapped her hands, then quickly settled down. "It's one of the TA's isn't it?

Candle shrugged her shoulders. "Name didn't ring a bell, but I'm not familiar with all the new TA's since the professor disappeared and the new school year started. When I get the report, I'll put it on your desk." She motioned to Gabby's old desk.

"Thank you."

"Understood. Molly and I are going to get breakfast down the street. I'll call you before we leave. Can we bring you anything?" Cayson asked.

Candle's eyebrow rose nearly to her hairline. "Taking Molly to breakfast. Huh?" She moved the mouse and tapped it. A map spread across the screen. "No, I had breakfast with Miacoh."

He frowned and pursed his lips. "It's not like that. We started work before dawn. Neither of us had much of a breakfast. So, it's only right." He handed her the green file and quickly filled her in on the installation.

"Sure, you keep telling yourself that. Now, get out of here before I change my mind." Candle's gaze locked onto the computer screen.

Cayson, his hand at the small of her back, guided Molly out of the office hurriedly. They nearly ran smack dab into Miacoh when he burst out of the police station, turned on his heel, and rushed for Terrabyte's office.

Cayson paused in the middle of the sidewalk. "Got a break on Ben's whereabouts?"

"Not sure. If we do, you'll be one of the first to know." Miacoh yanked open the office door.

Puffing his cheeks out, Cayson released a breath. "Better hurry, if we are going to get anything to eat."

Molly turned to see Miacoh disappear into the office. "Is it always this hectic?"

"Not in the beginning, but appears things are picking up, which is a good thing for us all. Sure hope they got a lead on Ben."

Chapter Nine

Lucky Break in the Case or False Hope.

Candle glanced up from the computer as Miacoh shoved through the door to Terrabyte. The crisp early morning breeze sent a chill through the office and swept papers to the floor. The pup jumped up from her blanket, all wiggles to greet him.

He paused to ruffle her fur and picked up the documents, putting them back on Candle's desk. "Got anything?" His boots squeaked when he came to an abrupt stop behind her, staring at the map on the screen.

"Yeah, but it appears they're off the shore of the Pacific Ocean." She pointed to the screen where a small red blip blinked. "Looks like they are returning to the coast."

"It's an airplane. They have him on an airplane. Only explanation for the location. Wouldn't be on a boat. Can't move fast enough if the police were closing in." He shoved his hands in his pockets.

She glanced up at him hopefully. "Are they?"

"Unfortunately not, but I did send a BOLO to all major airports, including LAX and Sacramento International Airport. Can't believe whoever they are would risk landing at one of those airports. Security is tight with enough manpower to assist us if…" He paused. The blip was now moving north hugging the shoreline then disappeared.

"No. No." She grabbed the sides of the monitor and shook it.

He put his hand gently on her arm. "Hey, not the monitor's fault." Suddenly, the blip appeared again, this time close to Sacramento appearing to make a large circle. "Hey, there is a small airport in that area. I've a friend that works or worked there." He yanked his cell out of his pocket and scrolled down the screen while pacing across the room. A smile spread across his face. "Bridger, how ya doing?" He paused for a long moment. "Know how that goes. So you're still working at the little airport near Sacramento?" Another pause. "I need a favor and it's urgent. There is a possibility a plane with a kidnap victim aboard is about to land at your airport. Any chance you got security?" Another pause. "I was afraid of that. No, I'm not positive. Don't know how many men are on the plane either. The victim's phone just came back online. We're tracking it and it appears to be circling above your location. There is a BOLO out. But the specifics on the plane are sketchy. I can send you a picture of the victim, Ben Alrich."

She heard Bridger's exclamation. "No shit."

"Yep, one in the same. He's married to my wife's best friend. Terrabyte Security, my wife's company, was hired by her to find him when he went missing. A multiple-agency situation with Pitkin County and a long story. I'm the police chief in our little town, Aspen Ridge. Is that enough info plus the BOLO for you to move on it?" Miacoh hit speaker phone as she tried to pull the phone into her hearing range.

"Yep, I'll see what we can do. At this point, I don't

see an airplane on the ground, but one is circling. We'll stall them while I get a police presence here without alarming the pilot. No promises."

"That's all I ask. Don't mean to put you on the spot, but rescuing Ben is priority one."

"Understood." Bridger disconnected the call.

"I hope he's on that plane." She chewed on her bottom lip. "What about Pitkin?"

"They're my next call." He strode out of the office and sprinted to the police station.

After he disappeared from her sight, she returned to the blip on the screen. "Please don't lose that connection." *It's got to be Ben.* Glancing at her phone, she scrolled to Gabby's name, hesitated, then swiped up. *Not going to get Gabby's hopes up until we are sure.* At this moment, California seemed a million miles away. She picked up Molly's employment paperwork off the desk and reviewed the background check she'd sent out yesterday. The woman was as she presented herself. *Good hire.* Taking out an order form, she wrote Molly's name across the top. That task would wait until tomorrow when she had Molly's size, preferred colors, and long or short sleeved.

Candle's glance returned to the computer screen. The blip was still circling. She crossed her fingers and looked down at Terrabyte curled up on her rug over in the corner. *Oh, to have a dog's life.* Shaking her head, she reconsidered. *Probably not.* Almost as if the pup knew Candle was looking at her, she rolled over, stretched kicking both hind legs, and yawned wide, her purple tongue lolling out for a moment. Her chocolate-brown eyes looked up at her person and gave a doggy smile and a tail wag before returning to her belly then resting her head on her paws.

She pulled out a crimson file folder, affixed a name tag on it, and arranged Molly's employee packet inside along with the background search, then slipped it into the wooden employee cabinet and locked it. Next, she slid all the paperwork Molly had given her, along with notes on the investigation so far into another folder, green this time, and filed it among the active cases in the blue filing cabinet.

Already open and spread across her desk, Candle rifled through Gabby's file, comparing her notes to Miacoh's, then picked up the background check on Ben's ex-partner. A knot formed in her stomach. On the surface he was squeaky clean, but the deeper you dug, the more suspicious his actions and acquaintances appeared in the months before the breakup. *Ben was right to cut him loose. Had some of those acquaintances been responsible for Ben's abduction? Why ransack Ben's office? Had the ex-partner promised something he couldn't deliver? That had to be it.* Unable to sit still any longer, she shoved up from her chair and glanced at the screen. The blip had stopped moving and the signal was getting weaker. From the hook on the wall, she grabbed Terra's leash, clipped it on her harness, and yanked open the door. She sprinted down the sidewalk toward the police department, the dog running to keep up with her. She burst through the front door, past the front desk, and raced down the hall to Miacoh's office. The officer she left in the wake of her appearance followed asking, "May I help you, Candle?"

"Nope, gotta see Miacoh." Skidding to a stop at her husband's door, she knocked, then rushed inside. "The blip is stationary and fading. We've got to do something."

Miacoh held up his hand to silence her, then motioned for her to sit in a chair opposite his desk. Phone to his ear, he listened to an excited voice on the other end. Candle couldn't make out the conversation only the tone. She edged closer, leaning far over the desk.

In order to keep Candle from crawling on the desktop, Miacoh interrupted Bridger. "I'm going to record this conversation and put you on speaker phone since Candle just arrived. Okay with you?"

"Sure."

Bridger gulped in a breath and excitedly continued. "Okay, so here's the blow by blow. There were four men on the plane. When airport security approached them, three of them fled, jerking one man along with them. The man broke loose and dove to the ground as another man fired at him on the run but missed. The man that broke loose rolled under the plane, jumped up, and ran for security, his hands raised in the air. Airport security tackled the shooter. Sirens blaring, local police arrived. Their cruiser skidded sideways in the path of the man with a beard who slid up and over their hood landing on his feet. Before he caught his balance, the officers jumped out of the vehicle and shoved him to the tarmac handcuffing him." The excitement left Bridger's voice and he sucked in another breath. "The other man dressed in a suit escaped. Police are still searching for him."

Miacoh paused for a beat or two. "If he gets to the main drag around the airport, he's as good as gone."

"I know it. There just wasn't enough time or manpower to—"

"I totally understand. Thank you for all your assistance, Bridger. I appreciate your efforts regardless of how it turns out. Please call me back when the men have been identified."

"You got it. This is the most excitement we've had around here in a long time."

"Gotta keep you on your toes." Miacoh disconnected the call and rubbed the back of his neck. "Now we wait. Pitkin County will take it from here. After all, it is their case. They'll be none too happy with me as it is."

"Was Ben on that plane?"

"Well, the occupants sure didn't want to cooperate with airport security from the time they landed. Or they were drug runners. We'll have to wait and see. Either way, Bridger had an exciting day." He glanced her way. "Want anything? Coffee, tea, me?"

"At a time like this—you joke?" Candle frowned hands fisted on her hips.

"Hey, gotta deal with the stress of the job some way. Humor is better than other avenues."

"True." She nodded. When her phone rang, she jumped. Checking the screen, she peered at Miacoh. "It's Gabby. What do I tell her?"

"Nothing until we can confirm whether or not Ben was on that plane."

"Okaaayy—" She tapped the screen. "Hey, Gabby, what's up?"

"I've dropped the kids at school reiterating the instructions they are not to leave with anyone but me and you. I've a meeting with the in-laws in thirty minutes at Rosemary's cafe, a public place. Hopefully they'll behave themselves. I can't stand much more drama. I feel like I'm living in a nightmare and can't wake up. You guys left the house mighty early this morning. Was the limo still there? When the kids and I ate breakfast and left, the limo was gone. But I picked up a tail after dropping the kids at the school. I circled back, stopped, and reminded the school again."

"Do you want me to attend the meeting with you? I want to make sure they don't attempt to kidnap you in order to get to the kids."

"Hadn't thought about that." Gabby paused. "Not a bad idea. Maybe you could arrive early, grab a table, and keep an eye on things."

"Done. I'm on my way." She stepped away from Miacoh's desk. "Guess I'm sorta meeting Gabby at Rosemary's. She has a meeting with the in-laws."

"Neither of you should go alone." He rubbed the stubble on his chin. "I've got to deal with the fallout from Pitkin County, so I can't leave. Are Cayson and Molly tied up for the rest of the day?" He walked her out of the station.

She paused outside her vehicle and opened the door. "They already finished Gabby's upgrades this morning and will knock out the other two service calls by early afternoon. But that's doesn't help us now. We'll be all right."

"I'll have Officer Camarono drive by the cafe on his route and stick close. Keep me in the loop."

"Copy that. You let me know the minute the men at the airport are identified." She hopped into the vehicle, rolled the window down, and gave her husband a smacking kiss.

"Hey, lady. Public appearance to keep up." He grinned.

She gave him a sloppy salute. "10-4."

Chapter Ten

Trust If Freely Given Could Be A Bust or A Boon—
Which Will It Be?

For Molly trust had always been buried deep. She fingered the spreadsheet in her pocket that listed possible suspects stalking her, the times, dates, and locations. Also it listed the possible suspects in Kinley Jaybird's disappearance. She'd contacted the authorities, but after the initial report, nothing happened, though she checked in daily.

The last time she checked in the officer in charge of the case told her, "Another college kid on a bender. She'll find her way home soon."

"You're only saying that because she was Native American. Kinley wasn't that type of girl." She'd gotten so angry she'd marched back to her apartment and grabbed a copy of her thesis on indigenous women going missing or murdered and the lack of resolution of these cases. Returning to the police station, she'd slammed the report on the officer's desk. "You're part of the problem. A woman is missing, could be a victim of foul play, yet here you sit on your ass—" She'd been escorted off the premises.

Cayson whipped the steering wheel left onto a dirt road. The jostling yanked Molly out of her thoughts.

"Next service call is Wolicks. They moved into

Aspen Ridge from Raven's Hollow shortly after the Jansen family. Kinda for the same reasons. Moon is an ER nurse and Peter is a contractor." He paused as if considering saying more, then stopped.

"What were you going to say?" She glanced in his direction. *The man was attractive in a rugged kind of way. Chiseled features, muscular build, large sapphire-blue eyes rimmed with thick lashes any woman would kill for, shaggy, shoulder-length surfer blond hair...and a relaxed air about him, as if he could do anything— Oh stop it. It's business.* She sighed.

"Nothing. You'll see. According to the work order, outside security cameras quit working. I installed their system a couple of months ago. Sometimes equipment is faulty, but not all at the same time." He scratched his head and readjusted his hat. "We'll start troubleshooting the conduit from the house to the first camera." He slowed to a stop in front of a Cape Cod style cabin, one and half stories with stone and aspen exterior. A front porch ran the full length of the home. A quaint porch swing gently swayed in the breeze at one end. "We're here."

Molly climbed out of the truck, put her tool-belt on, and followed Cayson who knocked on the door.

"Good morning, Cayson." A pleasant man with a full head of dark hair answered the door.

"Hey, Peter. Hear you're having trouble with your outside cameras." Cayson offered his hand, then nodded toward her. "This is my assistant, Molly. I was just telling her we would start the troubleshooting at the line that runs outside to the cameras."

Rather sheepishly the man shifted from foot to foot. "I'm afraid that after we called you, we confronted our oldest son. Apparently, Future and his little sister were playing in the back yard—He caught the wiring conduit, cut through it with his equipment, whether that be teeth or toy excavator. Gave him a bit of a sting but he didn't say a word. His sister Fantasy ratted him out." Peter motioned them around the house to the back yard where a roll of wiring lay next to an area that had recently been excavated and replaced. A toy excavator and yellow dump truck were parked outside the hole.

"Playing construction, huh?" Cayson chuckled.

"Apparently. Future helped dig the hole with his claws. Not sure what role Fantasy played in their endeavor, but both have been punished and vowed never to do it again." Peter blew out a breath. "Living in a mortal community is a challenge for the young ones."

Yipping and howling, a couple of large dogs rushed by them.

Molly furrowed her brow and glanced from Cayson to Peter. Her thoughts drifted back to the Jansen family. But Peter definitely wasn't a fairy. Then the dogs transformed into two human-looking children and raced into the house. *Werewolves?*

Peter cursed. "Excuse me." He loped into the house after the children.

"Let's get to work while Peter takes care of his situation." Cayson chuckled and wrote "supplied by owner" under the materials column of the work order.

"You suspected it was a severed wire. Didn't you?" She shaded her eyes with her hand and stared up at him.

"Yeah, werewolf pups at Future and Fantasy's ages have a propensity to dig."

"I thought werewolves didn't change until puberty.

Or at least that's what some of my ancestors passed down regarding the werewolf genes or myths."

Cayson glanced at her, eyebrow quirked as he cut the frayed wires, stripped the insulation, and added new wiring. "Molly, please measure and cut metal sheathing to run from the house underground to the first camera."

"Will do."

"Clearly, werewolves aren't myths. Both kids apparently took after Peter. Moon is mortal and much happier in the ER at Aspen Ridge's Hospital than in the emergency room at Raven's Hollow." Cayson shivered. "I can only imagine what types of cases she saw there. Not that I have anything against the paranormal, but from a medical standpoint the physiology alone…"

She finished measuring for the metal sheathing, cut and handed it to Cayson who pulled the wire through and buried it underground. He then climbed the tree to replace the original wiring to the camera. "All set." He jumped out of the tree to land beside her.

Peter stepped outside with two chagrined children at his side. He looked down at them. "Did you have something to say to Cayson and Molly?"

The children brought their gazes up to first Molly then Cayson. "We're sorry for the trouble we've caused." Future peered over at where the hole had been. "And for shifting in front of you."

Fantasy licked her lips and shook her head vehemently. "That's a big no no." She pointed to her brother then stepped behind her father.

"Last night was a full moon. It's hard when you're only eight and nine years old to resist the pull of the moon for change. One of the many things we deal with on a daily basis in a normal town. But we are adjusting and Moon is so happy here," Peter said wistfully. "We'll make it work."

"No problem here." Cayson nodded to Molly who nodded as well. "This is a very understanding town. You'll do fine. The damage is all repaired. I used a metal sheathing this time from the house to the first camera in line. If you'd just check your computer monitors to make sure everything is operational, we'll be on our way."

Peter turned with his two children and walked toward the house. "Won't you come in and have something to drink? I've iced tea, lemonade, and soda."

He followed Peter into the house and watched as he checked the computer monitors. "Looks great to me."

"We've a tight schedule today, so we'll be on our way. But a can of lemon-lime soda and a cola would be great."

Molly smiled and took the lemon-lime soda from Peter. *Can Cayson read my mind? Oh, that's silly.* Still, she watched as his back muscles rippled under his T-shirt when he reached for the drink. *He was fine.*

Cayson took the cola. "Thanks. Just give us a call if you have any more problems—with the alarm system." He grinned.

Peter bent down and hugged his children to him. "There won't be any more problems with the alarm system. Right, kids?"

Future and Fantasy peered at their father and shook their heads solemnly.

The next service call was a new install at the Turners'. They were an older couple who'd watched the town grow up around them after they put the well-kept, white house with sunny yellow trim, and a picket fence in the middle of town.

Cayson handed Molly a roll of wire. He picked up the box of equipment for the install. Three hours later, Molly demonstrated how the system worked to the couple. The woman wrote everything down then clicked her tongue.

"I hope we can remember all the steps." She glanced at her husband.

Mr. Turner laid a hand on his wife's shoulder. "We will."

Molly waved a hand in dismissal. "If you have a problem, don't hesitate to call me at Terrabyte. I'll happily walk you through the steps over the phone."

The couple walked them to the door. "Thank you so much."

She and Cayson waved as they walked out the door.

"Thanks for all your help today." Cayson smiled down at Molly, his arm around her waist as he gave her a squeeze.

She glanced up at him. "You're welcome. You're a great instructor." She held his gaze a little longer than necessary feeling a connection to him she didn't know what to do with. She dipped her head down, then stuck her hand in her pocket and again fingered the spreadsheet. *Should I share it with him? Or Candle? Or maybe Miacoh?*

Cayson yawned and stretched his arms over his head one at a time while still holding the steering wheel. "Last night was brutal. Today was busy but short—thankfully." He glanced at his watch. "Too late to drop you off at the office. I'll just let you off at the safe house."

"When you drop me off at the safe house, why don't you come in? I'll throw together dinner from the frozen food Candle and Miacoh left. Then you can go home and get some rest."

He yawned again. "I'm really beat. Can I have a rain check?"

"You gotta eat. Going to bed on an empty stomach is not smart. Especially this early. You'll wake up in the middle of the night starving. I bet there's not much to eat in your house either."

"Have you been to my house?" he countered. "But you're right. It's been a while since I've done grocery shopping. It's on my to-do list." After driving around the house, once, he slowed the truck and stopped in front of the safe house. "You talked me into it. I'll let you make me dinner. Then I'm off to bed." He snickered. "My bed. Just for clarification."

"Your bed. Of course." She hopped out of the truck and sprinted to the door. "Come on in and make yourself comfortable. I'll have dinner ready in a jiffy." In the freezer she found chicken Alfredo and garlic bread. "Perfect." She heated the oven for the garlic bread and popped the Alfredo into the microwave, then put on a pot of coffee. When she returned to the family room, he was sprawled out on the sofa sound asleep His phone was vibrating on the sofa beside him.

Should I wake him? She glanced at the screen; it was Candle. She tiptoed to the sofa, picked up the phone, and hurried to the kitchen. "Candle, it's Molly."

"Molly. Where's Cayson? Is everything all right?"

"Yes, yes, everything is fine. Cayson was so tired, I offered to make dinner for him and send him on his way, after a couple cups of coffee. I got things out of the freezer, put them in the oven and microwave, and put on the coffee. When I went to find him, he was sound asleep on my sofa, his phone vibrating next to him. If you need me to wake him, I will. Didn't mean to butt into his business." She paused and sucked in a breath. "I'm rambling, huh?"

Candle laughed. "Just a bit. I called to see how things went today and update him on Gabby's case. But it can wait. When you two finish dinner, have him call me on his way home. I need you both in the office in the morning."

"Will do." She plopped on the kitchen chair to wait for dinner to get done. Reaching into her pocket, she took out the folded spreadsheet and smoothed it on the kitchen table reviewing her entries.

A hand touched her shoulder lightly. She jumped out of the chair and squealed, fisting her hand and striking out blindly.

He caught her hand in his and smiled. His attention was riveted to the spreadsheet on the table. "What have we here?"

She tried to gather the paper to her and out of his sight to no avail. He leaned over and put his hand on her shoulder studying the sheets of paper.

"Looks like someone has done some investigation work on her own." He continued to study the spreadsheet.

His face was so close to hers, if she turned her head, their lips would meet, or at least her lips would brush his cheek. She sucked in a breath, then let it out slowly.

"Who's this Kinley Jaybird? Is she a friend of yours? She's missing? Did your report her disappearance?" He leaned away and turned his head to peer at her, his brow creased. The timer for the garlic bread went off.

She jumped. "Dinner is almost ready. Wash your hands and I'll set the table." She started to fold up the paper.

He glanced at the oven for a moment, then put his big hand on the paper. "Well?"

"We can discuss it after dinner, if you're interested."

"Hell, yes, I'm interested." He took one more intense look at the spreadsheet and pushed up from the table then walked to the kitchen sink. "You're going to want to share that spreadsheet with Candle."

She bustled around, setting the table, getting the garlic bread out of the oven, and opened the microwave when its timer went off. Everything on the table, she poured coffee in mugs, then turned around, mugs in hand, to find him staring intently at her and then at the spreadsheet.

"What secrets are you keeping, Molly? You know what Candle said." His expression seemed somber, but there was a twinkle in his beautiful deep-blue eyes.

"Nothing that I can't explain after dinner."

"I'll hold you to that." He smiled and caught her hand. "Thank you for dinner. I'm starved." He kissed her hand and slowly released it.

Flustered, she stuck her hand in her pocket. "Candle called. You were asleep. Candle wanted an update from you and had one on Gabby's case. It's all right to call her back after dinner."

"Thanks. I'll do that on my way home. Hopefully, it's good news. If it was urgent, she'd had you wake me."

"No, she said it could wait," Molly explained the spreadsheet in between bites of Alfredo noodles. She shook her head and took a bite of garlic bread. "Law enforcement spends lots more time, money, and resources on other missing persons than on missing or murdered indigenous women. It's astounding how law enforcement turns a blind eye to the situation." She waved her half-eaten piece of garlic bread around.

"It could be a matter of not enough resources and manpower, or you know, a case of the squeaky wheel gets the attention." Cayson scooped up the last forkful of Alfredo and slid it in his mouth. "Candle is one hell of a cook."

"She sure is. I've enjoyed every meal she prepared."

He covered his mouth as he yawned wide. "I'd better be on my way. Thanks for dinner. I'll pick you up bright and early in the morning." He stood, rinsed his dishes in the sink, and stacked them in the dishwasher.

She walked him to the door and opened it. A bright full moon lit up the horizon. "Mr. Wolick was right. Too bad it causes trouble for his family. The moon is beautiful."

"The full moon causes all kinds of behavior even in normal people. Nurses in hospital ERs and law enforcement will attest to that." Cayson paused on the porch to study her. He leaned over then tipped her chin up.

Standing on her tiptoes, she leaned into him and licked her lips as he gently brushed his lips over hers.

He backed away slowly. "See what I mean. It's the

full moon. I don't know what came over me. Sorry."

She smiled shyly. "I'm not. See you in the morning." She stepped into the house and started to close the door. Cayson's foot stopped her.

"Don't forget to set the alarm. If anything seems suspicious, hit the panic button." He removed his booted foot.

"Got it." She closed the door but peeked out the curtain watching him leave. Touching her fingers to her lips, she wondered at the desire zinging through her. Cayson was dangerous.

Chapter Eleven

Women, a Dangerous Breed. Good News on the Investigation—But...

That woman had put a spell on him. Never had he acted so impulsively with a woman. Not just any woman, but one he was working with or could even be considered a client. *I got to get myself under control.* He licked his lips. *But her lips were so full, soft, and moist. The memory...* He shook his head. It couldn't happen again. Leaning against his truck, he gazed up at the night sky where striated clouds floated across the full moon in the star-strewn night sky. Soon, sunset would be later. He looked forward to longer days. He sighed and pulled his cell out of his pocket. Suddenly, the wind tugged at his truck door when he climbed into the truck. He glanced to the west where storm clouds gathered. *We're in for a blow tonight.* Giving her house one last look, he punched in the number to Terrabyte. *What was it about the woman? I'm drawn to her like a moth to flame with the same consequences if I'm not careful.*

Candle answered on the first ring. "Spending a lot of time these days with Molly, aren't you?" She snickered.

"No. You assigned her to work with me. I'm doing as the boss says."

"A little defensive, aren't you?" Candle chided and snickered again. "You must be tired to let me get under your skin so easily. I'm putting you on speaker phone. Miacoh is standing here. We have great news."

"Spill it. Instead of—"

She filled him in, with Miacoh adding a few details. "The best part is that it was Ben on that plane and as soon as the officials are done with him, he'll be on a plane returning home. Gabby was so excited when we told her. It made up for her in-laws petitioning the court for full custody of her twins. They had her served at Rosemary's Cafe where she'd requested a meeting this morning. Those people are a piece of work. No doubt Ben will set them straight as soon as he returns. I'd love to be a fly on the wall at that meeting. So—tell me about breakfast and dinner with Molly."

"Candle, leave him alone. He's tired." Miacoh chuckled. "You can interrogate him tomorrow."

"I'm glad Ben is safe. Do we know why they kidnapped him?"

"We'll ask all those questions when he returns. His business partner is still at large. We think the other man on the plane, who escaped, was picked up on street camera not far from the airport getting into a sports car exactly like Ben's partner's vehicle."

"Wow, then Ben still isn't safe."

"No, we'll post officers outside his home and office until his partner and the other man are apprehended. Shouldn't be long."

"Good. I have news. Molly created a spreadsheet of suspects in her stalking. There is another facet of the situation. Her friend from college, Kinley Jaybird, is missing. She reported her missing to the authorities, but nothing's been done. It's a long story. I'll let her explain. I told her to bring the spreadsheet with her tomorrow morning. We need to do something about getting her transportation."

"At this time in the investigation, I'd just as soon she not be left alone too often. Unless it's too big an imposition for you to pick her up and take her home."

He knew that tone in her voice. She was looking for a reaction from him regarding Molly and he didn't like it. *Yet if I overreact, she'll know something is up between Molly and me. Not that there is.*

"She'll work in the office when I'm here. When I'm not, I'll depend on you to fill in or take her on service or installation jobs. Is that a problem?"

"No, of course not. She's a quick learner and good worker." *Oh, no, I answered that way too quickly.* Gave her just what she was looking for.

"Cayson, ol' man. Go home and get some sleep. You'll be better able to defend yourself against the inquiring, sneaky mind of my wife in the morning. Besides, if she's working at the office, I'm in the next building over. We have surveillance set up at Terrabyte where I or one of my staff can keep on eye on her."

"Gabby's case isn't closed yet. We need to interview Ben. As long as his ex-partner is at large with an accomplice, no telling what they will do. Ben has something they want and appear to be willing to go to any lengths to get it. Depending on the situation, that will spread your little police department too thin." Candle tapped her fingernails on the desktop near the phone.

"Already thought of that. Pitkin will be sharing the burden of protection until we get to the bottom of Ben's situation. It's also possible the FBI may become involved, depending on the nature of the software created at Ben's company and due to kidnapping across state lines. So—I believe it's in everyone's best interest to go home and get some rest. Reconvene in the morning."

Hearing the tapping of Candle's nails over the phone meant she was either thinking, plotting, or—and right now, he didn't want any part of what she was considering. "I'm all for that. Good night, all." Cayson ended the call before more questions came his way. Slowly, he circled around the safe house making sure there was no one lurking before heading home.

These feelings were new for him and dealing with them wasn't what he wanted to do. He'd always been a confirmed bachelor with no plans to change. *I need sleep. Everything will sort itself out tomorrow.* A jaw-popping yawn caught him by surprise. He rolled the window down to let the chilly night air help keep him awake. Lightning streaked across the sky in front of him, followed by a clap of thunder that rattled the truck, then big raindrops splatted on the windshield. *Well, so much for making it home before the storm broke.* He shrugged and turned on the windshield wipers. By the time he pulled in front of his cabin, the rain was so heavy he could barely see a few feet in front of him. Glad for the umbrella he stashed under the seat, he reached for it, opened the truck door and then the umbrella, kicked the door shut, and made a mad dash for the porch. Leaving an umbrella open in the house was bad luck, so his mother said. He unlocked the door and shook the umbrella prior to semi closing it. Before he could get inside, the wind blew the rain directly in the door and soaked him. He slammed the door and tossed the umbrella. He stalked across the floor, took the matches from the mantel, and lit the logs, kindling, and newspaper he'd prepared before leaving this morning. The flames raced up the fuel and soon merrily crackled in the fireplace. Standing in front of the hearth, he kicked off his boots, removed his wet shirt, socks, and jeans, then shook the rain from his hair causing the flames to spit and sizzle. Warmed by the fire, he yawned and eased onto the couch. *I'll only sit here for a minute.* Two hours later he awoke cold and shivering. All that was left of the fire had turned to embers. He pushed up from the couch, trudged toward the bedroom, and paused at the doorway. Too dirty to crawl into bed, he reversed course and padded to the bathroom. After a hot shower, he fell into bed. His last thought was how pleasant a warm, willing female body in bed next to his would be, then Molly's face swam through his mind. "Shit."

Chapter Twelve

Secrets Revealed and a Plan Created.

Candle swung her SUV into the parking lot at Terrabyte Security. Last night's rain left several puddles in the parking lot that needed to be resurfaced. The early morning golden sun's rays bounced off an unfamiliar vehicle parked in the lot. She circled her SUV slowly around the vehicle coming to a stop beside the suspicious car. Blackout windows and tricked out exterior of the SUV made her spidey senses go off. Quickly, she patted the gun in her holster at the small of her back, then stepped out of her vehicle and yanked on the door handle of the other car. To her surprise the door opened. Ben grinned up at her. *Thank God I didn't pull my gun.*

Gabby leaned over her husband. "Surprise. We're back."

Candle leaned down and peered into the vehicle. "Good to see you safe and sound. I see you have the whole crew with you."

"Yep. Kids haven't seen Ben for a few days. We're on our way to a meeting with his parents at our attorney's office. Dan set the meeting up to discuss their petition. What they don't know is Ben is back. When we walk into the office—" Gabby paused.

"—the shit is going to hit the fan and the kids are

going to know the whole story. Can't have this type of thing happen again. Not that I plan on getting kidnapped or anything." Ben shook his head. "Normally, I wouldn't involve the children. But unfortunately, my parents have put Nash and Natalya front and center. I've been far too lenient with my parents for way too long. Time to set out boundaries and consequences." He rubbed the back of his neck and scrubbed his hand over his haggard face. "Been a long few days. But I wanted to stop here first and explain what exactly is going on. Maybe formulate a plan or at least get you thinking on one."

"Ben, shouldn't you be home, maybe resting?" Candle peered at him anxiously then at Gabby.

Gabby threw up her hands. "Ya think. But no, he has his own agenda. Won't listen to me. So here we all are straight from the airport."

"Okay, let's get inside. I'll call Miacoh. He went in early today, something about Pitkin County and the Sacramento police." She shrugged.

"Yeah, Pitkin is arranging the protection detail. I made them aware I have my own security team. But police want to question my team—since I was kidnapped on their watch. Sacramento has a BOLO out on Ken, my old partner and his accomplice." Ben blew out a breath and opened the vehicle door. "What a mess. Do you always approach an unknown vehicle in that manner?"

"I like the element of surprise on my side." Candle grinned and shook Ben's hand as he got out.

Gabby exited her side of the SUV, bounded around the vehicle, and hugged her friend. "What a wild ride. Thank you for all your help."

The twins squealed in the back seat. "Hey, the doors are still locked."

"That's right. What did we discuss?" Ben turned, leaned into the vehicle, and paused.

Nash swung a leg over the front seat in an attempt to climb over and into the front. "You're already out of the car."

Natalya leaned over and peered at her dad. "Never get out of the car until Mom and Dad are out and the back doors are unlocked," she said smugly, smiling sweetly at her dad.

"Now get back in your seat, Nash, and sit down."

As soon as Nash plopped back in his seat, Ben tapped a switch on the dash, a click sounded, and the twins scrambled out of the car.

She let Terrabyte out of the SUV, then led the way to the office, unlocked the door, turned off the alarm, and motioned them to her office. "Hey, kids, there is a video game in the break room. If it's okay with your parents, you're free to play." She leaned over to Gabby. "The games are all rated PG."

Gabby grinned. "I figured. Go ahead, kids. But don't mess with anything else. Understood?"

"Yes, Mom," the twins chorused running through the office with Terrabyte yipping in hot pursuit.

Candle motioned Ben and Gabby to have a seat across from her desk, then pulled her cell phone out of her pocket. Before she could touch the screen, the front office door warning sounded. Miacoh strode in, took off his hat, and clapped Ben on the shoulder. "Good to see you again." He looked him over and scrubbed a hand across his face. "A little worse for wear, but I figure a good night's sleep should cure what ails you."

"I only wish it were that easy." Ben leaned back in his chair. His eyes closed.

She sent a worried glance at Miacoh for a moment, then pasted on a smile and shifted her attention to Ben. "Your partner and his accomplice being still at large must be a serious problem."

"Ya got that right." Gabby put her hands flat on the table.

Ben shot her a warning glance. "If we're going to make it to the lawyer's office on time, let me fill Miacoh and Candle in without interruption."

Gabby sat back with her hands in her lap.

"Go ahead." Candle eased into her chair behind the desk as Miacoh hiked a hip on the corner of it.

"I'll start at the beginning. Our partnership became rocky when Ken Miller, my ex-partner and I disagreed on the use and availability of the latest software I created. Ken was the sales end of our enterprise, while I was the programmer and creator. Ken did some programming, but not a lot in recent years."

"So did your partnership contract set out those parameters?" Miacoh asked.

"Yes. But apparently it didn't go far enough regarding settling disagreements. When we discovered that my ransomware blocker actually worked, Ken got extremely excited and wanted to release it to the open market, with an exorbitant price tag, when the first trials were successful."

"I can see where such software would be highly sought after." Candle tented her fingers and leaned elbows on the desktop. "Terrabyte Security would be quite interested in obtaining copies to keep our clients safe." She paused for a moment. "As would every other cyber security company in the world, not to mention our government as well as foreign ones."

"Yep, that was the problem. All Ken saw was dollar signs, even early on. He didn't care who paid the bill. I wanted to source the programs out to clients, like Terrabyte, maybe the U.S. government. So we put controls on the programs. Ken didn't like it but went along with it. Or at least I thought so. During final testing, a prototype came up missing, though the completed one was still in an encrypted file on my personal laptop in the safe in Aspen Ridge office. I found documents jammed in the shredder in Aspen, with Ken's signature on them, suggesting he'd been in contact with sketchy characters, offering them the programs and negotiating a price. I immediately locked him out of the computer system, changed the locks and entry codes to both offices."

"He was furious." Candle peered at Ben.

"You bet he was. When he broke into the Aspen Office and destroyed equipment in a fit of rage, I had him arrested and Dan, my attorney, dissolved the partnership. Ken filed a lawsuit in court. His claim to half the intellectual property was denied by the court. He failed to return a thumb drive containing the program files and claimed to have destroyed it. I moved everything to Aspen Ridge and closed the Aspen office. Ken threatened I'd not seen the last of him, but he was always a hot head, so I wasn't particularly worried. I'd had a bad feeling about him in recent months, so in order for the program to run, it had to have a patch I created. Without it the program was useless."

"So that's what Ken and associates were looking for when they ransacked your Aspen Ridge office and tried to gain entry into your home. Correct?" Miacoh stood and paced across the floor.

"I imagine the buyer discovered the programs wouldn't work and confronted Ken. He knew I made a practice of leaving out part of the code after testing to make programs work until we were ready to market it. Lots of problems with theft in the computer world. That was our way of protecting ourselves. Other software creators did the same."

"So where is this patch or missing code hidden? I assume they didn't find it." Candle's leather chair squeaked as she shifted.

"Your assumption is correct." He pointed to his temple. "It's all up here. Thought it was the safest place. Didn't anticipate Ken would figure it out and have me kidnapped. I'm still not sure he knows where it's at, but figured he'd force me to tell him once it was discovered the program didn't work."

"Which is why your life and your family's lives are in danger until Ken and accomplice are caught." Candle shook her head noticing Gabby's face was as white as a sheet. "Gabby, you didn't know all this?"

"No, I sure didn't." She turned to her husband, eyes blazing. "How could you put us in that kind of danger?"

"I had no idea Ken was so dangerous. I figured the less you and the twins knew about the business the safer you would be. I wasn't wrong."

"No, they kidnapped you. They could have killed you. What do you think would have happened if Miacoh and Candle hadn't acted on their gut feeling and contacted Miacoh's aviation friend at the airport? I'll tell you what—they'd come after the twins and me."

Gabby huffed, crossing her arms across her chest. "I believe being late for the meeting is the least of our problems."

"Not if they wanted the information. Toward the end of my captivity, Ken may have guessed where the patch is by now. Which is why I'm not sure what to do next. Stationed guards outside the house and office are good, but..."

"I tend to agree with the Pitkin County officers. Your security team could be a problem. If there is a mole in your team, your security is no good." Miacoh shoved his hands in his pockets and pulled them back out.

"I have an idea. There is a little town several miles from here that could possibly temporarily hide you and your family until we can locate and arrest Ken and his accomplice or the entity that bought the defective software. Hopefully, it won't have international ramifications." Candle pushed up from her chair. "One more thing. If the government gets wind of this situation, will the FBI become involved?"

Ben grimaced. "It's possible. Early on, the US government was interested in my prototype. I've not been in contact since its completion. But I don't think we are safe anywhere." Ben frowned and glanced in Gabby's direction.

Miacoh snapped his fingers and smiled at his wife. "You're right. Raven's Hollow is off the grid. The safe houses are unusual and undetectable— Let me contact Jason Jansen, the city attorney for Aspen Ridge. His wife grew up in that town and we'll see what arrangements can be made. If we move fast enough, we'll have this case wrapped up before the FBI gets wind of it, if they do. Until then, your meeting today needs to be moved to the Terrabyte Security office. We won't give any warning; we'll have Cayson and Molly escort your in-laws from the attorney's office with all the individuals concerned and driven here." Miacoh pulled his cell phone out of his pocket.

At the mention of her name, Terrabyte barreled up the hallway skidding around the corner into the lobby and came to a screeching halt in front of Candle, the pup's tail and body wiggling all over. Not far behind, Nash and Natalya rushed into the room.

"What's going on?" Nash fisted his hands at his sides and peered from one adult to another.

"Change of plans. Go on back and play your games. Meeting's been moved to here." Gabby ruffled her son's hair. "So who's winning?"

"I am." Natalya pumped her fist in the air.

"Only because she is cheating," Nash shot back. "I just can't figure out how."

With her hands on her hips, his sister stood her ground. "I am not. Beat you fair and square. You were so busy working on strategies to beat me that you failed to arm your players well. My players destroyed yours."

"Well, that's a first. Guess you better sharpen your skills, son." Ben patted his daughter on the shoulder. "Good job. Now go play. We'll let you know when the others arrive."

Natalya peeked up at her dad. "Will Grams and Pop be mad at us?"

"I won't lie to you. They're going to be unhappy. It's not your fault. We adults just have to get a few things straightened out. Boundaries and consequences. Then things will be great."

"Oh, kinda like the school issue. Huh, Dad?" Nash smiled brightly.

"Exactly. We all want what is best for both of you. Only a minor bump in the road of life. Now go play."

Terrabyte raced circles around the twins, then stopped to nose them in the direction of the breakroom.

"Good girl. Take the kids back to the games." Candle laughed and turned her attention to her husband who ended the call to Cayson.

"All set. They are on their way."

"The only hitch in your plan, Miacoh, is the apprehension of Ben's ex-partner and his accomplice. The FBI sources could be a valuable asset."

"The Sacramento police are searching for them." He paused for a long moment. "As long as we get Ben and family hidden away before the FBI come barging in, they may not be able to muck it up too bad. Like the murder investigation and the explosion at the school last year."

"That was Homeland Security and to be fair, we had more resources and knowledge of the area than they did. The agents didn't have time to get up to speed before all hell broke loose. All's well that ends well." Candle sidled up to Miacoh, put an arm around his shoulder and kissed him.

"So true. I'll visit with Jason as soon as the meeting with Ben's parents is done." Miacoh brushed his lips over hers one last time then turned on his heel and strode toward the front door.

Chapter Thirteen

Sharing Information Brings Unsavory Facts to Light.

The howling wind, lightning and thunder raged until well after midnight, keeping Molly awake. Finally, the storm subsided, and she fell asleep. A scratching, scuffling sound awakened her. She jerked up in bed and stared into the darkness outside her bedroom window. *Was a person's shadow moving outside?*

She blinked, grabbed the cell phone Candle provided, and slid out of bed onto the floor crawling over to the window. The cell's screen displayed two thirty a.m. Her finger hovered over Cayson's number. Another thud and scratching sound, and she slapped her hand over her mouth to keep from squealing. The phone went skittering across the floor.

Then she saw it. A large branch cracked from the tree next to her window and hung down, the smaller branches brushing against the windowpane. She puffed out her cheeks and blew out a breath, got to her knees, and searched the darkened landscape then retrieved the phone.

Adrenalin still raced through her veins making sleep impossible as she crawled into bed. After tossing and turning for what seemed like hours, she gave up. She dressed in a turquoise blouse and pastel print long skirt, brushed her long raven hair, then put it up in a braid that fell nearly to her waist. Turning this way and that in front of the mirror, she nodded. *That should do for office attire.* She packed an additional pair of jeans in the event she was sent on assignment with Cayson later.

Before dawn, Molly paced around the kitchen floor. She made a peanut butter sandwich, added a bag of chips, a cola drink, and slipped it all into her insulated lunch box. Her nerves still a bit jangled, she made hot chocolate and toasted a bagel. The thin orange line on the horizon was a welcome precursor to sunrise. She nibbled on her bagel, sipped the hot chocolate, and enjoyed the first warm rays of sun through her kitchen window.

She was still debating telling Cayson, when his truck slowed and stopped in front of the house. A calm washed through her as he got out of the truck and sauntered up the path to the door. Instead of coming inside, he walked around the house. She waited for him to come in. When he didn't right away, she went to the back door where she'd last seen him. "Whatcha doing out there?"

"Just checking things out. Quite a storm last night." He returned to the door and stepped inside, pausing to look her over. "Wow, you look nice today. Not that I mean you usually don't look nice— I removed that large tree branch before it does any damage to the siding or window."

She smiled. "I'll take the compliment. Storm was terrible, torrential downpour and lightning." She related the events of the night and he stared incredulously at her.

"Why didn't you call me?"

"For a broken tree branch?" She squared her shoulders.

"No. Because when I moved the broken tree limb, there were footprints outside your bedroom window. They lead across the property but were washed away the closer you got to the road."

"Someone was here. It wasn't my imagination playing tricks on me because of the storm." She licked her lips nervously. "Someone knows I'm here," she stammered.

"Now let's not jump to conclusions, yet. Could have been teenagers. Maybe neighbors saw lights earlier, heard the tree crack, and came to investigate."

"Oh, you're good. But you know none of those scenarios are plausible. But thanks for trying to make me feel better." Her face paled.

"How about we grab a couple of those bagels, pour the rest of the hot chocolate off the stove in a go cup, and head to the office? We'll fill Candle and Miacoh in and see how they want to proceed. I've already told them about your spreadsheet. They want to discuss it with you."

"I hope it will help." She grabbed her jacket, bag, lunch box, and keys and followed Cayson out the door, stopping to set the alarm and lock the door.

"I'll mention beefing up the security around the outside of the house to Miacoh. Add a few cameras. It's a different world now than when that safe house was originally commissioned."

The crisp mountain air was cooler than expected and she shrugged into her jacket before climbing into his truck.

Cayson remained outside the truck for a few minutes talking on his phone. When he opened the driver side door and hopped in, he glanced at her. "I filled Candle and Miacoh in on the events of last night. Miacoh authorized the new equipment to be installed at the safe house. But first, we have a short assignment. We need to stop by Gabby and Ben's attorney's office and escort their attorney along with Ben's parents and their attorney to Terrabyte's office. Apparently, a big pow-wow is going to be held at a neutral location."

"Doesn't sound like much fun." She frowned.

"It doesn't, but it's the job. Candle wants you to work in the office this morning. Sounds like Gabby won't be returning to work at Terrabyte anytime soon. We'll escort the parties to the office. I'll leave you there. I'll get the cameras and other equipment to update the safe house. Get that taken care of and see how the afternoon shakes out."

"Did they locate her husband?" She paused for a moment picking at her fingernail. "Don't need help?"

"Yes, they found Ben. Not my call. Candle's the boss." He shot her a reassuring smile. "Like working with me, huh?"

"Of course. I like learning new things and meeting the people in town. Quite a diverse population in Aspen Ridge."

He laughed. "Way to avoid the question. I'll just take it as a yes. I have to agree with you. Things have changed since I arrived and took this position." He hesitated while glancing at the address on the navigator and slowed the truck to a stop. "We're here."

"Shall I stay in the car?" She peered outside at the two-story brick building with large glass doors and a sign that read Law Offices of Goodwell & Brighton then back to Cayson.

"Nope. This is a joint operation." He jumped out of the truck and joined her on the sidewalk. "Follow my lead."

"Copy that." She drew in a breath and walked through the door he held open for her. There were two men and a woman sitting to their right in the plush lobby which included a small coffee bar stocked with pastries.

He walked in behind her and up to the reception desk. "Cayson Eriksson and Ms. Reacher. We are here to escort Mr. Goodwell and Mr. and Mrs. Alrich to a meeting scheduled in thirty minutes."

"Mr. Goodwell is expecting you." The receptionist picked up the phone and pushed a button. "Mr. Eriksson is here."

A large mahogany door opened across the hallway. "I'll be right out."

One of the men in the waiting room leaned over to the other one. "What's going on? Isn't Gabby supposed to meet us here?" The man glanced at his watch, then took his phone out.

Smiling, Mr. Goodwell strode into the lobby. "As I told your attorney, Mr. Waterford, there has been a change of plans."

"We didn't approve any changes," Mr. Alrich blustered then turned his attention to his lawyer. "Why weren't we advised so we could take the appropriate actions?"

"That's exactly why. This meeting is only for the two of you and me. No need for any outside interference." Mr. Waterford glared at his clients. "Now if you both will hand me your cell phones, we'll follow Mr. Cayson and Mr. Goodwell out into the parking lot."

"This is an outrage. I pay your fees, and I expect you to do my bidding as I direct."

"Believe me, I understand. However, over the course of the last week, you have defied my advice and now find yourselves in a situation of your own making. I strongly suggest you take this meeting."

"We aren't going anywhere. I demand that Gabby and the children be brought here as arranged." Mr. Alrich stood and pointed a finger at his attorney's chest.

Cayson walked to the door, opened it, and motioned Molly through it. "Shall we?" He glanced at the others.

"Yes indeed." Mr. Goodwell clapped Cayson on the shoulder. "I believe we will all follow you in separate vehicles. I have a court appearance after the meeting."

Mr. Alrich didn't move a muscle. His wife started to follow their attorney to the door. Mr. Waterford held out his hand. "Cell phones, please."

Mrs. Alrich began to reach into her handbag. Her husband blocked her action.

"We are not turning our cells over to you. What right do you—"

Mr. Waterford leaned over and whispered in Mr. Alrich's ear. His face turned bright red. "This is an outrage." He thrust his cell phone into his attorney's hand. "I'll be talking to the managing partner of your law firm. You can't treat me like this. I'll have you disbarred."

"I'm happy to withdraw as your attorney right now and return your retainer. If you'd like? However, the meeting will be canceled."

"If you—" At his wife's urging, Mr. Alrich stopped mid-sentence and mumbled something under his breath.

"I didn't think so. Now, let's get into my car and follow Mr. Eriksson and his associate to the designated meeting place."

Molly released the breath she'd been holding and walked out beside Cayson. Once inside the truck, she turned to him. "What the heck was all that about?"

He started the engine and glanced in the rear-view mirror to see both vehicles lined up behind him. "Not sure, but I suspect that Mr. and Mrs. Alrich had their hired security lurking somewhere around here poised to snatch the children once Gabby arrived. They're unaware that Ben has returned."

"Oh, that's why no cell phones. He can't relay the change in plans." Molly shook her head. "What a shame. Family is supposed to have your back, not stab you in it."

"Family matters are sometimes complicated." Cayson pulled into traffic and turned toward the Terrabyte office checking his side and rear-view mirrors for unauthorized vehicles.

Slowing, he pulled into the parking lot behind Terrabyte's office and hopped out circling once around the unfamiliar vehicle while waiting for the rest of the group to catch up.

Candle poked her head out the back door. "It's Ben and Gabby's new vehicle. The old one met its demise during the kidnapping." She smiled and motioned everyone into the office.

Ben's parents followed by their attorney burst

through the door accompanied by Cayson and Molly.

"What is the meaning of this?" Ben's father bellowed.

Gabby inched closer to Ben. "Now calm down, everyone. I had this meeting moved to avoid meddling by outside sources."

"Ben! You're back." His mother rushed to envelop him in a hug. "You have no idea what's be going on in your absence." Pointing to Gabby, his mother said, "She put the children in terrible danger—"

"I'm well aware what went on while I was gone. I guarantee it will never happen again. Mom, Dad, Mr. Goodwell, and Mr. Waterford, please step into the conference room." He pushed the door open to a room with a long oval oak table, eight padded chairs, a small refreshment table at the far end, and watercolor landscape paintings lining the walls. "Chief Zane will witness our discussion and any agreement reached."

After everyone entered the room, Miacoh closed the door behind them.

At the sound of voices, Terrabyte and the twins came racing into the office.

"Kids, your mom, dad, and your grandparents are in a meeting. You'll be called when it's your turn to join in. Okay?" Candle caught both twins by the back of the collars. "Terra, sit."

The pup's butt hit the floor, her gaze shifting from the kids to Candle. "Now everyone back in the breakroom. Cookies and chocolate milk coming up."

"How does she do that?" Molly stood there in awe.

"Lots of training." Cayson chuckled. "I'm going to get equipment and install it at the safe house. Candle will keep you busy here. I'll check in later this afternoon." He pointed to Gabby's old desk. "That's your desk. Go ahead and get comfortable. I'm sure Candle will be right back." As he pulled the chair out for her the phone rang. She stared at it.

He grabbed the phone. "Terrabyte Security. This is Cayson; how can I help you?" He paused for a moment. "She's with clients. May I take a message?" He grabbed a phone message pad from the desk and scribbled down a message. "Got it. She'll get back to you soon." He disconnected the call and made a ta-da gesture. "That's how it's done."

"Wow, is there anything you can't do?" She grinned at him.

"Nothing comes to mind. But we can explore that notion—" He waggled his eyebrows. "Later."

"Seriously?" She raised an eyebrow and took the message pad and pen from him. "Don't you have a job to do?"

"Actually, I have more than one. However, protecting your body is priority number one." He sent her a seductive smile.

"Oh, is it?" Candle returned from the break room a Cheshire cat's grin on her face. "Glad to know you take your assignments seriously."

"I'm out of here." Cayson, red-faced to the tips of his ears, scooted across the floor and out the door.

"The man is a puzzle. Talk about running hot and cold all in a matter of seconds." Molly tore her gaze from the door.

"This could turn into a real tangle, what with you working for me too, and a client—and he's responsible for your safety. But you are both consenting adults, so I'll just say watch your step. Cayson is a confirmed bachelor. Or at least he was. Now about your spreadsheet…"

Chapter Fourteen

Molly's Investigations and Indigenous Women Missing.

Candle's chair made fingernails on the chalkboard scratching sounds as she scooted it over to Molly's desk. Molly smoothed out the wrinkles in her spreadsheet on the desk in front of her.

"Let me take a look." She turned the piece of paper toward her and reviewed Molly's document. Pointing to one of the names on the sheet, Candle said, "This is the TA that took your place after you left the school. Right?"

"Well, officially, I haven't left the school. I'm still enrolled. I need access to investigate Kinley's disappearance. But yes. The TA, Greg, was one of the professor's right-hand men or women. Erin is doing time now, but numerous individuals were involved with the professor that went undiscovered. Of course, the minute the professor took off leaving Erin to take the fall, they all were in the wind. When the temporary replacement for the professor was appointed, I was reinstated as TA. However, Greg moved right in before his arrest, demeaning me and my work. Actually, shunning me as if the former professor's trouble was somehow my fault. Even though the truth of my original thesis had come out. Then another TA,

Murdock, and I got into a verbal altercation, and I was dismissed as a troublemaker. Don't know if the current professor believed him or not. Before I was dismissed, I caught Greg in my laptop when I stepped out of the office for a moment and quickly returned. Shortly thereafter, my apartment was broken into, and pages of my original thesis and my current one were scattered all over the floor. Threats were spray painted all over the walls."

"Before his arrest?" Candle scrunched up her face perplexed. "He wasn't one of the ones caught and charged along with Professor James for causing the explosion at the chemistry lab. Was he?"

"Not exactly. Rumors swirled that with the stolen IDs the professor left behind when he fled the country, someone created an identity theft ring in addition to stealing others' research papers. Oh, who knows? Prof. James may have been in on that too before he fled. There were so many rumors bouncing around shortly before and after the lab blew up."

"Like what?"

"His involvement in the sale of drugs, weapons, and all kinds of things. I'm not sure he was that brave to be involved with those types of individuals. Professor was pissed because of the tenure deal. Probably wanted to discredit the school and many of its prestigious students. But hard-core criminal activities? Questionable? Too narcissistic."

She raised an eyebrow and glanced at Molly. "People can surprise you. But he didn't seem the type. Now about the threats. What did they say?"

"To mind my own business or I'd be sorry. That kind of thing." She shrugged. "When I started getting bills for credit cards I didn't own and unauthorized charges on my own credit cards, I figured there must be more to the rumors, and the identity theft nightmare began again. I dropped an anonymous tip that led the police to discover the stolen identity ring operating on school property. It's my understanding the police found credit cards with my name on Greg's person. When they searched his apartment, the authorities found a vehicle purchase invoice with my name and forged signature on it, along with other items not connected to me."

"From other students or what?"

"Police didn't say. Thank goodness Greg never took possession of the vehicle. He supposedly took a plea deal to roll over on the others involved and give up the professor's location. I agreed to testify against him, which is when the stalking and threats began. Greg made bail and disappeared." She paused for a moment. "Didn't Prof. James flee to a country where he couldn't be extradited? Samoa or somewhere?"

"That was my thought too. But you never know what the authorities have up their sleeve." Candle leaned back in the chair and rubbed her eyes. "What about this Murdock? Do you think he's involved? Obviously, someone wanted to scare you from testifying against Greg. Correct?"

Molly nodded. "I guess. Funny, though, once I reported and started looking into Kinley's disappearance, things got worse. Maybe he or the others had something to do with that too. Or it may have been a coincidence."

"Was your friend also one who had her identity stolen?" Candle narrowed her eyes and flipped the spreadsheet over where Molly had outlined her efforts to locate Kinley.

"I have no proof. Though, she was an engineering and chemistry major under Professor James. He had access to her information, thus those involved in the ring would too. The authorities were pretty tight-lipped with me when they asked me to testify. I said no at first, unless they were more forthright with me. Didn't help much. It got worse when I started asking questions about what they were doing to find Kinley."

"You're sure Kinley didn't leave on her own?"

"I'm positive. She never would have left Mocha in her apartment alone without making arrangements for her care."

"Mocha?"

"Yes, Kinley's long-haired guinea pig. A neighbor is taking care of her until I get my world straightened out."

"Huh? And you told the police this when you reported her missing?"

"I did. Kinley got Mocha from a shelter and took her care very seriously. The officers looked at each other, then nodded. I felt they were placating me. As I said, I believe they chalked it up to a student on a bender. But that wasn't her." Molly got up, grabbed her backpack, and rummaged around in it. Finally, she pulled out a folded piece of paper. "Here is the police report. I requested a copy when I felt they wouldn't do anything about it."

Candle took the document, unfolded it, and read it. "The report is thorough. Did you ask for follow-up info?"

"Yes, all I got was they were working on it.

Nothing to report yet. Had she been blonde, blue-eyed—"

"—I know. I'm familiar with the statistics of indigenous women going missing and lack of follow-up."

Molly's voice rose. "Lack of follow-up— Did you know the National Crime Information Center reports that, in 2016, there were 5,712 reports of missing American Indian and Alaska Native women and girls— though the US Department of Justice's federal missing person database, NamUs, only logged 116 cases."

"Wow. That's a big discrepancy. I wasn't aware." Candle paper clipped the report to Molly's spreadsheet.

"Not the exact figures, but it's reported by the CDC murder is a leading cause of death for Native American women. It's a national tragedy that seems to have attracted a blind eye from law enforcement."

Candle nodded patiently waiting for Molly to finish her tirade.

"I'm sorry. I didn't mean to go all soapbox on you. Kinley Jaybird is another complication of my life and a separate case from the stalking one. I'd appreciate your help, but I can understand if you don't have time to get involved."

Candle stood and paced around the desk. "We are never too busy to help people in trouble. My husband and I both have Native American roots. I understand your strong feelings. We'll do everything in our power to find out who is stalking you and what has happened to your friend Kinley Jaybird."

"I appreciate your assistance." Molly glanced down at her hands in her lap.

"We are not going to get anything done if we don't

get you trained and up to speed. While you show great potential in investigation techniques—" She pointed to the computer. "—this computer and software will help your research a lot." Handing Molly a notebook, she grinned. "This details Terrabyte's practices and procedures. The password to your computer is under your stapler. Cayson has already taught you the security installation." She tossed a green expandable file labeled "Molly Reacher" on the desk. "Start building your case file. Add your spread sheet, Kinley's missing person police report, any other threatening notes, and if you took pictures of your walls when your apartment was broken into add those. Then set up your file on the computer. In the notes section, you need to document everything you've told me. Then add a section for Kinley Jaybird. Again, document everything that happened in the days or weeks leading up to her disappearance. List every document in your hard file in the computer file."

"Got it." Molly glanced at her watch. "I need to call Cayson and tell him I won't be available to assist him this afternoon."

"He'll be checking in soon. Oh, how we want you to answer the phone—"

"Cayson already went over that before he left."

"Oh, good man." Candle moved to her desk as Miacoh stepped out of the conference room. "How's it going in there?"

"Not bad. Ben set out rules he expects his parents to abide by and the consequences if they don't. There will be no unsupervised visits with the twins until Gabby and Ben feel his parents understand their meddling will no longer be tolerated. Whether Ben is here or not. He's pretty pissed, and Gabby feels vindicated. I'm going to bring the twins in now and get things wrapped up." Miacoh snapped his fingers. "Oh, yeah, I'm meeting with Jason Jansen at the City Attorney's Office this afternoon and will work out plans for Ben, Gabby, and the twins to disappear until we can find his ex-partner and cohort." Walking toward the break room, he paused. "Nash and Natalya, front and center." He pushed open the conference room door.

Terra came skidding down the hallway and around the corner, followed by the twins.

"They're ready for you." He closed the door after they rushed inside.

Terrabyte head-butted Candle. In turn, she scratched the pup's ears and pointed to her blanket. Then she returned her attention to Miacoh. "Sounds like a plan. If you have a chance in the near future, could you look into what the police have discovered in Molly's stalking case?"

"I'll get on that as soon as the meeting wraps up and I talk to Jason."

She grimaced. "And see what you can find out about the progress of Kinley Jaybird's missing person report?"

"Missing person report? Who's Kinley? You took on another case?" He frowned and rubbed the back of his neck. "You better be hiring some more investigators." He walked to the door. "I'll be back after I check in at the station. Seems a little too quiet over there."

She smiled sweetly. "Kinley is part of Molly's case. I'll fill you in tonight. Hiring more employees is on my to-do list."

The phone rang. Molly grabbed it. "Good afternoon. Terrabyte Security. This is Molly, how may I help you?" She was silent for several beats. "Um—I'm Candle's new receptionist. Gabby is taking time off. Let me get Candle for you." She pushed the hold button and blew out a breath. "Candle, your dad's on the phone."

Laughing, she picked up the receiver. "Dad, are you giving my new employee a hard time?"

"Of course I am. What happened to Gabby? Your mother and I are back. Do you need some help?"

"Well, we got Ben back. Thanks to Mom's vision, we kinda knew what we were looking for. Gabby's working for him. Ben's ex-partner and his accomplice are still at large. The Sacramento police are on it. I have a new complicated case—or two." She paused for a moment. "Yes, I could use your help. If you don't have plans."

"I've had enough traveling around for a while. Your mom says nothing dangerous." He chuckled.

"It's a stalking case and missing person. Mom hasn't had any more visions?"

"Nope. What, you got a missing person stalking someone?" He roared with laughter.

She puffed out her cheeks and blew out a breath in exasperation. "No, Dad. It's kinda two cases. I'll explain when you stop by Terrabyte."

"Fair enough. Why don't you and Miacoh join us for dinner tonight and we can discuss my fee. Your mom wants to show off vacation pictures."

"Let me get with Miacoh and I'll get back to you. Okay?"

"Your mom won't take no for an answer. Therefore, we'll see you tonight around seven. Come hungry."

"Of course. You bossy old man. Love ya." Candle ended the call before he had a chance to retort.

Molly answered the phone. "Hey, Cayson. I won't be able to help you this afternoon. Candle has me working on cases." She paused. "Oh, that sounds great. See ya later."

"Got a hot date?" Candle snickered as Molly's cheeks turned red.

"No. Not exactly."

"You and Cayson are an item. Don't you break that boy's heart." Candle turned her attention to her computer screen grinning.

"Break what boy's heart?" Miacoh pushed through the front door, striding toward Candle's office.

"Eavesdropping again, Chief?" Candle dissolved into a fit of giggles. "We're meeting Mom and Dad for dinner at seven."

"Oh, they've returned and already issuing demands?" Miacoh tucked his thumbs in his belt and grinned.

"Dad's tired of retirement and Mom always wants to feed us."

"Well, you could put him to work temporarily."

"Already done. We'll discuss the details over dinner."

"That's my girl." He leaned over and kissed her. "Gotta get back to the station and make those calls for you." He paused and turned on his heel. "What boy?"

"Cayson."

"Cayson is a grown-ass man. Don't you be playing matchmaker. He's a confirmed bachelor. You've enough irons in the fire right now."

"Now who's issuing the commands? FYI, so were you." She stuck her tongue out at him. Unprofessional as the action was, it gave her great satisfaction.

The phone rang three more times and Molly had to put the first two on hold. She turned to Candle. "Is it always this busy?"

Gabby stepped out of the conference room with the twins in tow. "Whew, what a day. Yes, Molly, business is picking up. If it gets out of control, turn it over to the answering service until you get caught up. I had to do that a few times. Then pick up the calls you missed from the service and off you go again. I told Candle we needed more help."

"Thanks for the tip. Candle, you don't mind?"

"Nope, soon you'll be running the office just like Gabby."

"Thanks for the vote of confidence." Molly glanced at her desk a bit overwhelmed.

"At the moment, nothing has rush or urgent on it. So take your time." She glanced at her watch. "Let's wrap things up here and call it a day." She snickered. "You have a hot date. I've got to get Terra home and fed, corral Miacoh, then get him moving toward home so we aren't late for dinner at Mom and Dad's."

"I don't have—" Molly stopped mid-sentence at the dubious look on Candle's face. "—thank you."

Chapter Fifteen

When the Cards are Stacked Against You, Sometimes You Gotta Fold.

After speaking to Molly on the phone, Cayson finished up his last installation late afternoon. *I've got time to go home and take a shower before I pick up Molly from work.*

An hour later, dressed in black jeans and a maroon and black striped mock turtleneck, he ran a brush through his shoulder-length blond hair and was on his way to Terrabyte Security. He strode into the office to find Molly sitting at her desk, file open and papers scattered all over, fussing at the computer. Her hand was held high in the air as if she was about to smack it.

"Looks like computer one, Molly none." He chuckled.

She picked up a stick eraser and threw it at him. He dodged right and caught the offending item in his left hand. "Wow you clean up nice." She did a slow appreciative glance at him up and down.

"Something I can help with?" He walked around the desk and stood behind her chair, his hands gently massaging her shoulders.

"I can't seem to add the additional info on Kinley and attach it to my main file." She pushed back from her desk and sighed, closing her eyes.

"Everyone gone?" He surveyed the office and went down the hall.

"Yeah. Gabby's family left a little while ago after hammering out an agreement with his parents. The parents didn't look any too happy, but…Apparently, Gabby and family will be spending another night at their home with guards stationed. Candle wasn't too happy about that. Mr. Jansen is checking with the town of Raven's Hollow about using one of their safe houses. Arrangements are to be finalized tomorrow. Candle and Miacoh are having dinner at her parents. Apparently, her dad is coming to work here part-time." She rolled her shoulders and glanced up at him. "I've had it. Computer wins. Let's eat; I'm starved."

"One moment." He leaned over and pointed to the screen. "Your file is already primary. Click here and make Kinley's secondary. That way it's attached to your file but has all the options and sub-files you need. Boss lady wrote the programs to fit her business needs. Not real user-friendly until you work on it a bit. Then it all makes sense." He backed away giving her room to stand.

"Wow. That works. Thanks." She gathered up the papers on her desk, sorted them into the proper places, and filed them in her desk drawer. "I can finish it tomorrow. Don't want to make mistakes because I'm tired." She pushed up from her chair, turned, and was face to face with him.

"I wondered how long Hunter would stay retired." Ignoring the little warning voice in his head, he pushed the chair out of the way, pulled her to him, lowered his lips to her full warm ones, and lingered. When he hesitantly pulled back, her warm brown eyes opened and held his gaze. "I've been thinking about doing that all day."

She traced her lips with the tip of her tongue. "Mmmm." She rested her head on his chest. "Just what I needed after today. Feels like I am barely treading water after the events at the lawyer's office then the tense situation with the parents, Gabby, and her family. Learning what Candle expects from me, then being assigned to work on my own files. Whew."

"Yes, around here it's kinda sink or swim. Not because Candle doesn't care, but because the company is growing so fast. And she knows you have the skills." He tipped her chin up and kissed her again. "I have a reservation at Angus Steak House in forty-five minutes. Wanta go home and change or go straight to the restaurant?"

"I'm ready." She turned off the computer, checked the other rooms, then set the alarm. "Lead the way."

He held the office door open for her. They walked hand in hand across the parking lot to his pickup.

At the truck she turned, her back to the passenger side door, wrapped her arms around his waist, and gazed up at him. "I've never known anyone like you. Don't push for personal information. Don't take advantage of my weak points. Treat me like someone special—"

He leaned down until his lips almost touched hers. His hands gently caressed the back of her neck. "I figure you'll tell me what I need to know in your own time. I wasn't aware you had weak points. I'll have to explore that further." A suggestive smile quirked his lips, then the tip of his tongue explored around her top lip. "You are someone special to me." He slipped his tongue between the parted lips and began a sinuous dance with hers as he crushed her to him. His hands slid from her neck, down her sides, brushing feather light touches along her firm breasts. She quivered at his touch, and he enjoyed the sensation.

She pressed more urgently against him and moaned in his mouth. She opened her eyes to find his gaze searching her face.

Hesitantly, he backed away from her and slid his hand behind her to grasp the door handle. Breathing heavily, he whispered, "Unless you want to end up in the backseat of my truck beneath me, we'd better get going or miss the reservation."

She heaved out a breath and rested her cheek against his solid chest. "You're right, but that backseat sounds pretty good right now." She snickered and moved out of the way so he could open the door.

The parking lot at the steakhouse was packed. He parked, went around to her side, and opened her door. She slipped out slowly, her entire body sliding against him until her feet reached the ground. "Tease."

She sent him a coquettish glance. "Nope. A promise as soon as my hunger for food is quenched."

"I'm going to hold you to that." What little relief he'd managed on the drive here immediately disappeared as his body bloomed in full arousal again. He took several deep breaths of the crisp evening air willing his body under control.

She flashed a knowing look at him and grasped his hand. "Come on, let's eat."

Inside, the hostess led them to a secluded booth in the corner. On the table, a candle flame flickered and reflected in the crystal vase containing a bouquet of long-stemmed yellow and red roses with a red ribbon tied at the top. A bottle of wine chilled next to the flowers. He waited for her to slide in.

"Oh—they're beautiful, Cayson." She turned to him and kissed him full on the lips. "This is what I mean. I've never—" Her cheeks pinked as she leaned over to inhale deeply of the roses before she eased into the booth.

"Lucky me to have found you." He slid in next to her.

Todd Cimerono, one of the officers from the police station waved as he walked by the table. The Wolick family sat two tables across from them and also waved. He and Molly smiled and waved back.

Small towns. No privacy. Word would be all over by morning including to Miacoh and Candle. He shuddered, hesitated to slide his arm around her shoulders, then went ahead anyway. She gently placed her hand on his thigh.

"Shall I pour the wine?" a waitress asked setting wine glasses on the table.

"By all means." Cayson glanced to see Molly nodding. "We're ready to order."

After ordering, Molly sipped at her wine. "This is one of my favorites. How did you know?"

"Lucky guess. It's one of mine as well." He tipped his glass to hers, the crystal making a tinkling sound. "To us."

The dinner of porterhouse steak, baked potatoes, and salad was perfect and served quickly. They took two pieces of cheesecake with strawberries on top to go.

Driving to the safe house, the rain sprinkled on the

windshield. The drops and wind increased when he turned into her driveway. "Guess we're in for another storm tonight."

"Appears so. At least you'll be with me this time. I do love to watch storms."

"I can stay for a while. The new security system will catch anyone messing around outside. Or if anyone tries to break in. You're safe. I promise."

She just smiled.

Inside the house, she shed her jacket, put the cheesecake and the remainder of the bottle of wine in the fridge, then stalked over to him.

He took his jacket off as she slid her hands around his neck and pressed against him. "This is how it's going to go?"

"Mmmm." She reached for the bottom of his shirt and pulled it over his head.

He hesitated only a moment, slipped his hands around her waist, then farther down to cup her fine ass pulling her to him.

She resisted, reached down, and unzipped his pants. She lifted her leg up, put her foot in the crotch, and brought the jeans to the floor. Next, she tugged his briefs down and they pooled inside the jeans.

He stepped out of his clothes "This isn't right I'm nearly naked. I'll have to do something about this." He chuckled. Taking his time, he removed her blouse, tugged her long skirt to the floor, and unhooked her bra allowing her soft rounded mounds free. "Oh, that is so much better." He breathed kisses down her neck. As she curved into him, his tongue teased the cleavage of her breasts until his mouth covered her hardened nipples.

She arched into him and moaned. "Now who's the tease?"

"Oh, believe me, I'm just getting started. I'm going to take you completely and have you begging for more."

"Sound pretty sure of yourself."

"You bet." He reached between her legs, slid fingers under her panties, and teased her intimate parts.

She squealed and arched against his hand. "Oh, Cayson." The storm nearly drowned out her voice. Rain pelted on the roof. Lightning streaked across the night sky as thunder continued to rock the house. She paused to glance out the bay window in the living room.

In a flash, he'd removed her panties and continued his ministrations. "Let's take this into the bedroom." He picked her up and carried her to the bed. *I gotta slow this down, or I'll not last long.* He eased down beside her and they watched the storm out the bedside windows for a couple of moments. The rain drops splashed in the puddles formed in the dry earth.

Lovemaking began slowly, tongues teasing and tasting, hands touching, caressing, exploring, and arousing intimate sensations. The sheer, raw, primitive power of the storm surrounded them, once again fervently fueling needs and desires.

Kisses were hot, deep imitations of their bodies' intent and desires. His lips moved from her luscious mouth to her breast, tongue teasing and gently stroking while his other hand returned to her most intimate parts. She wrapped her hand around him. Pushing it away, he slid down.

She arched against him. "Oh...Cayson...Please."

His fingers played in her heat and caressed until

she softened, melted, ready to make love. *The commitment I've avoided for so long isn't as scary as life without her. Tonight, I'll take her completely and make her beg for more. Tomorrow can take care of itself.*

Molly moaned while wrapping her long, beautiful legs around his. "Cayson, please, I want to feel you inside me."

"Patience...soon. If you're sure. Let's just enjoy each other for a little while longer," he murmured against her ear.

"I've never been surer of anything in my life," she whispered against his lips. Using the element of surprise, she flipped over and pounced, straddling him. "Not waiting any longer."

A flash of silvery lightning filled the room making her moist skin shimmer as she slid down on him. Thunder rocked their room once more as he grasped her hips and thrust, slow and easy at first then hard, fast, and deep. The strobe effect of the lightning flashes caused a sensation of slow motion.

The storm was directly overhead now, as the rain beat against the roof. The wind shook and bent the trees outside the windows. Lightning pierced the night sky, again and again, followed immediately by rumbles of thunder that shook the walls around them.

Feeling her shiver beneath his hands, he said, "It's okay. We're safe." He gathered her into his arms tighter. Her hips arched against him.

"Oh, Cayson," she moaned, "take me, now." She screamed. Ripples began from her center, caressing, and stroking. One final thrust into her quivering depth and their shouts of ecstasy were lost in the thunder rolling around them.

Panting, chest heaving, he savored the immense satisfaction as contentment and peace flowed between them. Wrapping his arms around Molly, he spooned against her, legs tangled together. He fervently hoped this had not been a mistake as sleep overtook them.

In the darkness, Cayson's phone's shrill tone split the quiet. He rolled over and sleepily yanked the phone off the nightstand, checked the time and caller. "What the hell?" He touched the screen. "What's up?"

Chapter Sixteen

Visions of Truth, Can They Save the Night, and Family?

Candle screamed. Shook Miacoh. Then she jumped out of bed tearing around the room. "Ben's partner is skulking around their house. I can see his face, and he's armed with a weapon. I can feel his malicious intent. Shit, I can't believe I said that." She yanked on a fresh pair of jeans from the closet, tugged on a sweatshirt, and grabbed her phone.

"Now hold on just a minute." Miacoh grabbed her arm and turned her to face him while he raised an eyebrow. "Are you sure this wasn't a bad dream? That is exactly what you've been worrying about. Could it have manifested in a dream?" He released her and began dressing.

She paused to scowl at him, hands fisted at her sides. "I know the difference between a dream and a vision, regardless of what I've alluded to before. My grandmother had the sight. My mother has it. No matter how hard I tried to ignore it, I do too. It was like I was there with him feeling his thoughts and emotions. He's going to kill them all. He's only a few blocks from the house." She stared at Miacoh. "Don't just stand there. We gotta get over there. I tried Gabby. She didn't answer."

"I'll call Cayson. The safe house is a lot closer to Gabby's house than we are. I'll alert Officer Smith at the station—he's on overnights. Besides, there is armed security on the grounds." Dressed, he jammed his weapon in his waistband while finishing up his call to Cayson.

"What if he didn't stay at the safe—" She grabbed her gun from the nightstand, shoved it in her backpack on the floor, and shouldered it.

"Trust me, from the town chatter, he's at the house with Molly. Now I want you to go to the safe house and stay with her. If anyone is monitoring the police scanner, they may take an opportunity to strike while we're all engaged elsewhere. I've already explained the situation and sent Cayson to Gabby's house." He hesitated a beat. "I can make better time cross country on four paws. He stripped, neatly stuffed his clothes and weapon in a canine saddle pack, and shifted to his wolf form.

Candle strapped the pack on him, and he streaked out the door, pausing to look back at her for a beat. "Be careful." She closed the door and opened the garage door.

****

A quarter of a mile from Gabby's house, Cayson discovered an empty sports car fitting the description of Ben's ex-partner's vehicle. As he reached to flip off his headlights, a figure darted along the street, dodging behind bushes and cars a couple of blocks from the house. Grabbing his phone off the seat, he called Miacoh to bring him up to date. There was no answer. So he left a message. "I can't wait for backup. I'm going after him."

Silently, Cayson crept up behind the intruder outside of the security perimeter of Gabby's home. He threw a roundhouse kick, connected to the intruder's head, and followed up with a front kick knocking the man's weapon from his hand. The gun flew into the air, landed on the ground, and skittered onto the patio. The perpetrator stumbled onto the patio after the weapon and the perimeter alarm wailed. Grabbing a wrought iron chair, the man swung it at Cayson. He sidestepped it, grabbed the chair, then landed a front kick to the solar plexus knocking the individual face down on the patio. The heavy chair caught him off balance for a moment. The individual slowly got to his knees, blood streaming from his nose, and reached for the gun.

Out of nowhere, a large silver and black wolf pounced. All four paws landed on the man's back and knocked him to the ground. As the man lay sprawled on the patio grasping for breath, the snarling wolf jumped off his back and bit down on the man's hand reaching for the gun. Blood pooled on the ground. The wolf gave one last tug and shook the hand, then let loose. With lightning speed, the animal raced behind the house, into the forest, and disappeared.

Regaining his balance, Cayson swung the chair full circle to trap the man under the chair face down and kicked the gun farther across the patio. Straddling the chair, he pinned the man's arms with his feet. Breathing hard, Cayson glanced down and raised an eyebrow. "Wild animals populate these woods. Should have invested in self-defense courses if you're going to engage in this type of activity." Security guards rushed across the grounds to subdue and collect the intruder.

Officer Smith, entering from the opposite direction,

shook his head. "Looks like I'm late to the party. You okay, Cayson?"

"Yep." He brushed at the dirt on his jeans.

Miacoh sprinted out of the forest's edge. "Got everything handled?"

Cayson glanced down at the muddy wolf tracks on the patio tiles and grinned at Miacoh. "Yep."

Ben, dressed in black sweats, flashlight in hand, stepped out of the patio door. "What in the hell is going on out here?

Cayson pointed to the man pinned under the chair. "Ben, can you identify this intruder?"

Ben strode onto the patio and shined a flashlight on the man wriggling under the chair. "Yes, that's Ken Miller, my ex-partner." He leaned closer. "What in the hell are you doing here, Ken? Haven't you done enough dam—"

"I'm going to ruin your fucking life and destroy your family, like you've ruined mine." Ken wriggled under the chair attempting to free himself.

"From where I stand, it looks like you did that yourself." Cayson cocked his head and peered down at the perp.

A security guard knelt on the patio, removed the man's arms from under Cayson's feet, and wrapped a bandage around the wound on Ken's hand. He screamed in pain while the officer placed the cuffs on the ex-partner's wrists and shackles on his ankles then helped him to his feet.

Miacoh faced Ken. "You have the right to remain silent. Anything you say can and will be used against you in a court of law. You have the right to speak with an attorney. If you cannot afford an attorney, one will be appointed for you. You have the right to have an attorney present with you while you're being questioned. Do you understand these rights as I have explained them to you?"

"Screw you," Ken spat.

Miacoh got to his feet. "I'll take that as a yes." Pitkin County officers arrived to pick up their prisoner. "He's all yours, officer. I've read him his rights. You might want to take him to the hospital first. He appears to have tangled with a wild animal sometime tonight."

The officer nodded and walked the cursing prisoner to the police car. "We'll be in touch."

Gabby and the twins tentatively crept out onto the patio. "Is it all over?"

"Almost. Ken's accomplice is still at large. I'll be checking in with the Sacramento Police Department in the morning. Meanwhile, I'd rather your security detail remain on duty." Miacoh motioned to the men standing around the property's perimeter.

"Sure thing." Ben shook his head. "Thank you so much. I'm in your debt. Never in a million years would I have believed dissolving my partnership would end like this." He peered solemnly over at Cayson and Miacoh.

"I did. I told you Ken Miller was untrustworthy scum." Gabby fisted her hands on her hips.

Ben wrapped an arm around his wife's shoulder and kissed the top of her head. "So you did." He gently turned her around along with the twins, who objected vehemently, and walked back inside. "Nothing to see here. Off to bed you go."

Miacoh and Cayson walked toward his truck. "Well, guess I'll see you over at Molly's house." He stretched an arm over his head leaning to one side and winced. "Been a while since I've done hand to hand combat. Not something I want to repeat too often."

Miacoh grinned. "From what I saw you cleaned Ken's clock."

He shrugged. "Got the drop on him with a little help from local wildlife. See ya at Molly's."

****

The next morning Miacoh strolled into the police station. Two people sat in the lobby. "Aren't you two quite a long away from home?" He grinned and stepped over to the pair offering his hand to Agent Jedediah Adams and Agent Caitlin Rossy from Homeland Security as they got to their feet. "What brings you to my neck of the woods—again?"

"Nothing as explosive as last time." Jed chuckled. "We'd like a word with Ben Alrich and his ex-partner. Didn't want to step on any toes, so thought we'd stop here and let you know we were in town."

"Little late. Ben's ex-partner was arrested last night. Attempted murder and kidnapping. Ben is at home with his family. I can give him a call and see if he wants to talk with you. What's this about?"

"We've been assigned to check out a problem with acquiring the anti-ransom software Ben created and subsequently offered the government."

Caitlin returned to the chair. "Apparently the government has decided to make an offer."

"Interesting. I hope you don't expect exclusivity. My wife, Candle negotiated a deal to purchase rights for Terrabyte Security. But I'm sure you'll work something out. Let me make that call." He walked out the back door, cell phone to his ear. "Hey, Ben. The feds are parked in my office requesting to talk with you about your anti-ransom software. Shall I send them out your way? Or would you rather meet here at Terrabyte?"

"Didn't think they'd have boots on the ground yet. Got an email. Normally, I'd rather meet in my office, but the repair crew said it'll be a couple weeks before it's ready for business as usual. We're kinda working out of the house, but I don't want the feds here. Gabby and the twins have had enough disruptions for a while."

"So Terrabyte's conference room it is. She doesn't have anything scheduled early afternoon. Will that work for you?"

"I can make that work. Won't take long. Either they'll accept a nonexclusive contract or not."

"I'll check with Candle. If you don't hear from me, it's a go." He disconnected the call and dialed Candle.

"Hey, charming, what can I do for you?" Candle purred into the phone.

"You'll never guess who was waiting for me at the station."

"Jed and Caitlin? Saw their government vehicle parked in my lot. Figured we'd be seeing them after everything that's gone down. Especially if the government is interested in the software."

"You know, you're scary sometimes. Way to take the wind out of my sail." He told her the arrangement Ben wanted.

"Sure. That works for me. Can't blame him for wanting to keep business out of his home. Send them on over."

Miacoh stepped inside the police station. "All set. You'll meet Ben at Terrabyte Security down the block

143

at one o'clock this afternoon. See if a deal can be worked out."

"Okay. We're going to grab breakfast at that little cafe. Want to join us?"

"Thanks for the offer, but I've had breakfast. I want to touch base with Sacramento police and get the latest on—" His phone chimed at the same time as his computer announced a new email. He waved as the feds let themselves out. Settling into his office chair, he opened his email and whooped.

Deputy Barry Smith turned to glance at his boss. "Good news?"

"You bet. Sacramento PD caught Ken's accomplice. Besides the various charges involved with the kidnapping, he picked up resisting arrest and assault on a police officer." Miacoh brushed his hands together. "Glad it's out of my hands. I'll print out a copy of the email and give it to Jed and Caitlin at the meeting this afternoon." He sauntered over to the front desk. "Reka, I'm going over to Terrabyte to tell Candle the good news. If you need me, call me there."

"Copy that, boss." Reka returned to her tasks.

He opened the door and saw his father-in-law crossing the street. "Hey, wait up." He sprinted out to greet Hunter. "Retirement not suit you?" Miacoh chuckled.

"Candle needs help at Terrabyte. I'm tired of sitting at home watching Pekabo paint. We have three months before our next trip. So I offered my services and she hired me." Hunter grinned.

"Pekabo doesn't mind you working in security?"

"Naw, as long as danger is off the table."

"Better not let her hear about the dust-up at

Gabby's last night."

"What happened?"

"A vision woke Candle out of a deep sleep. She was screaming so loudly, I'm surprised the neighbors didn't call the cops. Damn near scared the shit out of me. She saw Ben's ex-partner planned to break in Ben's house with murderous intent. Sent Cayson over to intercept. Long story short, Ken, Ben's partner is in custody over in Pitkin County. Sacramento PD picked up his accomplice. Oh— Jed and Caitlin are here. Something about the government wanting Ben's anti-ransom software. They're meeting in Terrabyte's conference room at one this afternoon. I was on my way to update Candle when I saw you." Miacoh opened the door to Terrabyte Security and held it open for Hunter.

Chapter Seventeen

What Does a Break-In, Stolen Identity, and A Missing Person Have in Common?

Molly peeked over her computer screen to see Miacoh and Hunter push the door open and step into the office.

"I hand the reins to the town over to you and all hell breaks loose. Thirty-five years I policed this town and nothing more serious than a domestic dispute involving a knot on the head caused by a cast iron skillet." Hunter laughed. "Better you than me."

"Now wait just a darn minute. Wasn't the last crime on your watch the murder of your newly appointed police chief? And didn't that whole episode bring the FBI, Homeland, and the alphabet soup of several other government agencies to your little town? Not to mention suspected terrorists blowing up the chemistry lab at School of Mines?"

Hunter frowned. "You know as well as I do, it turned out to be a disgruntled professor who didn't get tenure and his minions that did the damage."

"Be that as it may, no one's been murdered on my watch." Miacoh rocked back on his heels and raised an eyebrow. "That disgruntled professor is still at large. Fled the country. Right?"

"Not my—"

"Enough, you two." Candle straightened up from behind Molly's desk and brushed a stray strand of hair from her forehead. "Hey, handsome, what brings you to my doorstep?" She skirted around the desk and kissed Miacoh then turned her attention to her father. "Wow, two handsome hunks in one day. How do I rate?" Candle giggled and hugged her dad.

Terra came rushing through the door all wiggles and tail wags in greeting.

"Wow, that pup is getting big. She looks like a lion." Hunter bent down and scratched behind her ears. "You should have brought her to dinner with you last night."

"Terra was asleep in her crate when we left for your house. Given the night we had, good thing she got rest. She's still enough of a puppy to get cranky if she doesn't get enough sleep. Believe me you don't want to deal with a sleep-deprived dog. Took her over to Molly's with me while the guys had all the fun at Gabby's."

"I don't think Cayson had much fun," Miacoh interjected.

Candle looked thoughtful. "Probably not. Don't tell him I said that." Tugging Hunter toward Molly's desk, Candle introduced him to the company's newest employee. "She's our office elf, assistant installer, investigator in-training, and client."

Molly stood and flipped her long black braid over her shoulder. "Really? Office elf? I'm nearly as tall as you."

"I just like the sound of it. Might even put it on your job description." Candle dissolved into a fit of giggles. "Lack of sleep has caught up with me. I'll try to be more professional when the feds get here." She patted Molly on the shoulder. With the other hand she covered a jaw popping yawn. "Believe we'll close up early, if the feds don't take forever with their interview." She snapped her fingers and pointed. "Unless, Dad, you want to man the phones for a couple of hours?"

"Don't mind. You expecting important calls?"

"I got a couple inquiries out as to Molly's case, hoping they'll call back today. Give you a chance to study her files."

"I could also stay if the feds run late. Your whole crew looks a little worse for wear."

Her dad grimaced and jerked his thumb toward his son-in-law. "He told me about your dust up. Don't tell your mom. She won't want me working here with you."

A stiff breeze scattered loose papers again when a tall woman with long wavy blonde hair swept in through the front door. "You got that right. Dust up. You call guns, attempted murder, and heaven only knows what else, a dust up?" She shifted the awkward package she carried and rested it on the corner of Molly's desk. The woman studied Molly. "You must be Gabby's replacement." She extended her petite hand to Molly who firmly grasped it.

She peered at the woman. "That's right, I'm Molly. Would you be Candle's mom, Pekabo?" *Candle looks like a younger version of her mom only with cinnamon colored hair and her dad's big brown eyes and bronze complexion.*

"You bet I am." Pekabo untied the string and began unwrapping the brown paper from the large package, her gaze holding her husband's.

Hunter strode over and kissed her on the lips. "It wasn't as bad as all that. Which town gossip did you meet up with?" He peered at the package. "Is that the surprise you've been working on for Candle?"

"Yes. Don't try to change the subject. I talked with Gabby's mom this morning."

"It's my understanding last night's events were an uncommon occurrence for the town or Terrabyte Security." Molly shifted uncomfortably in her chair.

"Honey, everything is an uncommon occurrence in this town since Miacoh took over as Chief of Police." Pekabo's sapphire-blue eyes twinkled with mirth as she smiled wide and batted her eyes at Miacoh.

He harrumphed. "Not true."

Candle sidled up to her mom. "What you got there? A surprise for me?"

Pekabo tore off the remaining brown paper and held up a large painting. A mountain landscape of Pike's Peak sparkled with snow in the background along with evergreens. Lilacs and trees budded in the foreground, with a sprinkling of wildflowers and a couple of red-tailed hawks in flight.

"Oh, Mom, it's absolutely beautiful. We'll hang it right here in the lobby. The one you painted of Terra when I returned to Aspen Ridge is in my office." Candle peered at Miacoh. "Do you happen to have tools to put the painting up?"

Pekabo waved a hand in dismissal. "No need." She pulled out of her bag a small hammer and picture hooks then handed them to Miacoh. "Aren't you supposed to be at the police station?"

He grinned. "Yes, ma'am. I came over to give Candle the good news. Ben's ex-partner is in the custody of the Sacramento Police." He waved the copy of the email in the air. "Thought the feds might want a copy. So brought the paper over for the meeting." He went into the back room, brought out a level, and took the hammer and picture hanger from Pekabo. In a matter of minutes, the painting hung on the wall opposite the front door for all to see when they entered.

Hunter glanced from his wife to his daughter, then son-in-law, and finally Molly. "Hey, where's Cayson?"

"He's out on installations. It seems the whole town wants home and computer security systems these days. He'll be done about two this afternoon and will head home. He had a rough night."

"Where do you want me to work?" Hunter surveyed the room.

"Down the hall and to the left. Across from my office. We put a new desk and computer system in there. You'll share the space with Cayson. Plenty of room. I'll show you." She padded down the short hallway and motioned to the joint office.

"This will do fine. You have me for about three months. Your mother has another trip planned for a few weeks."

"No problem. Happy to have the help." Candle leaned on her office door frame. "I gotta update Gabby and Ben's case before I can leave. I better get after it."

Miacoh tugged his wife to him. "Could I have a few minutes of your time? You'll need to hear what I have to say and you can close out Gabby and Ben's case."

"Dad, Molly can bring you up to speed on her case, while I get an update from Miacoh." Candle smiled wide at her husband. "I assume that's why you're here."

"You never cease to amaze me." He leaned down and brushed his lips over hers, then deepened the kiss.

"I'll go to my office and give you two some privacy," Hunter grumbled.

Molly cleared her throat. "Unless you want to talk with the feds who are almost at the door. I set out water pitchers and glasses on the refreshment table in the conference room and added a few pastries from the kitchen. Anything else?"

"Good job, Molly. Shouldn't need anything else." Candle shook her head.

Miacoh huffed out a breath. "Duty calls. We'll finish this later."

"I'll hold you to it." Candle smiled up at him, then kissed him lightly. "Now go." She walked into her office.

He'd no sooner greeted Jed and Caitlin, than Ben strode into the office. "Let's get this party started. Ben, you don't need me here, do you?"

"No, I don't believe so. Simple negotiation that I believe the government will be amenable to." Ben held up his briefcase and walked into the conference room. "Shall we."

Molly answered the ringing phone. "Yes, he's here. Just finishing up with the feds." She turned to Miacoh. "Your office."

He took the phone from her— "Miacoh here." — listened for a moment. "I'll be right there."

Hunter returned to the lobby area. The door closed to the conference room and he drew a chair over to Molly's desk. "So you have a story to tell?" He grinned, his eyes glittering with mischief like his daughter's, putting Molly at ease.

"I guess so." She proceeded to tell him her history, what connected her to the earlier college case, the stalking, the threats, and Kinley Jaybird coming up missing. No one interested in looking for her. "You may get a better grasp of the situation after you read my files. According to Cayson, everyone in the office has access to the main server where all the files are stored. Did Candle give you a password?"

"Not yet. But I know where to find her." He started down the hallway and paused. "Rest assured, we will find your friend."

"I'll hold you to that." She sent him an unsure smile. "The more time passes after a person goes missing the worse the outcome."

"Well aware, but let's think positive." Hunter turned to go into his office.

Chapter Eighteen

Meddling Gossips, Spring Festival Planning, and Peaceful Evening?

"Well, as I live and breathe, it's Chief Bearclaw returned to public service." A plump woman with gray hair pulled into a bun at the nape of her neck, sparkling hazel eyes, a friendly smile, and purple nail polish bustled inside. She clutched a stack of brightly colored flyers.

"No, Clara. It's Hunter Bearclaw. My son-in-law, Miacoh is police chief as you well know. I'm just here helping out Candle for a few weeks."

"Chasing the bad guys again." She chuckled. "I knew retirement wouldn't last long. Oh, hi, Pekabo. When's the next trip?"

"Not for a while. Hunter gets bored easily." She laughed.

"Where's Gabby?" Clara gave Molly a pointed look. "And you are?"

"Molly. I'm filling in for Gabby while she—"

"Oh, I heard all about the kidnapping, break-in, and that awful ex-partner of Ben's. Just dreadful turn of events." Clara clicked her tongue. "These things never happened when Chief Bearclaw was in charge."

"Clara, times change. Chief Zane has things completely in control. I for one am extremely glad to hand the reins to the town over to him. Law enforcement is a young man's job." Hunter turned to Molly. "Forgive my manners. Clara is one of our outspoken town council members."

Molly extended her hand to grip Clara's. "Pleased to meet you."

Pekabo grinned. Her eyes sparkled with mischief. "If you ever want to know what's happening in Aspen Ridge, Clara will have the scoop."

Clara harrumphed. "Are you calling me the town gossip?"

"Well, if the shoe fits." Pekabo snickered.

Hunter sent his wife a warning glance. "Molly is Gabby's permanent replacement. You see, Gabby will be working with Ben for the foreseeable future."

Pekabo patted Clara on the shoulder and reached for the stack of papers. "Are these the flyers for the Spring Festival? May I?" She took a flyer off the top of the stack. "These are gorgeous. Did you create them?"

Clara waved a hand nonchalantly. "I took your example from last year and modified it."

"Great job."

Clara looked at her watch. "Oh, dear, I must be going. I have to deliver these flyers all over town. May I put one in your front window?"

Molly glanced at Hunter who gave a small nod. "Of course. In fact, you can leave a stack on my desk, and I'll hand them out to clients."

Clara beamed. "Thank you. The festival is going to be fantastic this year. Most businesses have floats in the parade. Though I haven't heard from Terrabyte Security. The high school marching band will be playing in it. Several food venders will be on hand in case anyone gets hungry. Games for the kids, early morning hot air balloon rides. Viola will be doing face painting, she used to be a professional makeup artist, you know, and…" She fluttered her hands around. "So much fun." She glanced at Pekabo smugly. "Oh, not that the festival wasn't fun when you were running it."

"Oh, no problem. You have a lot more time on your hands than I ever did," Pekabo shot back. "Besides Viola has more free time since she hired two more hairdressers for her salon, Aspen's Wylde Mane. It's wonderful her business is expanding. Don't you think?"

"Yes, yes of course. But—"

"Ladies. I'm sure the festival will be the best ever." Hunter put his arm around Pekabo leaned over and whispered, "She's baiting you."

"I gotta get going. Much to do." Clara waved and scooted out the door.

Terrabyte bounded out of Candle's office and pounced on Hunter. She was right behind the pup. "We were just about to go for a quick walk. My eyes won't stay open. Want to join us?"

"There you are. Hiding out while Clara was here, huh?" Pekabo stood hand on hips.

"Nope. Had work to do. Molly takes care of things up front. Sorry I missed her." Candle shrugged.

"I just bet you are," Pekabo shot back.

Hunter winked at his daughter. "I could use some air. Before I dive into Molly's files, I've some questions about her cases. What's your take on the situation?"

"My gut says the missing person has something to do with all of the rest. Obviously, her stolen identity and previous thesis papers are tangled up with the professor, his possible involvement in the identity theft ring, and the rest of his misdeeds. Someone took over the illegal activities from him and maybe Molly got a little too close to the truth for her own good."

"Think she stumbled across something?"

"Maybe. I'd like you to interview the current TA at the college. I've got a couple of names I'd like you look into. Something isn't right."

"It's a place to start." He glanced at Pekabo. "Care to join us, honey?"

"Sure. Can I leave my bag with you?" She peered at Molly.

Molly nodded and pointed to the empty chair in front of her desk.

"Also, she's pretty outspoken about the old practice of Native American and other indigenous children, as young as four years old, being taken from their families and put in Arizona boarding schools from 1807 through 1969. Many of those children died or were scarred for life. Apparently, her birth mother was one of those children."

"Hey, I'm sitting right here." Molly whirled around in her chair to face them.

"I know. Just making sure I have all the facts correct." Candle continued. "Not to mention the missing and murdered indigenous women plight. In fact, Molly's most recent thesis took a deep dive into that topic. Doesn't help that the police departments involved haven't been helpful."

"What's the connection to Jaybird? Other than she's missing."

"Leverage." Candle opened the back door. Terra barked and rushed at the end of the leash. "Molly, we're going to take Terra for a quick walk. Be right back."

Molly returned her attention to the computer. "Sure thing. Don't forget to give Mr. Bearclaw a password."

"It's Hunter—Molly. I feel old enough as it is." He chuckled and closed the door behind them.

The door to the conference room opened. Jed, Caitlin, and Ben strode out.

"Well, was it a productive session?" Molly smiled and scanned the faces of the participants.

"We have a starting point." Caitlin said. "Something to take back to Washington."

"Ben has a point. We'll work things out. Thank you for your time, Ben. We will be interviewing your ex-partner before we return home." Jed extended his hand to shake.

"Good luck." Ben waved to the feds as they left. "Hey, Molly. Where is everybody?"

"Hunter, Pekabo, and Candle are out back walking the pup. Miacoh returned to the police station. Cayson is working in the field."

The front door opened, and the light spring breeze attempted to scattered papers from her desk, again. She slapped her hands on top of the documents, gathered them all up in a pile, and plopped a police procedural manual on top.

"Nope, he's picking up Molly and headed for home." A weary Cayson trudged into the office. "Candle called to check on me. Said her dad was going to stay at the office until close and I should pick you up."

Ben rubbed his eyes. "I'm going home. If anyone needs me, they can contact me there." He fist bumped Cayson on the way out and closed the door behind him.

Molly gathered her stuff. "I have to admit last night was tough. I don't run on little to no sleep as well as I did when I was younger."

"Makes two of us."

Hunter and Pekabo returned to the office alone. "Candle and Terrabyte went home. He raised his eyebrows questioningly. "You both staying at the safe house? Cayson, did you get the upgrades done?"

"Yeah, Miacoh approved them. I picked up the material and finished it today. Going to do a run-through this afternoon with Molly's help. Computer was a bit cranky after I got everything online and updated."

She bristled. "Cayson is staying at the safe house with me because I failed to call him when an intruder skulked around a couple nights ago during the storm. I thought it was the fallen branch and twigs scratching the window." She raised her hands up and let them fall. "Last night, Candle and Terra stayed with me while— You know the story. Frustrating."

Hunter scratched his chin. "Sounds like Terrabyte Security is doing its due diligence to a client. Protect and investigate. Now both of you get out of here and get some rest. I've got this."

Pekabo stood by her husband and stroked his cheek. "Do you want me to stay with you? Maybe help."

Hunter took her hand and kissed the palm. "Nothing for you to do here. I need to read the case files and answer the phone. I'll be home right after I close the office at five sharp."

"Okay. I'll go home and fix supper." She gave him a smacking kiss and skipped out the door.

Cayson wrapped his arm around Molly's waist and guided her toward the door. "Night, Hunter."

"Night, you two."

"If you have any questions after reading my files…"

"I'll talk to you in the morning about it." Hunter smiled and made get-moving motions with his hands.

At his truck, Cayson lifted her into the passenger seat, reached across to clasp the seatbelt, then paused to gently brush his lips over hers. "How was the rest of your day?"

"Hectic," she said softly against his lips. "And yours?"

"I missed working with you." Slowly, he leaned away and closed the truck door. When he slid into the driver's seat, he grinned and shook his head. "That damn Wolick werewolf pup, Future, dug up the alarm line again. Chewed through the aluminum sheath we put on. Had to stop by, splice it, put a steel sheath on it, and rebury it. Told his dad, we'd have to charge a service call if it happened again. Then I told the pup that he was way too old to be digging up the back yard. Implied he'd get a bad rep if other werewolf juveniles got wind of his antics." Cayson slapped his knee and roared with laughter. "The boy's eyes got big as saucers. Then asked how would they find out? I smiled and walked to my truck not saying a word. I thought his dad was going to bust a gut. He had to turn and beat feet back into the house. We'll see if it worked."

"Quite creative of you." She giggled. "Would they really?"

"Hell if I know, but worth a shot." Cayson yawned wide. "Bed will feel good tonight."

"Couldn't agree more." She stretched her arms over her head and stifled a yawn. "What do you know about the Spring Festival?"

He started the engine and put the truck in gear. "Not much. I arrived after the festival last year. Pekabo would be the one to ask."

"A woman named Clara stopped by the office with flyers for the Spring Festival." She told him about the conversation between Clara and Pekabo. "She indicated that Terrabyte Security didn't enter a float in the parade. Does Candle usually do that?"

"Again, I don't know, but the company hasn't been open that long. I'll bet Candle would want the company to be included." He groaned. "Sounds like more work for us."

She giggled. "I'll send her a text. Tell her I'll follow up tomorrow morning. But Pekabo may mention it also. Those two women were like oil and water."

"Good idea." Cayson sighed as he slowed to make the turn onto Bear Paw Lane.

Chapter Nineteen

After Beefed Up Security...Another Attempted Break-in? Is She Hiding Something?

As they turned onto the safe house street, Cayson received notification of a breach of the perimeter alarm, then the front door alarm. He pulled into the driveway and saw a battering ram resting at the bottom of the front door as if someone had hurriedly dropped it. Off in the far distance, he noted two hooded figures running away. He grabbed his phone and called the police station. "Hey, Reka, I have an attempted break-in at the safe house. Please send whoever is on duty over ASAP."

"Are you in pursuit?"

"No. The perps are too far away, and Molly is with me. Can't leave her alone. I'm going into the house now."

"10-4, I'll send Barry right out. Should I call in Todd too? Chief left orders not to be disturbed until the morning. But..."

"Don't bother Miacoh. Barry should be enough. The alarm system scared them off coupled with our driving up the driveway. Could be evidence with fingerprints on the battering ram though."

"Battering ram?" Reka repeated.

"Yeah, installed a heavy-duty steel front door this

morning."

"Barry is on the way."

"Okay. Thanks." Cayson turned to Molly. "Stay here until I clear the house and lock the doors."

"By yourself?"

"Don't think anyone else is here. Another officer is on the way." He stepped out of the truck, made sure the doors locked, then stealthily checked the perimeter before advancing into the house, weapon drawn. A few minutes later he emerged and signaled her to come inside.

"What do they want?" Molly asked, frustration evident in her voice.

"That's what we are going to find out. We are going to search through all your things. You've got something, or they think you have something, they are desperate to get their hands on. Any idea?"

"None. I don't have that much. I left most everything behind."

Cayson caught movement outside from the corner of his eye. He breathed a sigh of relief when he saw Barry's police cruiser. Yanking open the door, he greeted Officer Smith. "Glad to see you."

"New porch decoration?" Barry touched the battering ram with his toe. "Mind helping me get it into the cruiser? We'll dust it for prints at the station. The windblown dirt here is going to obliterate any prints."

"Yeah, looks like we're in for another storm tonight." Cayson put on gloves and helped Barry get it into the vehicle.

"Want me to stay close tonight? I can call Todd in," Officer Smith offered.

"No. We should be fine. If not, I'll call."

The officer shrugged. "Okay, it's your decision. Chief won't like it."

"Copy that." He closed the door and glanced at Molly.

"Bring all your stuff into the living room, including clothes, intimates, every single thing." He followed her into her room and helped move all her stuff into the living room.

"There isn't anything here." She dropped the last of her textbooks and binders on the floor.

"Where is your laptop?" Cayson glanced around.

"In the safe at Candle and Miacoh's house. It has all my research and thesis on it. Candle thought it best to be stored there until the case is over or I need it."

"We'll search it tomorrow."

After three hours, Cayson got to his feet, blew out a breath, and paced.

"I told you there is nothing here." She kicked at a binder that held the hard copy of her recent thesis, then picked it up. The notebook slid out of her fingers and landed on the floor with a thud. The rings popped open, and papers flew everywhere. She buried her face in her hands.

Cayson leaned over and picked up a neatly folded piece of cream-colored paper unlike any of the other sheets now littering the floor.

She peeked between her fingers at him.

He put his index finger to his lips, walked over to the stereo system and turned it on. Pulling out an electronic device from his equipment bag, he walked around the living room, kitchen, and bedrooms. "No listening devices detected." He tucked the device back inside his bag, but he left the music playing. "What is this?"

"I don't know." Her interest piqued, she dropped her hands to her lap and peered up at him. "It's not mine. All the pages for the thesis were hole punched and bound in the binder."

He unfolded the paper to find two handwritten sheets. His eyes widened. He started to wave his hands in the air, then reconsidered, letting out a low whistle. "This could be what they're after." He handed the papers to her.

"This is Kinley's handwriting on the outside. The list inside is in the professor's handwriting. It's a list of the participants in his schemes, from identity theft, buying grades or papers, to heaven only knows what. Must have been before he set the explosion in the chemistry lab and disappeared." She turned to the second piece of paper. "This is in someone else's handwriting. A list of students with some names marked off, and others with check marks beside their names." Both her and Kinley's names were on the list. Kinley's had a line through hers with an arrow pointing to Molly's. "If I didn't know better, I'd say this is a hit list. Several of these students left school after the incident. A couple are missing like Kinley."

"And you're being harassed, stalked, and threatened. But to what end? You didn't even know this list existed. Did Kinley mention it?"

"No. But she had to be the one that secreted it inside my thesis binder which was only for backup. She also knew my thesis was complete and stored on my computer. Kinley seemed restless the days before she disappeared. She called me a couple of times but never left a message. I turned my phone off when I was studying online after I transferred schools."

"Well, we turn this list over to the authorities. Have them round up the culprits still at the school and see who breaks first. We could guess all day what all this means." He took the sheets of paper from her, scanned copies from his printer to his laptop, then emailed the documents to Miacoh with a short note of explanation. Tapping the originals against the side of his leg, he glanced around the room, tucked the papers inside his shirt, and tucked the shirt tail into his jeans.

She watched with wide eyes. "Don't feel this place is safe, even after the security upgrades?"

"Battering ram. If we'd not shown up when we did, he could have forced the door framework to splinter."

"But the alarm would have gone off. Right?"

"Yep, and the video system should have caught the perps."

She stood at the computer command center and flipped screens between current feed and the older feed. Pausing at the front door feed, she zoomed in on the intruder with the ram. Dressed in a black hoodie, he had his face turned from the camera. "He knew where you installed the cameras." She continued surfing through the video feed, but the individual skirted the camera's eye leaving only backs and sides of him at the edge of the frames.

"Must have watched me installing the system this morning. But why didn't he attack me to gain entrance?"

"Because he still didn't know where to look. If they think I have the list, you may not know about it. Didn't want to show his hand or get caught. I still say Murdock is calling the shots. Greg is the fall guy. I don't think Greg has the brains to pull this off on his own. Murdock wouldn't get his hands dirty. I could be wrong, but…"

Cayson's phone rang at the same time there was a knock on the front door. He answered the phone. "Miacoh, did you get the list? Hang tight for a second. Someone is at the door."

Molly stood in the center of the room staring at the door. Finally, taking a step toward the door, Cayson intercepted her. "Wait."

"Cayson? Officer Barry Smith here."

Cayson checked the monitor. "Be right there." Sprinting over to the door he let Barry in and returned to the phone call. "Miacoh, Barry is here. I'll get back to you."

Micoah interrupted. "Just wanted to let you know we got the file and are moving on it."

Barry waited while Cayson finished his call. "Todd heard dispatch over the radio and joined me. He's checking out the grounds. Didn't see a soul here when I arrived. Todd thought he saw a character sauntering down the side of the road. The person's gait increased after spotting the squad car, then he veered off the road and disappeared into the woods. You know he could circle back and end up behind the safe house."

"Well aware. How long has Todd been gone?" He moved the curtain in the front room and stared outside at the darkening sky then turned on the security lights.

"About fifteen minutes." Barry shoved his hat back on his head. "I'd better go check on him. He should have been here by now."

Cayson opened the door. The bright security lights showcased Todd walking up the path from the forest prodding a man in front of him. He had his weapon trained on the individual. "Looks like Todd had better luck than you."

Molly slipped out from behind Cayson. "Greg, what are you doing skulking around here? A battering ram? Really?"

Greg stared menacingly at her. "This is all your fault. If you'd just mind your own business."

"My friend is missing. You had something to do with it?" She took a couple of steps forward and jabbed her finger in his chest. "What about stealing my identity? Breaking into my house, leaving threatening notes, trying to steal my thesis? You behind all of this too? What did I ever do to you?"

"This is bigger than just you." Greg struggled against the tie wraps restraining his hands behind his back, but he said nothing else and returned his gaze to the floor.

Cayson stepped between them and gently returned her arm to her side. "Go back inside, Molly. Let the police handle this."

"But if he knows what happened to Kinley, he has to tell me," Molly insisted attempting to push Cayson aside and raising her fist in the air.

Greg raised his gaze to her and sneered.

Cayson pressed Molly's arms to her sides and propelled her into the house and shut the door with his foot. "You're making the situation worse. Let Todd take him to the jail. Miacoh will have a go at him in the morning before anyone else gets involved. He's really good at getting information out of people. Besides, Greg cooling his heels in a jail cell might be just what he needs."

"I don't like it. Besides, there could be another person out there waiting for the excitement to die down and take another run at the house."

"You don't have to like it. That's the way it's going to be." His tone garnered no argument. "As far as another accomplice—" He patted his weapon holstered at his waistband. "The alarm system will give us plenty of notice as well as the police."

Molly jerked out of his hold, stared at the door, as if considering a run at it, but turned and stalked to the alarm system's bank of computer screens. "Did you test the direct connection to the police station?"

"Yes, but the connection failed. I was going to have you test it while I check the connections." Cayson stepped out of the door in time to watch Todd put Greg in the back of the squad car and close the door. He pulled out his cell and punched in Miacoh's number. It went right to voice mail. He left a message as to what happened, then turned back to Molly. "Try the connection again. We'll trouble shoot it right now." He stepped inside and closed the door then dialed dispatch. "Cayson here. We're checking the connection from the safe house to the police station. Barry is still here, so no need to send anyone. It's just a test."

"10-4. You're clear," dispatch responded.

Cayson stared at the data connections, then unplugged the router and plugged it in again. Then he checked the wi-fi then the cellular connection and password. The cellular link blinked red. He re-entered the passwords and the light switched to green. "Molly, set off the alarm."

She made sure both doors were closed, then set the alarm, went to the window, opened it, then opened the front door. The alarm wailed. Her cell phone and Cayon's rang simultaneously. She peered at him as he answered his phone.

"Yep. We're all set. Thank you." He disconnected the call and joined Molly at the front door.

Barry caught his attention. "I'll see to it that Chief has time to question the prisoner before anyone knows he's here."

"Thanks. I don't think Greg acted alone. He's someone's puppet."

"You don't think Professor James is pulling the strings from out of country, do you?"

"No. The feds are monitoring him in case he tries to re-enter the US. But I don't believe we have all his henchmen. Molly believes Greg isn't smart enough or has enough balls to pull this off alone." Cayson turned to see Molly had returned to the open window watching the events. "Still, time is of the essence if we are going to find Kinley Jaybird alive."

Barry raised his eyebrows and shrugged. "It's possible it's already too late."

He lowered his voice. "Don't you let her hear you say that. Positivity is what we need right now."

"But you know—"

"You'd better get back to the station and prepare the incident report for tonight. Thanks for your assistance. But I don't want to hold you up any longer."

"Sure you'll be all right the rest of the night? Todd can come back out here tonight."

He patted his weapon and pointed to the security system. "We'll be just fine. Molly's packing too. Besides, Todd's got paperwork."

Barry adjusted his hat on his head. "Chief

Bearclaw didn't see this much action in the whole thirty-five years he served. Chief Zane takes over and…" He made an explosive sign with his hand.

"If I were you, I wouldn't let Miacoh hear you say that." Cayson chuckled. "It's called job security. Besides it's a different world now, even in small towns."

"Yep. Night." Barry waved and sauntered out to his squad car. The radio squawked as he opened the door.

Chapter Twenty

Spring Festival Plans, a Float, and Further Investigation Nets More Suspects.

Molly awoke refreshed after the rest of the night was uneventful. She quietly dressed and padded out to the kitchen where the automatic coffee maker hissed and sizzled the last drops of coffee into the glass pot. She inhaled deeply, enjoying the aroma of fresh brewed coffee. *Too bad it didn't taste as good as it smelled.* By the time Cayson found his way downstairs, she'd put a pitcher of orange juice on the table, prepared scrambled eggs and bacon warming on the stove, and began buttering the toast that just popped.

"Wow. How long have you been up?" Cayson glanced over the stove and table.

"Not long. I woke up rested and hungry. Figured I'd let you sleep since you tossed and turned most of the night. Have breakfast ready, and we could get an early start at the office. I've a feeling that float creation is in our future after the challenge Clara left hanging with Pekabo. Though I don't know Pekabo or Candle well, they're gonna bite."

Cayson laughed. "You can bet on it. The gauntlet dropped." He plopped into a kitchen chair and gulped down orange juice. "I'm surprised you slept as well as you did, after the commotion last night."

"I guess I'd reached my limit of worry and sleeplessness. I was asleep almost before my head hit the pillow." She scooped up a forkful of eggs and slid them into her mouth, then washed them down with orange juice and reached for a piece of toast. A golden ray of sunlight struck the silver and turquoise bracelet she always wore. On her wrist it appeared to glow.

"Hey, what's with your bracelet?" Cayson reached out for her hand, turning it this way and that. "Guess it's the sunlight." He released her hand.

She took a bite of toast, chewed thoughtfully while observing the piece of jewelry. The bracelet continued to faintly glow out of the sunlight. Curious, she twisted the band and removed it. The glow disappeared. "Isn't that strange. Never happened before."

"Where did you get the bracelet?" He reached out his hand. She put the piece of jewelry in his hand.

"I always wear it. My grandmother gave it to me. Said it was for good luck and protection." She shrugged. "She must have been mistaken."

He turned the bracelet over and over in his hand. "There's an inscription inside."

She leaned over the table to get a better look. "The magic decides." Taking the bracelet from him, she shook her head. "One of my prized possessions, I have examined, cleaned, and polished it. There was never an inscription inside it."

"Well, there is now." Cayson grinned. "We'd better get going. Talk to Candle or Pekabo about it later today. They're good at solving mysteries and woo woo things."

She peered at the bracelet again, then slid it on her wrist. *Still felt the same.* "Woo woo things?"

"Things not of this normal world. The Bearclaws have an interesting history. And Miacoh…well there's more to him than meets the eye. Stick around long enough and you'll see what I mean." He winked and shrugged into his jacket then held hers out. "Gotta go."

The sun had just risen over the small town of Aspen Ridge when Cayson and Molly arrived at the Terrabyte office. He parked beside Candle's SUV in the parking lot.

"Boss lady is here early this morning," Cayson commented.

The street was already buzzing with activity. People were milling about, measuring for booths and decorations for the upcoming Spring Festival. Clara had certainly put a bee in everyone's bonnet to make this festival something special.

Cayson, Molly, and Candle stood at the front window of Terrabyte Security. "Well, I guess we'd better get to work on our float for the festival parade." Candle sighed glancing down at Terra who sat on the floor squeaking her toy loudly.

"I cleaned out and organized the warehouse last week. There's room for creating an elaborate float, if that is what you're after." Cayson grinned at his boss. "I have a couple of early installations, but I could be back by mid-morning."

"I've never created a float before. I'm at a loss where to start." Candle glanced at Molly, who had been typing furiously on the computer prior to joining them at the window.

"I've a few ideas," Molly said hesitantly. "In college, I was on the float committee. A huge task of coming up with a theme, design it to fit the parameters, and cost to come in under budget. One year the dang thing caught on fire. Quite a fiasco that year."

"Sounds like. Let's take a look at what you're thinking." Candle followed Molly to her computer. Molly printed out a listing of ideas, then pulled up a 3D rendering program.

"Let's see what you got." Candle stood behind her.

Molly pointed to the screen. "First the theme, Spring into Security should be a banner across the front. Second, decorate the float with all kinds of security tech equipment like shells of cameras, computers, keypads, etc., surrounded with flowers."

"Flowers?" Cayson screwed up his face in mock disdain. "We're a serious security firm."

"Of course. But we need to appeal to the softer side too. Wives and girlfriends influence their men. Heck, the company is owned by a woman."

"Yes, but she's the daughter of the former chief of police," Cayson argued.

"I like it so far. You have quite an imagination Molly." Candle leaned over and peered at the computer screen as Molly created a rough image of how the float would appear.

"Next, a colorful desk at the center with all four of us sitting or standing around it, with logo T-shirts on and blue jeans. Terra could sit under the desk or wherever she's comfortable. Then use an aluminum framework, bottom weighted, to create a second story, French doors open to a balcony, base of the railing computer shells with twinkling lights inside. A banner draped across the balcony that says "Your Security is Our #1." The idea is to showcase our talents to the community."

The front door squeaked open. Hunter strode in with Pekabo at his side. "Good morning." He glanced at the three then at his watch. "Am I late?" His attention zeroed in on his daughter. "You said nine this morning. Right?"

Terrabyte brought her toy over to Hunter and dropped it at his feet. He bent over, scratched the pup's ears, and threw the toy.

"Yep. But after Clara threw down the gauntlet yesterday, we decided to make our float the talk of the town, not to mention the window decorations for the festival." Candle winked at her mom. "Molly designed floats in college. Take a look."

Hunter and Pekabo crowded around the computer. "Nice," murmured Hunter.

"Aspen Ridge has never seen anything like this." Pekabo clapped her hands together and bounced from foot to foot. "Clara will be so shocked."

"To tie in the front window decorations with the float, we could use old keypads, shells of desktop computers, cameras, and other tech equipment we use and fill them with twinkling lights. A couple of fake schematics or plans printed out in colorful ink and leaned against the equipment should tie it all together."

"Excellent." Candle danced a jig.

Molly puffed out her cheeks and blew out a breath. "We could put up a "Have You Seen Her" poster of Kinley in the window and maybe on the float?" She rushed on. "It would bring attention to her plight and other MMIW, also may flush out the individuals that are harassing me or calling the shots."

"Yeah, I talked with Miacoh last night. This morning he's interrogating the perps that broke into the safe house. They caught the other on the road." Hunter shook his head. "Thinks they are just minions and they're not talking."

"Finding that list—at least we have a motive now. Don't we?" Molly peered questioningly at Hunter and Cayson.

Hunter nodded. "Seems to tie everything together."

"But I didn't know anything about the list. Why single me out?"

"I have several thoughts simmering on that," Candle interjected. "But right now, let's get to work on the float. I think better with my hands busy."

"After reading over the files and Molly's statements, I have a few hypotheses I'd like to share." Hunter slid his glance over the group. "We can discuss it further between your working on the float and answering the phone."

The group walked the short distance to the warehouse on Terrabyte property and stepped inside, pushing the door shut.

Suddenly, the door to Terrabyte Security warehouse flew open. Miacoh caught it by the edge before it hit the wall. "Boy, the wind is kicking up out there. Did I hear mention of the list?"

"We were tossing around ideas." Candle grinned at her husband.

"Greg isn't going anywhere until he talks. Won't be long." Miacoh shot her an encouraging smile. "Meanwhile, we've rounded up most of the people on that list, apart from a few that left town after the explosion. The feds are handling them. Break-ins and harassment should cease unless we have loose ends, but the trap is set. The individuals we don't have enough on to hold were released after overhearing that Greg is singing like a songbird and that they will be rearrested if he implicates them in the case."

Over the next week, the float took shape, over twenty feet high and adorned with a dizzying array of lights, shells of computer components, flowers, and signs. Banners and posters proclaimed the company's various services, from background checks to cyber security and investigations. Front and center on both the float and window decoration was Kinley's poster.

Candle stood back and brushed her hands together. "Great job, everyone."

Pekabo tilted her head. "Kinley's poster is going to make some people squirm. Rightly so. Maybe even push-back from the authorities? You up for that, Candle?"

"Yep. Time is of the essence if we are to find Kinley before it's too late. If they'd done their job, this wouldn't be necessary."

Molly swallowed hard. "I hope these help."

The door to the warehouse flew open again. Gabby and her twins rushed in. "I heard you were building—" She skidded to a stop, Nash and Natalya crashed into each other, then into her and stared up at the huge float. "We came to help. Guess we're too late. What a fantastic creation." She walked around the float, then stopped at the poster of Kinley and sucked in a breath, her forehead creased in concern. "Still missing, huh? Anything I can do to help?"

Candle grabbed a stack of smaller fliers. "Distribute these. Put one in your office window, if it's all right with Ben."

"Will do. The kids and I will distribute the fliers in

the crowd watching the festival parade." She gave Candle a side glance. "I didn't know you were so creative."

Candle waved her off. "Not me. It's all Molly's doing."

Molly's cheeks heated. "I learned a little about floats in college."

Miacoh shoved open the door. "What the heck are you all doing still here? Get this monstrosity to the staging area. I pulled some strings to get your float at the front of the parade. And, I might add, Clara is not one bit pleased to hear you have entered a float and she's not seen it yet." He rocked back on his heels, thumbs in his belt loops grinning like a Cheshire cat. "That'll teach her."

A woman standing in the doorway cleared her voice. "Holy Moley! This will take first place in the contest hands down."

The group whirled around to see city council madam chairperson, Tressa Harper, standing wide-eyed and slack jawed.

"Tressa, what are you doing here? What contest?" Candle strode toward the door with her hand outstretched.

Tressa shook her hand. "Clara decided to get more participation in the parade she'd add prize money and a guarantee to be first in line next year. Personally, I believe it's Clara's competitive personality that's putting people off. I told her to back off when the council approved the monetary request. Ruffled her feathers pretty bad." Tressa turned to Pekabo. "Big favor. Could you have a word with Clara? Maybe unruffle her feathers?"

Pekabo covered her mouth but couldn't hold back the roar of laughter. "I'm the wrong person." She relayed Clara's recent visit and actions.

"See what I mean? If you won't talk to her, we'll have to—" Tressa raised an eyebrow and grimaced. "Pekabo, you always did such a great job over the past twenty years with the parade. I'm afraid you'll have to take over until I can find a replacement or no parade or festival."

Pekabo slammed her fists on her hips. "That's blackmail, Tressa."

Tressa shrugged. "Desperate times require desperate measures."

Hunter raised his hand and stepped between the women and slinging an arm around Pekabo. "Whoa! We can schedule our vacations around the Spring Festival next year, if necessary. However, Pek and I will discuss the situation with Clara. Offer Pek to co-chair the festival committee with Clara for next year. Hopefully, the year after Clara can handle it on her own. She's overzealous to do a good job in Pekabo's footsteps."

"You mean to show me up." Pekabo crossed her arms over her chest.

"No one can do that." Hunter patted her arm. "And you know it. Now how about it?"

His wife let her arms slip to her sides. "Okay. I'll try. If nothing else, Candle can fill in."

"Oh, no. You're not roping me into this." Candle shook her head vehemently. "I have a growing business to run."

Cayson blew out a breath, walked to his truck, and backed it up to the float. He hooked it up, checked the tires, and glanced at the group. "Time to go, if we're to be first. I'll meet Candle, Molly, and Hunter at the staging area. You'll be prepared to climb aboard. Right?"

"Yep." Candle called Terrabyte, who came running, skidding around the edge of the float and stopping in front of her. "Molly, send the phones to the answering service. See you there."

"Will do." Molly sprinted into the office, switched the phones, and joined Cayson in the truck. "Whew, what a morning."

Throngs of townspeople wandered the streets and sidewalks as Cayson took the back roads to the staging area. He stopped one street over from the starting point and jumped out of the truck. "I'm going to make sure where they want us. I'll be right back." Reaching over, he caressed her neck, pulled her to him, and kissed her. "We'll find her."

"I hope so." She fingered the fliers in her lap.

Chapter Twenty-One

Spring Festival in Full Bloom and a Surprise Revelation.

The float was a sight to behold, an impressive and imposing display of security technology and expertise. Candle, Cayson, Molly, Pekabo, and Hunter beamed with pride as everyone but Pekabo and Cayson climbed onto the float. Miacoh hoisted Terra up on the float handing the leash to Candle.

After everyone was set, Cayson maneuvered the truck and float into the staging area and to the head of the parade and waited until he was signaled to proceed.

Cayson waved out the window as the float proceeded through the streets of Aspen Ridge to ooohs and awwws and loud applause. While pausing at cross streets, he'd turn and check everything was all right on the float. Approaching the last cross street a woman screamed and pounded on his passenger side door. He hit the brakes and leaned over. "Pekabo, what are you doing?"

"Open the dang door, now." She yanked on the handle, and he released the lock and waited for her to climb inside. "I was leaning over there against the wall waiting for the parade to reach here. A vision of Kinley formed. I must have passed out for a moment or two. When I came to, there was a group of people leaning over me." She waved her hand wildly. "Doesn't matter. Saw the woman being dragged from a house basement and loaded into a dark blue SUV, license plates started with CBK-2 I couldn't make out the rest. She was kicking and screaming until one man struck her. The vehicle turned out of a residential area, passed by a sign— Golden, Colorado then turned onto Colorado Highway 58, and the vision faded." She made a starburst with her hand. "We gotta go."

"Pekabo, I'm towing a float. Roads are blocked off. I can't just go busting through them. I understand the urgency. Contact Miacoh. He's in the squad car in front of us." He tossed his phone to her. "I'll stop at the next opportunity to get Hunter down here with us. Calm down. Are you sure this is happening now, or…"

Pekabo closed her eyes and was silent for a beat. "As the SUV drove it passed a building with time and temperature sign. Time flipped to 12:45." She opened her eyes. Panic written on her face. "We gotta go. Now. That was twenty minutes ago." She bounced up and down on the seat.

"Call Miacoh. Tell him to turn on his lights, bump his siren, and pull over so I can follow him." Cayson flipped on his four-way flashers, glanced behind him to see Molly on the edge of the float motioning with her arm to pull over, her bracelet glowing. As he slowed to a crawl, Hunter hopped off the float and began to direct the rest of the parade around him.

"Done." Pekabo handed the phone back to him. "You know, I have my own phone." She pulled a pink cell out of her pocket and wiggled it back and forth.

"Quicker to toss you mine." Cayson kept his eyes on the street.

The squad car ahead turned on lights and siren, pulling to the side of the road. Miacoh jumped out of the vehicle racing toward Cayson and the float. "What's the emergency?"

Molly too hopped off the float and sprinted to the truck. "Something is seriously wrong. I can feel it. My bracelet started glowing subtly then brighter a while after we began the parade. The strangest feeling came over me at the same time. An urgency."

Cayson pulled the truck and float to the side of the road, Candle and Terra joined the crowd around the truck.

After putting Terra in the truck, Candle jumped up on the hood. "Nothing to see here. Technical problems, just get back on the sidewalk and enjoy the rest of the parade."

Miacoh and Officer Cimerono, who was riding with him, directed the crowd of spectators back to the sidewalk and away from the float. Leaving Officer Cimerono in charge of the crowd control, Miacoh returned to the truck. "Again, I ask what in the hell is going on?"

Pekabo attempted to climb out of the vehicle all the while repeating what she'd told Cayson.

"Stay inside and tell us what happened. I don't want wind of this to get into the community, yet."

"We gotta go." She stared imploringly at Miacoh then grabbed the shirt sleeve of her husband, Hunter. "Now."

"Calm down, everyone," Miacoh said in a commanding voice. "Won't do anyone any good, if we go off half-cocked. I'll issue a BOLO for the vehicle, citing an anonymous tip. Molly, go with Cayson. Take the float back to the warehouse then join me at the police station. Hunter and Pekabo, ride with me to the station. I'll send someone to pick up Todd Cimerono after the parade is finished. Candle, you drove your own vehicle. Right?"

"Yep. Had a strange feeling this morning I'd need it."

He gave her two thumbs up, then strode over and kissed her. "This case may be about to break wide open."

****

Ben and Gabby with the twins in tow strode up to the truck. "Can we be of help?"

"How much did you hear?" Miacoh snapped.

"All of it," Gabby admitted. "We were among the group that assisted Pekabo. We skirted around the float when you chased the others away. I had an inkling as to what might be going on." She turned to Ben then shifted back to Miacoh. "We want to help."

"Could you stick around and give Officer Todd Cimerono a ride back to the station?" Miacoh peered at his officer still keeping the crowd's attention on the parade and out of the way as Molly moved roadblocks and Cayson negotiated his way out of the parade route to Terrabyte Security.

"Sure," Ben offered.

Candle interrupted. "Gabby, could you retrieve the messages from the answering service at Terrabyte Security? Let me know if there is anything earth-shattering or pertaining to Molly's case. I sent Kinley's flier to news agencies across Colorado last night. Terra and I'll be at the police station."

"Of course." Gabby corralled the twins and stood

behind Ben.

The twins squealed and wiggled in an attempt to escape their mother's grip. "We want to watch the rest of the parade."

Gabby gently shook the twins. "We'll watch the rest of the parade, then I'll take care of it."

"Fair enough." Candle jogged toward her vehicle, the dog keeping pace with her. She opened the passenger door and assisted Terra inside. After hooking her to the seatbelt, she scratched the pup's ears. "I've a feeling things are about to get interesting."

"I'll meet everyone back at the police station." Miacoh climbed into the police cruiser, turned off the lights, backed up, and followed the route cleared by Molly and Cayson.

Once at the station, he checked on the BOLO he'd requested Officer Barry Smith put out and called the jurisdictions that might be involved. He grabbed a map to try to figure out where they were heading. *North for sure, but how far? Making a run for Canada?* He typed Murdock Welsh's name into the computer. "Shit."

Molly, Pekabo, and Candle converged on the station and began talking at once. Terra joined the chaos by barking and running circles around the group. Hunter let out a loud whistle. "Calm down. We need a plan and to include other agencies in it. Golden is approximately one hour and thirty minutes from here. We can't catch them, assuming it is who we think it is. They can't outrun the telephone or police radios. I believe Miacoh has everything under control. Let the man work." Hunter walked over and clapped a hand on Miacoh's shoulder and whispered, "Better you than me, son."

Candle grabbed Terra by the collar. "Sit and quiet."

Miacoh glanced up at Hunter. "Damned Murdock has dual citizenship for the United States and Canada. If he's got a plane stashed at some little airport somewhere in Colorado or Wyoming—" He shoved back against the chair." What if Pekabo is wrong?"

"Son, her visions are never wrong. Besides, you have two other psychics backing her up. What's your gut telling you?"

Miacoh stared incredulously at Hunter.

"Why would he take Kinley with him? Why not let her go and flee alone or with whoever is helping him? He's figured out by now we're on to him and he has no one to do his dirty work."

Or kill her and dump the body in the Canadian tundra. Miacoh glanced up at Hunter.

His father-in-law winked. "We both know that is not going to happen. Won't let it." *Yep, our link as werewolves is still as strong as when you were a teenager. Pack mentality will share thoughts. Remember.*

Molly sat slumped in a chair, wringing her hands. "I feel so helpless."

The bracelet on her arm pulsed slowly at first then more quickly. "What does it mean?"

Candle's phone played a tune about the devil in Georgia. "Yes, Gabby?" She listened then pumped her fist in the air. "That's fantastic. Did you tell her to contact the Golden Police Department?" Silence for a few more beats. "Perfect. Thanks. I owe you." Candle disconnected the call. Terra, who settled at Candle's feet, now got to her feet, picking up on the excitement in her owner's voice. The dog's tail wagged uncertainly back and forth.

Candle pointed to the floor. Terra plopped down on the rug and huffed.

Bracelet momentarily forgotten, Molly perched on the edge of her chair, her hand finding Cayson's and gripping tightly. "What's happened?"

"Well. Someone called the answering service. She saw the flier on the news, then witnessed a man drag a woman kicking and screaming out of a house in her neighborhood. The woman fit Kinley's description. The witness also called the police department to report it. Bless her heart, she got the whole license number and description of the car they left in."

Candle looked up to see Miacoh on his phone. He was nodding. After disconnecting the call, he grinned at her. "Got confirmation we're not on a wild goose chase. Those fliers were a great idea, Molly. Sending them to the news stations was genius, Candle."

"So what do we do now? Wait for him to take her across the Canadian border?" Molly threw up her hands, then let them drop to her sides.

"Police agencies in northern Colorado, Wyoming, and the four corners area are all looking for the vehicle and Kinley. Agents Caitlyn and Jed of Homeland Security have joined in the search accessing their database and cameras. The airports have been alerted. It's only a matter of time. Murdock has to stop for gas, food, and bathroom breaks. If he uses a credit card, we got him. If he pays with cash, he'll be picked up on the store's surveillance camera. We got him." Miacoh paced the room.

"What if he makes it to an airport? Maybe a private one. What's to stop him from jumping in a plane and

187

taking off?" Molly continued wringing her hands.

Cayson hiked his hip on the corner of Molly's desk. Leaning over, he put an arm around her. "What if pigs fly?"

Molly's eyes flew wide open, a soft chuckle slipping out.

He played with a wisp of black hair that had escaped her braid. "Let's not play the what if game. If you want to start traveling north, we can use my truck. But I have to tell you, with all the agencies searching, they'll pinpoint his location shortly. Then we'll know where exactly to go."

"I just can't sit here and do nothing." Molly wiped her hands on her jeans.

Miacoh's phone buzzed again. He glanced at the screen. "Gotta take this." He stepped into his office and closed the door. A few minutes later he burst out of the door. "Caitlyn and Jed have procured a helo from Homeland. It'll be in the air in ten minutes. The car's been sighted at a gas station on I-25 south of the Wyoming border. Wyoming State Police have been alerted. Roadblocks will be put in place."

Cayson hugged Molly. "See, no need to go anywhere. We couldn't get there before they capture the vehicle."

"If everything goes according to plan, Kinley will be returned to Aspen Ridge via helo after they've interviewed her." Miacoh peered at Molly. "Best if you sit tight here and wait for her."

"If things go south?" Molly asked even as a feeling of calm washed over her. For the first time in a while, she glanced at her bracelet when the light pulsing slowed, barely visible to those around her.

"Please, a little positivity. You still wouldn't be anywhere near her. And you would have done all you could for her. Don't forget that." Miacoh glanced at her bracelet. "What is your talisman telling you?"

"I've no idea."

Pekabo stepped over to Molly and put her hand on her shoulder. "I'm aware this is the first experience you've had with the bracelet, or any type of psychic abilities, but let's backtrack for a minute. I've watched you and the bracelet on and off since you jumped off the float. It's gone from a bright orange glow to a subtle pulsing glow to a peaceful pulsing rhythm. How do you feel?"

"I panicked at first, then was anxious to get on the road. Now, like you said, a feeling of calm washed over me a few minutes ago." Molly's forehead creased. "How could the bracelet know an outcome?"

"The talisman doesn't. But the connection between you and Kinley is so deep, now that you're tuned into it, you sense her wellbeing. Scared. Yes. But she feels the light at the end of the tunnel, through you."

"If the police agencies would have acted on the info I gave them earlier, she'd be—"

Pekabo quickly put her finger to Molly's lips. "No negative thoughts." She glanced at the bracelet barely able to make out the calm pulsing glow. "It's going to be all right. I can feel it." She blew out a breath slowly then turned to her daughter. "You feel it too, don't you?"

"I do." Candle glanced at her husband who frowned deeply at her. "I know, I know, only cold hard facts. But you and others are aware there is more in this world than what can be explained by the facts."

Miacoh opened his mouth to retort when his phone buzzed again. This time he didn't bother to go in his office. "Chief Zane here." He was silent for several minutes. "Are you sure?" Again silence. "And Murdock?"

Candle took a couple of steps toward him. He held up his hand in a waiting motion.

Candle puffed out her cheeks and released her breath.

"I see. Do you have an ETA?" This time he paused only a beat. "You can interview her here at the Aspen Ridge Police Department. I'm sure she'd like to see some familiar faces. After all, we are the ones that brought her abduction to light when other agencies just swept it under the rug or worse yet, looked the other way. I don't mean Homeland, this time. I'm aware you just learned of the situation and moved quickly to assist. We are extremely grateful. You may have saved that young woman's life."

Molly's head fell back against the back of her chair cradled in Cayson's arm. She closed her eyes.

Candle and Pekabo began a respectful celebration dance, including quiet high fives. Of course, Terra was on her feet again, this time prancing beside Candle quietly.

Miacoh continued to listen for a few moments. "As far as we're concerned, Homeland or FBI can have Murdock and his associates. We have Greg and another associate in the jail here. Golden Police are also involved. Might want to copy them in. We're more than willing to turn them over to the proper authorities along with the evidence we've collected. This whole thing is an extension of the professor's crimes at the School of

Mines last year. So you think about an hour?" He nodded. "We'll be ready." Disconnecting the call, he grinned over at Molly, then his wife. "Kinley will arrive here by helo in about an hour. The feds will want to complete her interview, but they are willing to do that here."

Exhausted, Molly got to her feet and joined in Candle and Pekabo's celebration dance, pulling Cayson along with her. He stood there like a fish out of water, looking to Miacoh and Hunter to assist. Both raised their hands, palms up in a gesture that said you're on your own, buddy.

Officers Smith and Cimerono trudged through the well-worn front door of the police station. "Parade is over. Everyone is at the park speculating as to what happened. You might want to give an update?"

Gabby, Ben, and the twins rushed in behind the officers. Gabby burst out, "Any news?"

"Yes. Most of it good." Miacoh smiled. "Have the bandstand in the park cleared. I'll make an announcement shortly." He turned to the others. "I want all of you on the bandstand with me. Including Molly. This was a joint effort."

Gabby bounced from one foot to the other as if about to explode. "I can't hold it in any longer. Terrabyte Security's float won first place. And Clara is none too happy." She exhaled loudly grinning from ear to ear.

"Been a rough day for a woman who can't keep a secret, huh?" Candle wrapped an arm around her best friend and squeezed.

"You betcha." Gabby still bounced on her toes. The twins located Terra and raced after her.

Candle grabbed the pup by the scruff and sat her down at her feet. "Stay. We'll play later."

Gabby grabbed the twins by their collars and yanked them to her sides. Ben took hold of Nash's arm. Gabby grabbed the other. "We're going home after your announcement. Please make it quick."

Miacoh corralled the whole group and headed for the bandstand at the south end of the town square. Hunter and Pekabo beat them to the bandstand and cleared the area.

Hunter motioned toward the stage. "It's all yours."

"After you." Miacoh deferred to the retired chief.

Once they were all assembled Miacoh stepped up to the microphone and tapped on the mic. "Is this thing on?" A loud thump followed by a squeal came across the speakers. The audience covered their ears and Miacoh laughed. "Guess so. I have wonderful news for you. Kinley, the indigenous woman's picture on our float and that all of you put in your store window fronts, has been found alive and is on her way back here via the federal government's helicopter. I'm not at liberty to say any more at this moment because there are lots of loose ends to tie up. Thanks to our employee, Molly, and her suggested poster campaign, then with each and every one of your help, tips came in that led to the recovery of the young woman. Thank you all so much." He looked over at Clara who stood on the bottom step of the bandstand tapping her foot impatiently. "Now I believe Clara has an announcement."

Clara bustled up the steps to the stage and took the mic from Miacoh. "As a town, we are extremely proud to have assisted in that young woman's rescue." She clapped her hands at everyone in the audience. "Even though the Terrabyte Security float was unable to finish the parade route, due in part to the emergency, it was voted best float in the parade, with Viola's float from Aspen's Wylde Hair, coming in second, and the Nuts and Bolts float from the hardware store nailed down third place." She chuckled as the crowd let out a groan. "The winning float pictures will be on display at city hall for about a week. Congratulations to all the contestants, and the winners. Thank you all for your participation. We had an additional fifteen floats this year, bringing the float total to forty-five making this the best Spring Festival in Aspen Ridge's history." Clara held her arms open to the audience then clapped her hands. "I have meal certificates from the Angus Steak House for the winners. And there's a free cherry pie from Echo bakery for all the float entries. Simply present your entry number at the bakery. That's all I have. Everyone, reconvene at the town square park where all the vendors have set up. Enjoy!"

"That's our signal to join the festivities." Cayson took Molly's hand and tucked it through his.

She shook her head. "Not sure I'm feeling like—"

He paused and took hold of both her hands and squeezed. "If there's one thing I learned in the military, you have to take fun or enjoyment where you find it. You never know what is waiting around the next corner." Cayson stared into her eyes. "We've got something special together and in a town that has embraced both of us. Good friends are like family. Don't keep waiting for the next shoe to fall."

"I've spent most of my teenage and adult life waiting for the next shoe to fall. Maybe I don't know how to move on." Molly frowned and peered at the ground.

"That's hard to believe but let me show you." He gently caressed her chin, tilted her face up to his, and captured her lips. He sunk into her like there was no tomorrow until several individuals loudly cleared their throats.

"Hey, guys, get a room or come join the fun. The latter would be the preferred action." Miacoh jerked his chin toward the werewolf family loping in Cayson's direction.

Peter reached out his hand to shake Cayson's. "That was quite a float Terrabyte Security built."

"Thanks. It was a team effort."

"Spurred on by Clara." Candle chuckled glancing at her mom, who promptly fisted her hands at her hips and appeared to pout.

Hunter grinned at his wife. "Don't act like you didn't enjoy every minute of Clara's challenge. You were just lucky that Molly had experience in float building, then Candle and company were up to the task."

"And won first place, I might add." Candle rubbed her polished nails against her blouse.

Cayson swung his arm around Molly and turned his attention to the young werewolf pulling on his sleeve. "What is it, buddy?"

Future motioned Cayson a few steps away from the crowd.

Cayson followed, arm still slung around Molly. He leaned toward Future whispering, "Whatever you have to say is safe with Molly too."

The boy dug the toe of his boot into the soft earth. "You told anyone about our secret talk—?" He hesitated for a couple beats glancing around.

"No. Of course not. Holding up your end of the bargain kept my mouth shut. Why?"

"Hum— Dad invited some of the werewolf families from Raven's Hollow to join our festival." He shrugged. "I was a bit worried."

"No need to be. It's our secret." He gave the boy a slight shove. "Now go on and have a good time with your friends."

As the boy loped off, Molly turned her back and laughed. "You left that threat hanging over that poor kid's head all this time?"

Cayson rocked back on his heels, huffed out a breath on his fingernails, and polished them against his shirt. "Yep. Worked too, didn't it? Saved his parents a ton of money in the process."

"You are incorrigible."

"Yep, that's why you love me." Silence reigned for several moments. *Did I just make the worst mistake of my life?*

Molly's eyes widened, and she licked her dry lips.

Chapter Twenty-Two

Festival Surprises and a Homecoming.

"Well— You going to leave me hanging or finally admit what's in your heart? It took me a while to come to terms with my feelings, being a confirmed bachelor and all. But when you want something bad enough, you are willing to throw caution to the wind and take that leap."

She straightened. "Now wait just one minute. Seems I'm the one on the hook, not you. I didn't hear a declaration from you."

He took her tenderly in his arms and kissed her with wild abandon, then whispered against her lips, "You are the only one for me. I love you to the moon and back. Would you consider spending the rest of your life with me?"

She backed away and sucked in a breath. "Are you serious? You'd ask such a life changing question in the middle of all this chaos?" Holding her hand to her heart, she squeaked, "And expect an answer?"

"You betcha." He continued to hold her close.

"What's going on over here?" Candle sidled up to Molly. "You all right? What did Cayson do now?"

Molly whirled out of his arms to face Candle and blurted, "He asked me to marry him."

Candle waved her hand nonchalantly. "Oh, is that

all."

Miacoh stepped up behind Candle, his hand sliding around her waist. "Well, don't stand there. Give the man the answer he deserves." Miacoh clapped his friend on the shoulder. "It happens to the best of us. You got a good one there.

"Not yet. I'm still waiting."

Miacoh shrugged. "Come on, wife, I'm starved. Time to feed your man."

Candle gave him a seductive side-eye. "Depends on what you're hungry for."

"Oh, you know me. I'll take whatever you offer. With the caveat that dessert be served at home and naked." Miacoh chuckled and nuzzled his wife's neck.

Miacoh's phone broke through the reverie. He glanced at the screen. "Now what?" He touched the screen. "Chief Zane here." He listened for a moment. "Yes, she's here, one moment."

"Molly, someone wants to speak with you." He handed the phone to the stunned woman.

"Hello?" She was silent for a beat then grabbed the phone with both hands. "Kinley, are you all right? It's such a relief to hear your voice." Molly slumped into a chair. Another silence. "No. you want them to bring you to Aspen Ridge. We can get your stuff from Golden later. There are lots of people I want you to meet. I mean, if you're up to it. Besides, I had Mocha brought here. She's waiting at my house—the safe house." She paused to listen again. "Yes, I believe they've rounded up most of the bad actors. But I'm not sure, and I don't think they know the extent of the corruption. Goes all the way back to when we were at college. You'd be safer here." Another slight pause.

"Okay, see you soon." She hung up and threw her arms around Cayson. "Kinley's on her way here. She claims she's okay."

"Great to hear. Let's get something to eat. You've not eaten since our early breakfast. You don't want to fade away before Kinley arrives."

Miacoh raised an eyebrow. "Did I hear you say Kinley is on her way here?"

"Yes. I hope it's okay. I kinda figured she could stay with me—" She glanced over at Cayson. "—and him at the safe house until all the loose ends are tied up."

Hunter cleared his throat. "You realize that all the loose ends won't be tied up until we get the professor? Which could be years or maybe never."

"But we will shut down his network of illegal activities and arrest his cohorts." Miacoh stood straight, thumbs tucked in his belt loops. "It might be a bit difficult to live day to day without an income stream. We'll see what Murdock has to say once he's the only one standing. His minions will roll over on him once they discover he has no means to protect them. A threat of a healthy stint in the federal judicial system should bring their cooperation." A wicked grin spread across his face.

"Provided Murdock is the kingpin. Below the professor." Hunter licked his lips as his wife handed him two teriyaki chicken sticks.

"These are to die for." Making shooing motions with her hands, she chased the others to the vendor tents to grab food.

Candle took two more skewers from her mom and handed one to Miacoh and nibbled on the other. "She's right. These are great. Let's go get more." She tugged her husband toward the line at the vendor.

"Smells really good." Molly tilted her head toward the vendor tent.

"There is still the little matter of an answer." He blew out a breath. "You aren't going to give me one, are you?"

"Yes, there is no doubt I love you. But marriage is a big step for me. With everything that's happened today, my head is spinning. And you're asking me to make a decision that will affect the rest of my life. Could you give me a little time to make my decision?"

"I didn't realize it would be that hard for you." Cayson's voice cooled.

"It's not that it's hard, it's…"

"Come find me when you figure it all out." He took several steps and ran into Miacoh.

Miacoh tugged him toward the vendor's tent. "Don't blow it. Cool your jets. She's yours. Let her come to that decision when it all settles down." He handed him an ice-cold adult beverage. "Take the edge off. Your pride will be fine."

He turned to glance back at Molly to see that Candle and Pekabo, who had appeared out of nowhere, were escorting her to the food tents. "It's not pride."

"Sure it is. You'll survive, just like I did. You put yourself out there and don't get what you expect. But great things come to the man that waits."

"When did you become so all-knowing about the matters of the heart?" He smirked.

"When I married the love of my life," Miacoh said smugly. "Come on. Time to get you something to eat. You have a long night ahead of you guarding the woman of your dreams and her best friend. Been there, done that. Not an easy task."

As the men turned around, a small child with wings buzzed them then landed hard on the ground. A pair of adults rushed after him. Jason and Calliope Jansen screeched to a stop in front of Miacoh and Cayson, each grabbing an arm of the young fairy, and hoisting him to his feet. Calliope pulled a carriage closer to her, letting her husband handle the boy.

"Young man, you do that again, you'll be grounded for life. We'll clip those beautiful wings."

Jason paused and turned to Miacoh. "Sorry about that. It won't happen again. Didn't really want to freak out the townspeople not in the know. Besides, I'm not sure my boss would be too happy our family being outed this way."

The young fairy batted away tears from his huge turquoise eyes. "I just wanted to say hi to Mr. Erikkson before he left. I kept my promise." The young boy quickly tucked his wings in switching his gaze from one parent to the other. "I haven't touched the panel since you left. Neither has my baby sister." The boy smiled down at the baby sitting in the carriage babbling happily and floating tiny toys back and forth between her chubby hands.

"Oh dear." Calliope snatched up the baby and threw a cover over the toys. "I guess we'd better take these children home." She looked longingly at the chicken on the skewer.

Pekabo rushed over. "Don't you dare cut your fun outing short. Don't worry about the town. Everything will be fine." She patted the baby on the cheek as the child batted her violet eyes at her. "Isn't that right,

Hunter?"

"Darlin', I'm not chief of police anymore. But I'll bet Miacoh will handle the situation if it becomes necessary." He turned his attention to Jason. "Your boss knew what your family was when he hired you."

"I assured him they wouldn't cause problems."

Hunter threw his head back and roared with laughter. "Your boss has four children of his own. He'll understand."

Molly stood on the sidelines watching this almost comical situation unfold. She silently compared her recent escapades to those of the young fairy family and the young werewolf family. There were no guarantees in life. Cayson was right—you find love, you need to hold on tight, because you don't know what is headed your way. Not that she expected to deal with the outing of fairy or werewolf children—but...neither did she know her exact linage. *Native American lore told of shapeshifters—didn't they?*

The whir of helo blades caused a pause in the conversation and interrupted Molly's train of thought. A dust cloud rose at the far end of the park as the helo's skids settled on the ground. She raced to where Cayson stood, a beer in one hand, four sticks of teriyaki chicken in the other, and grabbed his arm.

"She's here. Come on."

He handed his chicken to Miacoh. "Don't you eat those." Then he followed Molly nearly bobbling his beer. He took a long swig as they arrived at the chopper and covered the bottle top with his hand. The dust settled and the blades slowed then stopped. He held Molly back until the door opened and a petite bronze-skinned woman with waist-long raven hair pulled back in a braid hopped out of the helo and made a beeline for Molly. They embraced, tears sliding down both women's cheeks.

"I didn't think I'd ever see you alive again," Molly said softly. "I couldn't get any cooperation until Candle, Cayson, and Miacoh jumped in. They were the main ones, but several others were also instrumental in your rescue." She gulped in a breath.

"So I've heard. The feds filled me in as much as they could or would. Jed is so kind. Not that Caitlyn isn't great too. But...I refused to answer their questions until they answered some of mine." Kinley blew out a breath and sagged against Molly. "I need to sit down."

Cayson shook his head. "Those women are cut from the same cloth." He swept Kinley off her feet and carried her over to tables arranged around the vendor trucks. Molly followed close behind. Easing Kinley down in one of the chairs, he motioned Miacoh over who still held the four skewers, then handed one to Kinley. "Eat."

Daintily, Kinley took the skewer and nibbled. "This is really good. I didn't realize how hungry I am." Finishing the chicken, she wiped her fingers on a napkin Molly handed her and reached for more.

Hunter and Pekabo joined the group with plates of chicken skewers, deviled eggs, chips, soft drinks, and beer. They shoved two tables together. Everyone sat down and ate, listening to Kinley recount her capture and release. Molly added her part of the tale. Cayson and Miacoh did the same. Candle patted her mother's arm and added their contribution to the rescue.

Caitlyn and Jed ambled toward the group. Candle glanced up and waved the duo over to the table. "Got time to eat before returning the helo?"

"If we feed the pilot, he'll stick around. Besides, we have to finish Kinley's debriefing, if she wants to spend the night here. The original plan was to return to Golden. But we've taken lead in the cases."

"I hope you plan to give Kinley's case more attention than you all did originally. She'd still be missing or worse if it hadn't been for Molly's tenacity and coming to work for me." Candle shook her finger at the feds. "Shame on all of you."

Terra wandered around the group, nose in the air sniffing hopefully.

"Believe me, behind the scenes DHS has been working on this situation for a while, but it's a long-standing problem that won't be corrected overnight." Jed shoved his hand in his pockets. "DHS has taken steps in the right direction."

Caitlyn stepped forward. "Let me bring you up to speed on what DHS is and has been doing, which is how we were able to step in, get backup, move things along so quickly. Department of Homeland Security has established the first-ever Tribal Homeland Security Advisory Council. Last I knew, membership nominations were being taken in October of 2022. Not sure where that's at now."

Miacoh's head swiveled around, his eyes wide. "How is it I didn't run across this during our investigation?"

Jed smiled smugly, rocking back on his heels. "Guess you're missing a few new investigative tools. But seriously, connecting all the parts and getting them to work together is a tough task. The good old boy's network is alive and hesitant to report, which is the first breakdown. This Council will enable Tribal leaders to advise the Secretary on Homeland Security policies and practices that affect Indian Country and indigenous communities, including emergency management, law enforcement, cybersecurity, domestic terrorism and targeted violence, and border security. Including missing indigenous persons." He stared directly at Candle. "A good place for you to become involved. If only at a local level."

Molly got to her feet slowly. "Sounds like a good place for Kinley and me to check out as well. DHS needs to hear first-hand experiences." She stomped her foot.

Terrabyte jumped up and barked peering from one person to another.

"Sit." Candle pointed to the ground. The dog grumbled but sat next to her glaring at Molly.

Molly continued. "Jam a spike in the cogs of the good ol' boy network. They've put our lives at risk long enough. Proper punishment should be available to those refusing to comply." She clenched her teeth, but a jaw-popping yawn escaped before she was able to cover it with the back of her hand.

Cayson slid an arm around Molly. "How about we put your soapbox away for tonight. Go back to the safe house where Jed and Caitlyn can finish up with Kinley after which we can all get a good night's sleep before the both of you face plant on the ground."

Kinley blinked sleepily. "I'm all for that." She glanced at Jed as his chair crunched on the gravel when he stood, excused himself, and walked away from the group with his cell to his ear.

"Where's he going?" Miacoh peered at Caitlyn.

"Don't know. We've all had a long day. If I had to guess, I'd say he's attempting to decide to spend the night and keep the helo. Unless it's needed for an emergency."

Chapter Twenty-Three

Again! Paying the Price.

Well after midnight, Cayson set the alarms and checked the outside doors at the safe house. After finishing up with Kinley, Miacoh took Jed, Caitlyn, and the helo pilot to Aspen Ridge's bed and breakfast inn for the night. He could still see the red taillights of Miacoh's squad car bouncing down the road. Yawning, he pulled the shades, then blinked. *Am I seeing things?*

Slowly moving to another window where the shade was still up, he saw a beam of light across the road, in an open field behind a neighboring house. *What the hell?*

The beam of light cut vast swathes across the open field and moved toward the safe house. Pausing only a minute to make sure of the trajectory, he shook his head tiredly, took out his cell, and punched the programmed number to the police station. Office Cimerono answered. "Cayson?"

"Yeah. Got a possible intruder about quarter mile away and closing in fast. Send backup including the chief and feds if he's still with them. It's going to be a party."

A brief pause and the officer returned to the line. "You hold your position until backup arrives. I'm on my way. The others have been notified."

"Yeah, yeah, I know the drill." Cayson ended the call, slipped his boots on, and herded the women into the basement safe room. Turning off all the lights, he silently ducked out the back door. The beam of light slowed as it approached the road in front of the safe house. He fervently hoped there was only one person as he circled around behind the figure with the light. Pausing, he listened for additional footsteps, broken twigs, grass, or vegetation movement, and heard none.

Just a few more yards. He covered the ground quickly. Something metal gleamed in the sliver of moonlight. *Great, the idiot's got a weapon.* He pounced, aiming to knock the gun and flashlight out of the hand of the intruder. The intruder squeezed the trigger before the gun flew out of his hand. The shot went wild. Cayson hit the ground and swept the person's legs out from under him before he had a chance to retaliate, crashing the perp to the ground face first.

The suspect spit blood and gravel then glanced up at Cayson. "Didn't mean to cause trouble. I was looking for a couple of acquaintances that indicated they had business at this address. They've been gone a couple of days. Afraid something bad happened to them."

"That wouldn't be Greg and Dwayne would it? And who might you be?"

"I'm Ubasi Bayo. I had orders to stay behind and wait. Yes, I'm looking for Greg and Dwayne."

"They are cooling their heels in the county jail. For now. Mr. Bayo, what did you have to do with the kidnapping?"

"Kidnapping." His voice trembled. "Don't know nothing about a kidnapping. I swear. We had a side hustle since Professor disappeared. Borrowed a few IDs and college papers. Nothing more."

"Sold them to highest bidder among other things?"

Ubasi's lips set in a thin line. He nodded slowly.

A barrage of red and blue lights flashed in the distance as Cayson zip-tied the young man's hands behind his back. *College kids have no business playing mobster.* He pressed his boot in the small of the man's back. "Stay down. Don't give me a reason to bury you. You can tell your story to the feds." When the lights approached, Cayson let out an ear-splitting whistle, his signature communication when on military assignment. He knew Miacoh would recognize the whistle.

Miacoh slid the vehicle neatly crossways in the road, then jumped out followed by Jed and Caitlyn running to Cayson's location. Officers Cimerono and Smith slammed on their car's brakes behind Miacoh's, sending gravel spewing in all directions. Todd jumped out and yelled, "I told you to wait for backup."

Cayson shrugged. "Sorry. Didn't want him or the fight anywhere near the safe house. My gut and surveillance said only one. Better I get the drop on him than you guys come charging in lights flashing giving him warning what was coming. Besides, remember, I am a backup officer, if needed." He brushed the gravel from his hands and dirt from his jeans, then glanced toward the safe house.

"You know that's not what I mean," Officer Todd Cimerono shot back, shoving his hat on his head.

He jerked his chin toward the prisoner. "This guy claims to be Ubasi Bayo. He's mixed up in the identity theft ring, and stolen college papers. And he's all yours." He nudged the man with the toe of his foot.

"Anything else we should know?" Miacoh stared at his friend.

"I'm going to check on the women. I believe you law enforcement types got this." He shot a cheeky grin to Miacoh, knowing he'd hear about it tomorrow.

****

Back inside the safe house, Molly and Kinley waited at the front window.

He slammed through the front door, planted his feet shoulder width apart, and fisted his hands on his hips. "What part of safe room in the basement didn't you women understand?"

Kinley glanced nervously at Molly who rushed at Cayson, flinging her arms around him and wrapping her legs around his waist. She clung tightly and buried her face in his chest.

"Whoa." He took a step back to balance himself and Molly. "What's this all about?"

"One too many close calls in my life recently. I just don't have another brave face to put on." She wiped her face on his shirt and sniffed.

Kinley returned to the window. "So there was only one individual out there and you subdued him? He's in custody?"

"Yeah, I believe he may be the last former college student mixed up in this mess."

"Until you catch the professor, you won't know for sure." Molly unwound her legs and stood on tiptoe, still clinging to Cayson.

"True. But I doubt those kids will hesitate to roll over on each other. Although the one tonight seems to have a lot to say. Only one that concerns me is Murdock. He doesn't seem to blend in with the others.

209

Maybe he's an opportunist. When he stumbled upon their criminal activity, he shored it up with his cunning and leadership." Cayson leaned his cheek wearily on the top of Molly's head for a couple of beats. "The others don't seem to have the leadership or confidence to pull this off with the professor gone. Especially kidnapping. Still, they'll go down for accessory, unless one or more of them cooperate fully with the feds. I imagine that Miacoh and Pitkin County will be only too happy to turn the cases all over to the feds for prosecution."

A soft knock on the door brought Kinley bouncing over. "It's Jed, I mean Agent Jed— May I open the door?"

Cayson nodded. His eyebrows arched forming question marks.

Molly pulled his ear down to her lips and whispered, "It's possible that Kinley is sweet on Jed or vice-versa. Did you see them sneaking glances at each other at the park? But I would never suggest such a thing at this juncture of the investigation. Kinley is still a victim and witness in their investigation."

Kinley pulled the door open and smiled wide. "Jed, I thought you'd have returned to DC by now."

"Turns out Homeland is sending other agents to transport the prisoners. Cait and I have orders to tie up any loose ends here and report back in a day or two. Which brings us to finishing and reviewing your interview. Tomorrow morning after breakfast work for you?"

"Sure." Kinley glanced at Molly uncertainly.

"That works as long as you buy us all breakfast at the cafe. Say about nine in the morning. Since we're all getting to bed a little late tonight or rather this morning." Molly's face split into a wide grin. "Candle will be happy to let you use the conference room at Terrabyte Security to wrap up your interview."

Kinley's cheeks blushed and she smiled. "Okay by me."

Jed stood there, his mouth hanging open, but nodded slightly.

Molly totally ignored Kinley and bulldozed on. "Great. All set." She tugged Cayson's shirt. "We're going to bed. See you all in the morning. Kinley, lock up and set the alarm, like I showed you, when Jed leaves." She wiggled her fingers at them. "Night, everyone."

"That was a bit forward of you," Cayson whispered.

"Sometimes you just have to give your friends a kick in the pants. Kinley hasn't shown any interest in anyone for a long time." She brushed her lips over Cayson's then deepened the kiss before reaching her bedroom door. "Besides I've never seen her look at anyone that way. It's a good thing." She pushed the door open and pulled him inside. "Time to give you the answer you've been waiting for." She closed the door, pulled the shirt over his head, and unbuttoned his jeans.

Cayson grabbed the top of his jeans as an evil grin spread across his face. "Oh, no you don't. I want your answer before we engage in extra-curricular activities."

Molly huffed and stuck her lower lip out in a pout.

"While that's cute—" He kissed her bottom lip. "—It's not the answer I'm looking for." He pulled her shirt over her head and flipped open her bra.

"Fine. I'll marry you, but only 'cause I love you."

She giggled.

He dropped to one knee and pulled out a blue sapphire and marquee cut diamond ring. "Molly Malone Reacher, will you spend the rest of your life with me? Start a family with me?"

She sucked in a breath while he slid the ring on her all-important finger. "It's beautiful. Cayson Erikkson, I already said yes. But I'll say it again. I love you and want to be your wife. The rest we'll play by ear."

He stood bringing her with him and closed the door.

Chapter Twenty-Four

All is Well that Ends Well—With One Exception.

The next morning Molly and Cayson were the last to arrive at the cafe. She slid into the chair next to Kinley and patted the seat next to her for Cayson. Leaning over to her friend, she whispered, "How did you get here this morning?"

Kinley's entire face turned red. "Uh—Jed picked me up early this morning. We didn't want to wake you."

"Hmm— A little suspect. But I'll let it slide for now." Molly smiled.

Cayson stopped by Miacoh's chair. "Did you have a chance to investigate that issue we discussed a few days ago?"

"I did." Miacoh smiled smugly. "We'll discuss it later. Jed and Cait want to get through breakfast and finish up the interview. They've received an urgent assignment and will be leaving this afternoon."

"Fair enough." He slid into the seat next to Molly.

She reached for her glass of water as the waitress stopped to take their order.

"Oh, my, Molly. Do you have news for us?" Kinley grinned widely while pointing to the engagement ring.

"Yes, I guess I do." She beamed at him holding the

213

ring out for all to see. "Cayson and I are engaged. No date set yet, but you all will be the first to know. We'll be married in Aspen Ridge and make our home here."

Congratulations were offered around the table.

"See, patience did the trick," Miacoh teased.

"Says the man who has none." Candle roared with laughter.

Miacoh turned his attention to Jed and Cait. "Did you get anything out of the suspects?"

"As it turned out, Murdock was pretty chatty after he discovered he could be facing life in prison on the federal charges alone. Still, he won't give up the professor's location or the way he communicates with him," Jed offered. "Yet. Not sure what the professor has over him that keeps him tight lipped, but we'll find out."

Cait continued, "I talked to the agents this morning that picked up the prisoners last night. When confronted with the kidnapping charge, the suspects couldn't talk fast enough. Apparently, the others were just pawns in the identity theft ring and stolen college papers. The sad part is that Kinley was kidnapped because they thought Molly had the list of suspects and their jobs, when Kinley had it all along and passed it on to Molly when she got scared. Murdock didn't want to deal with Molly and her big mouth. Figured Kinley would roll over on Molly easily." She huffed out a laugh. "He couldn't have been more wrong. That's the crux of the investigation as it stands now. I'll let you know if I—" She cleared her throat. "—we hear anything else. Though our part of the investigation is done. It's been turned over to another set of agents." She shrugged.

"Thanks for the information, Cait, and thank you

both for your hard work to rescue Kinley." Miacoh stood and shook hands with them both. "Couldn't have done it without you."

"You mean our resources. You were well on your way. Those fliers broke the case." Cait chuckled.

The waitress brought the food to the table.

"Let's dig in. Miacoh's right. We've got a lot to do before we take off for the next destination and case." Jed picked up a fork and began shoveling food from his plate to his mouth. His eyes strayed to Kinley only once with a melancholy glance.

Cayson put his hand over Molly's and whispered, "If it's meant to be, fate will find a way."

"I know, but fate can take way too long without a bit of prodding from us humans." Molly fidgeted in her chair.

The meal was consumed quickly. Everyone from around the table got to their feet at the same time. Jed took care of the check, while Kinley and Cait walked out with Miacoh and Candle.

"See you at Terrabyte." Miacoh waved at Cayson and Molly. "Cayson, we got business to take care of before you start on your installs. Meet at the station."

"Hey, you wouldn't be trying to steal my employee would you?" Candle chided him.

"Well considering he was my part-time officer—still is backup—before you got your hooks in him, I'd say you're out of line." Miacoh tweaked her nose, then leaned in for a quick kiss before closing the passenger door. Jed, Cait, and Kinley piled into the backseat.

Cayson's face turned a bit red. "No need to fight over me. There's plenty to go around." He puffed out his chest and crooked his arm, then let out a hearty laugh. Wrapping an arm around Molly, they walked to his truck. "I'll meet you at the station after I pick up today's assignments and drop Molly off at Terrabyte."

Miacoh sent him a thumbs-up sign and drove off.

"If you don't mind my asking, what kind of business do you have with Miacoh?" She shrugged one shoulder nonchalantly.

"It's hard to tell. A job to poke at Candle. Maybe a real need for PI work on a police case. He's a little understaffed on detectives. Candle snatched her dad to help at Terrabyte now. I don't imagine that Pekabo is happy about the arrangement. But in her eyes, it's less dangerous than being chief and he's free to go globetrotting any time she wants. Or he's going to ream me for going out on my own the other night rather than waiting for backup. My bet— Probably the latter." Cayson grimaced.

Candle stepped out of her office. "Well, I see we all finally reported for work." She glanced at Molly whose forehead creased in concern. "Only kidding. Don't be so serious."

"Just the person I wanted to see." Cayson wrapped one arm around Candle's shoulder. "Got my schedule of installs for today ready?"

"Been a bit occupied this morning but give Molly and me twenty minutes and we'll have it put together.

Cayson raised an eyebrow in an unspoken question.

"I'm handing off your scheduling to Molly. We are getting so busy that Miacoh, bless his heart, thinks I'm spreading myself too thin. Not that he isn't doing the same. Anyway, he's probably right. Molly takes the calls for service anyway—she might as well schedule them too."

He scrubbed his hand over his face and grinned. "Good idea. If you two are going to be a few minutes, I'll run over to the station and see what Miacoh wanted to talk about." He picked up a donut, put it on a napkin, and poured a fresh cup of coffee, raising the cup toward Candle. "You really need to teach that man of yours to make a decent cup of coffee. It's worse now than when I served with him."

Candle huffed. "Officer Barry Smith makes the coffee at the police station. Take it up with him. Miacoh complains about it all the time. Unless Reka, the new dispatcher/receptionist, gets to it first. On another note, don't you dare tell him I conceded he was right. Understood?"

"Yes, boss lady." A cheeky grin spread across his face. "Was that a threat?" He winked at Molly who stifled a giggle and stared at her computer screen.

"I saw that. I mean it." Candle wandered over behind Molly and pointed at the keyboard. "Let's get into the programs I use to schedule Cayson. List the installations according to importance or urgency."

"See you in a few." He strode across the floor, waved his donut, took a bite, and disappeared out the door.

Twenty minutes later he swept into the office, kissed Molly on the cheek, snatched the work assignment schedule, and started for the door. "Hey, I get an hour for lunch?" He waved the paper. "That's a first. I'll pick us up lunch and be here as close to noon as possible."

"It's the law with the hours you work. And I insisted." Molly felt her cheeks heat a bit.

Candle shook her head. "Don't let me regret my decision." She sent a stern glance at both Cayson and Molly.

Ninety minutes later, Jed, Cait, and Kinley walked out of the conference room. Jed held up a document. "Who wants to sign as witness that Kinley signed the document under no duress or collusion."

Candle rose from the seat beside Molly and stretched while reaching for the piece of paper. "Oh, I'll do it. Might be a bit suspect if her best friend witnessed her statement." She signed the document and handed it back to the agent. "Do you always have a witness on a victim's statement?"

Jed took the paper. "Not always. But there are so many agencies involved in this case that I want to make sure our part is airtight before we pass it off to the next agents."

Terrabyte rolled over next to Candle's chair and yawned. The pup watched her with sleepy eyes, then got up, trotted over to the front door, and pawed it.

Candle shook hands and nodded to the dog. "Gotta take the dog out. You two stay in touch, maybe visit under better circumstances."

"You bet." Jed's gaze wandered over to Kinley. He winked. She blushed and walked out the door with him.

Chapter Twenty-Five

A New House and Changes Galore.

Molly, for the fourth time, put the phone on hold and blew out a breath moving the stray hair across her forehead.

Candle stepped out of her office. "Molly, just send the phone to the answering service. We need to review a couple of new cases that I contracted. Quickies, but you need to be informed if my dad takes off on vacation with Mom."

"Sure thing. I'm about ready to send the phone flying out the window." Instead, she tapped the button on the phone sending the calls to the answering service. Molly stood, stretched, and walked into Candle's office.

"Before we get started, I'd like to know how the wedding preparations are going. Have you picked a date? My mom is driving me crazy with questions. You are aware she is willing to help in any way?"

Molly laughed. "She beat you to the punch. Pekabo called the house this morning offering to bring over research she'd done on Hopi customs and wedding ceremonies."

"Oh, I'm so sorry. I was hoping to cut her off at the pass." Candle shook her head.

"It's all right. I reached out to my grandmother earlier. Brought her up to speed with the changes in my life. She'd love to help with the wedding, though her age and mobility inhibit her a bit." Molly lowered her voice. "Don't tell her I told you that." Molly's voice returned to normal. "Anyway, with her permission, I put Pekabo in touch with her. So, I imagine the wedding will take on a life of its own. I told them simple ceremony."

"Oh, Molly, I don't think you want to do that. Mom will steam roll—"

"You don't know my Grams. She may be elderly, but her spirit rivals anyone. Besides I'm too busy to plan a wedding, keep up with work, and leave time for Cayson. It's for the best. I'll check in on them occasionally and I told Grams and Pekabo I need to approve everything, even set out a budget. I made it clear, no over budget expenditures. Keep it simple."

Candle clicked her tongue. "My mom will blow right through your budget, if it doesn't fit her vision."

"Then I'll pay her back." Molly smiled. "I think the two of them will respect what Cayson and I want."

"Maybe. Now about the date? Or venue?" Candle pressed.

"Actually, four weeks from Sunday, on the fall equinox. Invitations go out end of this week. Pekabo said she could get it done. The ceremony will be private at your parents' home. The reception will be at Aspen Ridge Community Center. The entire town will be invited. Pekabo insisted. Kinley called Jed with the date and asked him to invite Cait. We didn't have an address to send their invitations. Besides it gave Kinley a reason to call Jed." She rolled her eyes. "As if she needed one."

"I was just going to ask about Kinley. She and Jed

are still going strong?"

"Oh yes, Kinley is convinced that he is the one. I only hope he feels the same. We'll have one less government agent if he breaks her heart."

"By the way he looks at her, I don't think we have anything to worry about." Candle snickered. "My mom gets wind of it, and she'll be trying to plan another wedding."

Cayson pushed through the door to Terrabyte. Terra greeted him at the door with a woof.

Molly stuck her head out of Candle's office. "We're back here."

He paused to scratch behind the pup's ears and strode through the front lobby to Candle's office. He kissed Molly on the lips. "Got any more installs for me?"

Candle stood up at her desk. "Nope. You can call it a day. But tomorrow installs and repairs will begin early to get them all in."

"Works for me. As soon as she gets off work, Molly and I are going to look at a good-sized cabin on five acres outside of town. The house is a few miles from your house. It's not on the market yet, but I have the inside track." Cayson grinned.

"We figured the town didn't want me to call the safe house home since the danger passed. A customer of Cayson's told him about the older couple that would be moving to Arizona to be closer to their kids and grandkids," Molly added.

"Besides, my place is a bit small for two, considering I have to go outside to change my mind." He hesitated, glancing at Candle. "Don't get me wrong. It was fine for me when Miacoh offered and I was unsure what was next for me. But more things changed than I could have imagined." He chuckled.

Candle snickered. "No problem. Is that cabin the Silvertons'? I'd heard they were considering moving closer to their children, but you got a jump on that before I did. That property should be perfect for you two. Good luck."

"We'll let you know." Molly smiled wide, nearly vibrating with excitement. She held up her fingers crossed on both hands. "We drove by the cabin last night."

Candle picked up a few files and handed them to Molly. "Let's go over these files and get you out of here."

Within thirty minutes, she emerged from Candle's office, put the files in her cabinet, and locked it. She looked across the quiet lobby, where Cayson relaxed in a lobby chair waiting for her. "Wow. This is the quietest I've seen this office in a long while. Best get out of here before things change." Molly grabbed her jacket and bag, pausing to pull the office keys out of her bag. "Candle, want me to lock the front door?"

"Sure, I'll go out the back in a few."

"I'm not leaving you alone here. We'll wait until you're ready to go." Cayson pushed out of the chair and stretched both arms over his head.

Candle turned the light off in her office. "I'm a big girl. You don't need to wait for me. However, I'm ready to leave now. Good luck with your cabin." She shrugged into her sweater and exited the back door, then Molly set the alarm and walked out the front door with Cayson. He circled around through the parking lot and waved to Candle as she drove her vehicle out the exit gate.

At Molly's raised eyebrow and questioning expression, he simply shrugged. "Better safe than sorry." He started the engine, turned out of the parking lot and onto Main Street through downtown, and took a left at the gravel road to the outskirts of town. He followed the circular driveway to the front of the well-maintained cabin and cut the engine. He swung around in the seat and slid an arm around her shoulder. "Are we ready to make an offer, if negotiations go that way?"

"I'll know for sure once we are inside, but from the vibes I'm getting out here, it's a yes." She shifted in her seat and opened the passenger door. When she stepped out onto the driveway, she noticed her bracelets were pulsing a faint amber. "Well, would you look at this?" She held an arm out for Cayson to see. "What do you suppose that means?"

He reached for her arm, gently turned it over, and then righted it shrugging. "You're the one with the woo woo power. How are you feeling? Good vibes?"

They climbed the few steps and onto the wrap-around porch. "Yep."

Mr. Silverton greeted them at the door. "You want to buy our humble abode?" He held the door open for them.

Cayson waited for Molly to walk through before him, then closed the door. "We think so. Could you show us around? The cabin sits on five acres, right?"

"Yes. As you can see, part of the acreage is set out in grass for front and back yards. The back yard is fenced-in for pups or children. As you can see, there is a multi-colored cobblestone path from the street to the house and paved circular driveway. My wife insisted on those amenities when we bought the property." Mr. Silverton motioned them through the cabin into the family/living room featuring a cathedral ceiling and full wall of moss rock. "We had a fireplace insert installed to avoid the drafts and keep the ambiance of that rock wall. The insert has a battery-operated fan and blower, so if the electrical goes out, you still have heat."

"Wow, it's beautiful and energy efficient to boot." Molly touched the moss rock. It was moist to the touch. She rubbed her fingers together.

"You'll need to lightly spray the rocks once or twice a week if you want the moss to survive." He pointed to the corner where a copper valve exited the wall inconspicuously behind a small, coiled tan hose resting in a hand-painted basket.

"Not a problem. I love the effect." Molly touched the rocks once more then turned her attention to Mr. Silverton.

"There are four bedrooms, including the master, and two full bathrooms, not including the master bath. We just remodeled the master bath. You'll love it. There is a loft with a huge floor to ceiling window. We used the room for our own hideaway. Not that we need it anymore with the kids gone and the grandkids growing up. Stairs get tough as you get older. But you two have nothing to worry about right now." He handed Cayson the recent appraisal. "What do you think?"

Cayson perused the document for a few minutes then handed the paper over to Molly who nodded emphatically. "It's sold as far as we are concerned. I can put half down in cash and procure a mortgage for the rest."

"Wonderful. We are glad to leave our house we've loved and raised our family in with two people that will care for her as we did." Mrs. Silverton joined them, wrapped an arm around her husband, and wiped a tear from her eye.

"Even though we know this is the best decision, it's still hard." Mrs. Silverton gave a wan smile.

"No hurry. Take your time. We understand." Molly patted Mrs. Silverton's shoulder.

"Our children are anxious for us to make the move. They will be ecstatic we've sold the house. The kids have already found a house for us a couple blocks from where they live." He rubbed his chin with his thumb and forefinger. "Guess you can take possession of the house and property by the first of next month."

"That's only two weeks away. Are you sure?" Molly tried to keep her face neutral, but a slight smile turned up one corner of her lips.

"The kids will want to get down here and get us moved the minute we tell them the house is sold."

"I'll talk to Katie at Aspen Title Company and have her prepare the paperwork. The bank will be no problem. When did you want to close?"

"We'll call the kids when you leave and let them know it's sold. I'll call you with a confirmed timeline. Still believe the first of next month will work. Okay?"

"You bet." Cayson reached out and shook Mr. Silverton's hand. "Thank you, sir."

"None of this 'sir' stuff. I'm Tayson and my wife is Julie." There were handshakes and hugs all around before Molly and Cayson left.

No sooner than the door closed behind them, Molly had her phone out of her pocket calling Candle. "We bought it," she squealed into the phone.

"Great. Tell me all about it," Candle said.

"I'll fill you in tomorrow. I want to call Kinley and tell her the good news. She can stay in the safe house if it's all right with the town. Just until she gets settled."

"Of course." Candle ended the call.

Molly dialed Kinley's number. She answered on the first ring. "Did you get to look at the house?"

"We did. Better yet, we were able to agree to terms to buy the house. The owners want to leave soon, so things are moving really fast. I'll tell you all about it when I see you. I gotta go." She disconnected the call then threw her arms around Cayson's neck. "Wow, we'll be homeowners soon and—"

"Husband and wife a few weeks later. I can't wait." He pulled her into his arms and kissed her. "Never expected those words to ever come out of my mouth." He stared into her eyes. "You are such a special person. How could I not fall for you?" He squeezed her tighter.

She smiled and snuggled into his warm chest then scooted over in the seat. "You might want to start the engine and drive to the safe house," she teased.

"Call me selfish. Didn't want to share this moment with anyone but you." He started the engine and put the truck into gear.

Chapter Twenty-Six

Interesting Turn of Events on Moving Day.

The weeks flew by as Terrabyte Security gained clients. Molly handled the front desk with ease, handed out the work assignments each morning, and worked on case files the rest of the day. This morning, she was at a cake tasting and would be a bit late.

Candle interviewed for installers and additional front office staff. With Molly and Cayson taking a few days off for the wedding and honeymoon, Candle was beginning to panic.

Whirlwind Gabby whisked into the office in her usual chaotic fashion. The breeze from the open door caught loose papers, and unsecured documents on desks fluttered to the floor. Terrabyte jumped to her feet, stretched, and barked her announcement someone had entered the office.

Candle poked her head out of her office. "Hi, Gabby. How are things going?"

"Great. I've hired a new receptionist and a secretary for Ben's office. I'll still fill in when necessary and do the books, but with the twins and their mounting schedule of afterschool activities, I'd need to be three people." Gabby paused. "You look worn out. What's going on?"

Candle waved her hand. "Molly and Cayson are off

this morning. Wedding stuff. Dad is taking Cayson's installation and repair jobs."

"Oh, how's that going?" Gabby stifled a giggle.

"I have one full-time and one part-time employee hired. They start next week, but decent help that can pass a background check is hard to find."

"You don't have to tell me. I went through applications until my eyes crossed. I had you do background checks, and we know how that went. Finally, I hired what we needed, even if we had to steal them from another company." Gabby polished her nails on her sweater. "We could afford better pay and benefits, not to mention flex time. The workforce isn't what it used to be."

"So I've discovered. Mom is coming in to help on the days Molly is busy with wedding stuff. Mom was already committed elsewhere this morning." She threw up her hands. "Not sure how that'll work. But I'm desperate. I've decided to close the office on Molly and Cayson's wedding day. Most of the town will be at the reception anyway. Oh, I'd better get that sign printed and posted in the window."

"Slow down, Candle." Gabby took off her sweater and hung it on the back of a chair. "I've got a few hours before I need to pick up the twins. I'll make the sign, print, and post it in the window. Looks like we have quite a bit of filing to do. I can get that out of the way in a jiffy."

"Oh, Molly would be grateful. Heck, I'm grateful. So much has happened in the last few months. I can't believe it."

"I told you the business would take off. But I'm part of the reason you got so far behind, so I can help you catch up." She sat down, patted Terra on the head, and got to work on the filing box. "I heard Molly and Cayson bought the Silverton place."

"Don't remind me. Miacoh offered our help and Mom and Dad's help to get them moved. Our little town is growing. The moving company in town is all booked up. Guess they're feeling growing pains too. Thank goodness, neither Molly nor Cayson have much to move."

"When are they moving?"

"This weekend."

"You mean like tomorrow and Sunday?" Gabby gasped.

"Yep."

"Ben and I can help with the moving. You'll just have to put up with the twins underfoot."

"Oh, that would be wonderful. One more thing off all our plates."

The door banged open, and Molly rushed in. "Sorry I'm so late. Who knew there were so many flavors of cake? Hey, Gabby. How's it going?"

"Good. And you?"

Molly spread her arms and turned in a three-hundred-and-sixty-degree circle. "Crazy. But we are still keeping our heads above water. Thanks for the offer to help move. We'll take it. In fact, Natalya and Nash can entertain Terra while we get things moved. She doesn't like changes in her world." Molly peered down at the fur ball wiggling all over and stroked her smooth shiny coat. The dog pranced back to Candle.

"You've spoiled her so badly. She thinks the world revolves around her." Candle glanced down at her pup with a wide smile. "By the way, where is Cayson?"

"As if she wasn't spoiled when I got here." Molly crossed her arms across her chest. "On our way over here, Cayson got a call from Hunter. So, he dropped me off and went to help your dad at the Falcon's place. Something about a wiring problem."

Candle nodded as Molly wrote the Falcon appointment on the schedule.

"She's got you there." Gabby gave Candle a challenging stare then switched her attention to Molly. "I'll catch the phones while you get your other duties caught up. Then I'll be on my way and see you all tomorrow." She snapped her fingers. "Hey, let's have a barbecue. Make moving day like a barn raising. I always loved those things in stories. Everyone gathered around helping out and a big feast at the end."

"Who's going to do the cooking?" Candle wanted to know.

"You leave it to me. I've got it under control." Gabby smirked and answered the ringing phone. "Terrabyte Security, Gabby speaking. How can I help you?"

Molly and Candle glanced at each other and shrugged. "Gabby always was a force of nature to be reckoned with." Candle chuckled.

"I'll bet the two of you were something to be reckoned with as teenagers." Molly giggled.

"You both realize that I am sitting right here. Right?" Gabby frowned at the women, putting the call on hold. "It's for you, Candle. Something about T-shirt orders."

"Of course." Candle winked.

****

Moving day morning dawned sunny and crisp with

a promise of a clear warm afternoon. A typical fall day in Aspen Ridge. Trucks, SUVs, and a small flatbed trailer were parked in front of the safe house. Ben, Gabby, Pekabo, Hunter, Miacoh, Candle, Cayson, and Molly stood in a circle setting out the day's duties.

Kinley and her guinea pig Mocha stood on the porch. "Do you need my help?"

"I don't think so. Hunter, Miacoh, and I all moved what personal belongings and bit of furniture I had to the cabin. All we have left is what's here," Molly said.

Candle glance around at Terra and the twins playing chase. "You know what? Kinley, you could pack up Mocha, the twins, and Terra in the spare SUV from Terrabyte. Take them over to the cabin, where the back yard is fenced, and let them run off their energy under your watchful eye."

"Done." Kinley went back inside, grabbed a hoody, put Mocha in her travel house, and piled Terra, Nash, and Natalia into the spare vehicle. She rolled the window down. "See you all there."

Pekabo flitted from item to item in the safe house like a bemused butterfly. She stopped and ran her fingers then her hand over a desk that Molly had set in the corner. "This is an exquisite piece. Where did you get this?"

"My grandmother gave it to me when I started college and needed a desk in my dorm room. It's been in the family forever."

Pekabo continued to run her fingers over the wavy top on the back of the desk. "What went here?" She tapped her fingers in the grooves.

"I don't know. All I got was the desk."

Pekabo clicked her tongue, tapping her finger to

her lips. Her other hand still caressed the back of the desk. "There's a matching hutch." Another minute or two passed before Pekabo spoke again. "I know where the hutch is." She blew out a thoughtful breath.

Candle stared at her mother. "Where is it?"

"Candle, dear, where did you get the hutch in your office at Terrabyte?"

"At Jade's antique store in Raven's Hollow."

"You've never been able to open all those wonderful little drawers. Have you?" Pekabo glanced at Candle then Hunter.

"No. But, Mom, I've not had the time to explore it fully."

"That's because the hutch is missing its other half." Pekabo tapped the top of Molly's desk. "I bet those grooves fit the hutch. Does your hutch have grooves?"

"I never noticed." Candle ran her fingers through her hair. Her mother could be exasperating at times. This was one of those times. "Mom, we'll take a look after we get Molly's stuff moved.

"No. No. That won't do. You must reunite the two pieces to restore the magic and learn the secret."

"Mom. We need to get Molly moved. We're burning daylight."

"Come on, Hunter. Let's get the hutch from Terrabyte and see if it matches. The rest of you can move the desk to its new place of residence." Pekabo grabbed Hunter's arm and started to tow him toward their vehicle.

He dug his heels in the gravel pathway. "Wait just a minute. You can't just go about taking others' possessions without their permission. We'll do as Candle says. Finish up moving Molly's things, then return our attention to the desk and hutch."

"But you don't understand. The hutch has something important to tell us. It's time sensitive."

"Honey, it's waited this long. A few more hours can't hurt." He wrapped an arm around her waist and propelled her toward the center of the room while the others packed and toted boxes and the few other pieces of furniture Molly owned out to the trucks.

Pekabo wasn't having any of it. She crossed her arms and dug her heels in. "I don't want to cause a scene, but this is important."

Molly, who had been standing in the corner of the room, put her hand up. "Stop." She paused. "If it's all right with Candle…" She peered at her boss. "Can Hunter and Pekabo go to the office and take a look at the hutch? I don't have that much furniture to move. The safe house was furnished when I arrived. My personal things are packed."

"Sure." Candle knew what a pain her mother could be if her mind was set on something.

"If it turns out the hutch does belong to the desk, then I'll pay Candle for it." Molly glanced at the parties involved for agreement.

"Nope. If the hutch is yours, it's a wedding gift. We'll all see what it has to tell or show us together. If not, Mom has to set up Molly's kitchen for wasting so much of our time."

"Fair enough. I know I'm right." Her mom flounced out of the safe house with Hunter in tow. "You'll see soon enough."

Chapter Twenty-Seven

Desk, Hutch, Surprises Abound.

Another hour later, all Molly's furniture sat in the appropriate vehicles. Molly's boxes of personal items were stowed in Cayson's pickup. The little caravan made its way to the cabin on the outskirts of town to find Hunter's vehicle parked in front of the cabin and Pekabo standing in the doorway, grinning like a Cheshire cat.

The vehicles parked and everyone disembarked. "Spill it, Mom." Candle stood, hands planted on her hips.

"I told you so. The desk and hutch were so happy to see each other they formed a rainbow over the entire piece of furniture right here in this room. I took a picture to prove it." She passed her phone around so everyone could see.

"What do we do now?" Molly picked at a string on the bottom of her sweater.

Cayson stepped forward. "In the consideration of time, let's get everything moved in and set up. Then we'll deal with the desk and hutch. We're still burning daylight standing around and there's a barbecue to be prepared."

Gabby's parents pulled up in their van and jumped out. Opening the back of the van, her father pulled out a huge barbecue and smoker that smelled delicious. "Don't mind us; we are the caterers. Give us a little room to get everything prepared. Dinner will be ready when you all have the house set up. Just like a barn raising." They looked over at their daughter.

Gabby ran to her parents and hugged them. "Thank you so much!"

Ben stood staring at Gabby. "The apple doesn't fall far from the tree. Does it?"

"You got that right." Candle hugged Matt and Rita, Gabby's parents.

"So was Pekabo right?" Rita wanted to know carrying an ice chest full of soft drinks and beer.

"Isn't she always?" Candle puffed out her cheeks and blew out a breath while helping Rita with the ice chest.

Cayson and Miacoh moved to help Matt get the barbecue and smoker set up. "Be careful. The smoker is extremely hot. I have these mitts to use the few times I've moved it before the meat was ready." He tossed a pair to Cayson and Miacoh. Once the food prep was set up, Miacoh and Cayson went back to getting everything in the cabin and arranged.

"Tour for those who want it, after we have it set up and before dinner," Cayson said.

"Not before we address the desk and hutch in the corner," Pekabo insisted.

Molly smiled to herself as she walked by the desk and felt an unfamiliar pull to the piece of furniture. She couldn't help but brush her hand lightly across the desktop. A golden glow zipped around the edges of the desk and hutch. Every drawer glowed in the recesses. Her bracelets pulsed in a subtle amber as if in welcome.

Tena Stetler

Cayson strode over the living room floor and wrapped an arm around her. "You couldn't wait. Could you?"

She slid an arm around his neck, nuzzled his ear, and whispered, "The pull was too strong. I never felt anything like it from the desk before. I'm not going to let Pekabo know, yet."

He glanced at her. "Really?"

"Yes. Really."

"Well, we're about done. Let's give the desk and hutch their due, then eat. The food smells wonderful." Pekabo touched Rita's shoulder. "You always could throw together a shindig at a moment's notice."

"We did that a lot when the girls were younger," Rita said wistfully.

"We should revive that tradition, now the girls and their families are back in town," Pekabo insisted. "We'll talk more later." She winked at Rita then looked pointedly at Molly. "Let's see if the desk and hutch recognize you." She rubbed her hands together excitedly.

Molly gently touched the desk. A golden glow emanated around the seams in the hutch. She touched the drawers in the hutch, and they pulled out easily.

"Would you look at that? I couldn't get half those drawers to budge when I tried," Candle mumbled.

Molly ran a finger over a slight indentation in a shelf, and a concealed drawer popped out from beneath. She squealed, then peered inside before sticking her fingers in and pulling out a rolled-up piece of brittle animal skin. Carefully unrolling the hide, she sucked in a breath. "There's a name, Stony Windwalker, a date, and Moenkopi, Hopi Nation." She held the hide up to the light, moved it at different angles, then walked to the door to hold it in the waning sunlight shaking her head. "Part of the date is unreadable. The handwriting is very similar to my grandmother's. In fact Moenkopi is the village where Grams lives."

"You need to contact your grandmother," Pekabo said.

"She's quite elderly. I wouldn't want to call her out of the blue and tell her what has happened here. I'll call her in the morning and make arrangements for her to attend, if she wants or is able to."

"I've been visiting with her a little about the wedding and a Hopi ceremony. She seems just fine to me." Pekabo piped up.

"Still, I want to see how she is doing in person. She needs to meet Cayson. If everything is good, I'll bring up the desk, hutch, and rolled up hide. She may not know anything about it. It could be my mom's. If that's the case, it's a lost cause and may bring up distressing thoughts for her."

"All good points. Maybe we should see if there is anything else in the drawers?" Candle walked closer to get a better look.

"I don't know." Molly gently put the rolled-up skin on the desk and glanced in the little drawers.

Candle did the same to the cubbies on her side of the hutch. "I found something." She held up a little girl's bent ring, a tiny ruby set in a star-shaped indentation on the ring, then handed it to Molly.

When Molly touched the ring, the stone glowed red, her bracelets pulsed amber, and she sat as if in a trance. Suddenly Candle was shaking her by the shoulder. There were wet patches on Molly's cheeks.

"Molly, Molly are you all right?"

"I think so. It was terrible. Two men and a woman came to Grams's place. They tore a little girl and boy right out of Grams's arms. There weren't any bags or anything, just the clothes on the children's backs. Grams followed them to the door, but the men pushed her back. She fell to the floor, and they slammed the door. When she opened her hand, this ring was in her palm." She wiped her cheeks as the tears still trickled down them.

Cayson strode to her and enveloped her in his arms.

Rita bustled in the back door. "Dinner is served." Her tennis shoes squeaked as she abruptly stopped and surveyed the scene. "What'd I miss?"

Pekabo rushed to her friend. "You aren't going to believe what just happened. Molly had a vision." She shooed her friend into the kitchen where the table was set and Forest and Miacoh brought in the platters of meat.

Matt followed them in and stopped. "What's going on in here?"

"We'll fill you in when everyone is seated around the table." Pekabo pulled out a chair for Rita, then went back and ushered the rest of them into the kitchen.

Molly shook her head when offered food. "Not really hungry right now."

"Come, you gotta eat. You've had nothing but breakfast all day." Cayson put a small slab of barbecue ribs, baked potato, and baked beans on her plate. "Eat what you want, but keep in mind that Rita and Matt slaved over a hot barbecue and smoker all day to put on this feast."

"We prepared dessert too," Rita added eagerly.

"Okay, when you put it that way, how can I refuse?"

Candle pulled out two bowls, filled them with water and puppy kibble, then set them on the floor for Terra. She stepped out the back door and called the twins, Terra, and Kinley into the house. The kids sat at a small table next to the adults. Terra rushed to her bowls and proceeded to crunch her kibble. Kinley took Mocha into the other room and fed her in her travel house.

In between yawns, Molly filled the guys in on the items discovered in desk and hutch. "The best place to get information would be Grams. I'll call her tomorrow and poke around in her memory, if she's up to it."

"I have a better idea. How about you and I drive up to your Grams's place tomorrow. I could meet her. We could spend a day or two with her. See what she knows about the desk, hutch, and note." He glanced over at Pekabo. "Maybe discuss what Grams and Pekabo have come up with in regards to a Hopi wedding ceremony and what you want in the ceremony. Then make the travel arrangements." Cayson grinned.

"You two are expecting a lot from an elderly woman." Pekabo frowned uncertainly. "I've been discussing the Hopi ceremony and a few things with her, but not so as to burden her."

"Oh, don't underestimate Grams or you'll see what a conniption fit an elderly woman can pitch." Molly snickered. "She can be a force to be reckoned with too, so I understand."

Kinley cleared her throat. "Umm."

"It's settled." Molly glanced at Kinley. "We'll get

my car out of hiding and you can use it while we are gone. We can return Terrabyte's extra car, in case it's needed. Will that work?"

"It should. I hoped to take a drive to Denver regarding the establishment of the Tribal Homeland Security Advisory Council. Jed passed on who to speak with and other information he had to me. I got a text from Jed that someone would be expecting me. I forgot the name, but I can look it up." She paused. "I don't know Denver very well, but…"

"Hold on. I can take you to Denver," Candle offered. "I want to find out more about this Advisory Council and how it plans to operate anyway. I'll get Gabby to cover the office for a few hours."

"I'll be at the office," Hunter's voice boomed. "And your mother can help out too."

"I don't have an I-9 or other employment paperwork for Mom." Candle rubbed her chin with her forefinger. "I have new employee packets prepared. Gabby could have her fill one out as a temporary employee. But, I sure don't want to derail any travel plans you two have."

Pekabo waved her hand dismissively. "With Molly's wedding and holidays coming up, we'll be staying through the first of the year. Happy to help. If the pay and benefits are right?" Pekabo raised an eyebrow and gave Candle a pointed stare.

Hunter leaned back in his chair and laughed. "You get to work with me. What else can you want?"

Pekabo picked up a pen and threw it at him.

"All right, kids, now play nice." Candle coughed to disguise a giggle, but to her chagrin, the fit of giggles burst out.

"On that note, I believe we have all the loose ends tied up for now. So Hunter and I will take our leave." Pekabo shrugged into her jacket.

"Believe we'll join you." Miacoh helped Candle into her coat. She paused and glanced at Kinley. "We can drop off Terrabyte's SUV and pick up Molly's car."

Molly nodded and tossed the keys to Candle.

"About that." Kinley shifted from foot to foot. "I don't want to sound like a scaredy cat, or wimp, or even invade Molly and Cayson's first night in their new home. But given the events of the past weeks, I don't feel comfortable staying alone in the safe house."

Molly moved to her friend. "Don't worry. You're free to stay with us as long as you want. But we'll be gone tomorrow night and maybe the next night."

"In that case, we'll take Terrabyte's SUV, return it, and drop off Molly's car. That way you'll have a car while Molly and Cayson are gone. Miacoh and I'll check in on you. We live only a few blocks from this house." Candle opened the door and motioned down the block.

Terra rushed to the door, tail wagging, nose in the air sniffing. "No, you don't." Candle moved her leg between the dog and outdoors. "Stay." She clipped the leash on and held the door for Hunter and Pekabo, following them out.

"Thank you all. I'll work on being a big girl and should be fine."

"Good night, everyone." Molly started to close the door. "Now, let's get you settled in the guest room, Kinley."

"I'll get Molly's vehicle and leave it in the driveway for Kinley." Miacoh peered out the front door before closing it. "Needed a good run tonight anyway."

"Great idea, hon." Candle put her arm around her husband as they exited the door.

Chapter Twenty-Eight

Road Trip Nets Unexpected Results.

Up before dawn, Molly was quietly muttering to herself as she prepared two bacon, egg, and cheese biscuits for herself and Cayson. She poured hot black coffee into one thermos and hot chocolate in the other. It was a little over a nine-hour drive from Aspen Ridge via I-70 and US 191S to the Hopi Reservation, where her grams lived. So many questions swirled in her mind, it was hard to sort them out and focus on one.

"Hey, beautiful," a quiet male voice greeted her. Cayson leaned down and kissed her forehead. "What a fantastic day for a road trip." He leaned over the map they'd spread out last night on the counter, smoothing out the wrinkles. "It appears that Moenkopi is on the Northeastern side of Arizona on Hopi Nation." He turned to peer at her then back to the map. "Did you know there are more than 13,000 citizens on the reservation which occupies part of Coconino and Navajo counties? The reservation itself is made up of twelve villages on three mesas."

"No, I didn't." She paused. "The first time I went to visit her I had one heck of a time finding her home. All I had was a hand-drawn map that was included with the letter and papers I received when my parents died." From her pocket, she pulled out a folded, worn piece of paper and waved it in his direction. "I still have the map and can find it easier this time, since I know what all the symbols mean."

This time, he turned and studied her. "What is plaguing your thoughts on this gorgeous morning?"

"Oh everything. I can't seem to get my thoughts to settle on one item. The wedding, the note, telling Grams, what she will say, and a Hopi wedding ceremony. Do I even have a right to request a Hopi ceremony? I've only been Hopi since I was eighteen and my adoptive parents died and shattered my world."

Cayson grabbed the coffee pot, poured the remaining coffee into a go mug, and took a long gulp. "Whoa, hot."

"Gee, imagine that. You just stole fresh brewed coffee, poured it in your mug—" She raised an eyebrow. "Investigator, what did you think would happen?"

He grinned and took a smaller sip, blowing over the top of the mug first. "Now wait a minute. You have been Hopi all your life; you just didn't know it. Not your fault. From what you told me, your grandmother is a kind woman who has endured much in her lifetime. She's due happy moments. Don't you think? After all, she helped you piece together your shattered life after your parents died. She'll be just fine."

"Yes, but dumping all this in her lap all at once?"

"She may find it a refreshing challenge. Besides, look at the grandson-in-law she is getting." He puffed out his chest and spread his arms wide. Then he roared with laughter.

Molly tried to stifle a giggle but ended up in a fit of laughter. "So true. What was I worried about?" Finally catching her breath, she peered at him. "You're right. I'm overthinking everything. What will be will be. I can't change it."

"Sounds like lyrics to a song." Cayson brushed his lips over hers, then pulled her tight against him and deepened the kiss. "I'm telling you everything will be fine. Look at that. Your bracelets are glowing a light amber. The little girl's ring on the chain around your neck has a soft red glow to its stone. All good omens."

By late afternoon, Cayson pulled his truck in front of a tiny but well-kept home. An old, wizened woman sat on the front porch in a rocking chair, as if waiting for them. She smiled wide and slowly got to her feet when Molly burst from the truck not waiting for Cayson to help her out.

"Grams. You look great." Molly hugged the old woman and kissed her leathery cheek.

"Granddaughter, what took you so long? I had a vision yesterday. In it, you were troubled and would be paying me a visit. It's good to see you." She switched her attention to Cayson. "Who is this handsome young *bahanna*? Is he yours?"

Molly laughed. "Not exactly. We are each other's. I guess. He's asked me to marry him. But he wanted your blessing. So here we are."

A mischievous grin spread across the woman's face. "You said yes?" Her grandmother nodded slowly.

"I did, Grams. He's good to me and I love him."

"All I need to know." Her forehead creased in concentration as she glanced back and forth between them. "Of course, you have my blessing. We will prepare a traditional Hopi wedding ceremony as best we can. I've been in contact with Pekabo about the ceremony. She claims no problem." She shrugged then glanced at the diamond ring on Molly's finger. "Hopi weddings are more about joining together of families, clans, and communities than shiny baubles. The ring is beautiful. Unfortunately, you have missed out on most of family, clan, and community."

"But I have a new family, clan, and community of sorts in Aspen Ridge. Won't you come back with us? Meet everyone and help plan the wedding?" Molly fidgeted with the bottom of her jacket. "The wedding is only a few weeks away, on the autumn solstice."

Her grams's eyes widened. "You're not with child?"

"No. No."

"Good. I thought my vision left out an important detail." She shuffled around the back of the couch and pulled out a well-worn cloth bag and a carved walking stick. "I'm all packed. You can fill me in on the desk and hutch on the way to Aspen Ridge." She touched the gold chain that hung around Molly's neck. "The ring is back where it belongs." She reached down again and pulled out a box. She opened it. A beautifully painted hand-made vase that had two drinking spouts lay within. It was marbled terra-cotta in color with inlaid turquoise winding around the bottom in a two-inch pattern interwoven with a blood-red to orange, pink, and a speckling of white coral. "This was my wedding vase. I have so few items to pass down to you, but this one and—" She tugged a larger flat box out from under the couch. Inside wrapped in various types of paper was a pristine white full-length leather cape. The garment appeared untouched by the ravages of time. "—this. It's yours."

Molly gently reached out and gently caressed her fingers over the cape. "How? So soft. It looks like—"

"Hopi magic of a mother and grandmother. It was to be your mother's but she never—" The old woman wiped a single tear from her eye. "We'll never speak of the sadness again. Your new life will be filled with happiness. I will share."

Cayson yawned. "I hate to bring this up, but we need to get going and find a motel. It's been a very long day. We'll be back tomorrow morning around dawn to pick you up. If that's all right?"

"When I foresaw your arrival, I prepared a mattress for you two." She shrugged. "It's all I have. Clean sheets and the blanket, which is yours, child. Afraid the mattress might be a bit lumpy. Not used to having overnight company." She pointed to a mattress covered with a colorful hand-made quilt pushed up against the far wall. As if the matter was settled, slowly she got to her feet. "If you plan to leave before the sun is up, this old woman needs to go to bed. It's been an interesting but tiring day. Good night." She shuffled into the other room and pulled the curtain closed.

"Guess we are staying here tonight." Molly glanced at the makeshift bed. "You can take the mattress. After all, you'll be driving all day."

He wrapped his arms around her and pulled her to him. "There's plenty of room for the two of us."

Awaking before dawn, Cayson rolled over to see Molly staring at him. "How long have you been awake?"

"Dozed on and off most of the night. Between the coyotes and wolf song, and other unfamiliar sounds, I couldn't really relax completely."

"I know the feeling. We'll pack up and buy breakfast on the way." Cayson folded up the quilt and added it to the other items.

"Grams has been moving around for the last half-hour or so. She'll be out here soon." Molly crept out of bed, washed her face, and brushed her teeth. Cayson followed suit.

Grams slid the curtain open, made a stop in the bathroom, and hobbled into the main room. "Are we ready to go?"

"Is this all you want to take with you?" Cayson picked up the woven cloth bag, folded quilt, and the two boxes.

"Oh, be careful." Molly took the wedding vase from him and clutched it to her heart.

"Yes," Grams said quietly waiting for everyone to exit before shutting the door. "The rest is food prep and it's stored up here." She pointed to her head.

Suddenly a small fluffy dark-red puppy skidded around the corner of the house and began to howl. A heart-breaking howl.

"Get away, *pooko*. find someone else to bother. I won't be here to care for you. Go on now." She gently pushed at the pup with her foot. "Someone dumped a few very young puppies on the road. Most the families along here took them in. But this one insisted on staying here, even though I discouraged her." The old woman was silent for several moments. "The pup is yours." Grams tottered out to the truck, leaning on her walking stick, and waited for Cayson to help her inside.

Molly stood there dumbfounded as Cayson shrugged and picked up the pup that nearly jumped into his arms. "I guess you'll have to hold her until we can get a crate. We'll stop at the first pet store we see."

"What? I don't know anything about caring for a puppy."

"I guess you'll learn." Cayson's lip twitched as he waited beside the passenger's door for Molly to climb in. "We have a big back yard in our new home. Not to mention the five acres. Must patch up the fence a bit. She'll make a great playmate for Terra." He traded her the excited puppy for the wedding vase box and closed the door.

Her grams, a smirk on her face, settled in the backseat all by herself while Cayson put the luggage and boxes in the truck bed then closed the lid. He carefully placed the wedding vase box on the floor in the back.

True to his word, Cayson stopped at the first pet supply store they saw and picked up a crate, food, bowls, harness, leash, shampoo, and brush.

He rummaged around in the bag until he found the harness and leash.

Molly hesitantly took the harness and leash from him. After a bit of a battle, she had the harness on the pup, leash clipped on the harness, and took her for a walk.

Meanwhile, he slid the crate into the back seat, the crate door facing toward the truck door. He tossed in the pillow, attached two bowls, filled one with water and the other with a bit of kibble from the store, and brushed his hands together. "That should hold her for the rest of the trip with a couple more pit stops." He pointed to the little café where someone had just flipped the closed sign to open and pulled up the shades. "Shall we?" He motioned to the eatery.

"Sure. I'm starved." Grams pushed her door open. Cayson helped her out and handed her the walking stick.

By the time Molly wrestled the pup back into her crate and checked the kibble and water in her bowls, Cayson and Grams were seated in the tiny café. The wooden floors and tables were polished to a shine reflecting the bright sunlight. Molly plopped into a chair and blew out a breath. "Not sure who is winning, the pup or me."

"It's not a contest, dear." Grams gave a little smile. "Pup's already is committed to you. She's only testing you to see who's going to be boss."

The waitress took their orders. "Food will be out shortly." She bustled away.

"You'll need to set down the rules and make her adhere to them, or you'll have an unruly pup on your hands. Candle did a beautiful job with Terra. I'm sure she'll be happy to give you pointers."

Quickly the waitress returned with steaming plates of eggs, hashbrowns, toast, and blueberry muffins. She made another trip for glasses of orange juice and cups of black coffee. "If you want sugar, it's on the table. I'll have the cream right out."

Finishing their meal in record time, Molly asked to have the blueberry muffins bagged up to take with them. Cayson produced a thermos. "Can you fill this up with coffee?"

"Of course." The waitress took the container and poured freshly brewed coffee in it.

"Thank you." Cayson paid the bill and they all headed to the truck.

Grams climbed into the backseat with a wide grin

on her face. "Looks like you know more about pups than you let on."

"Only from watching other people." Molly huffed, checking on the little fur ball. To her surprise, the pup had curled up in her crate and was sound asleep.

"Watch and learn." Grams rested her head against the headrest. "Now, tell me about the desk and hutch. They've been reunited?'

"Yes. You know Pekabo, Candle's mom, part of my claimed family and clan, felt the longing in the desk and matched it to the hutch in Candle's office." As they drove, Molly reiterated the story ending with the discovery of the note.

"I'll like your new family/clan. It's terrible to be the last or next to the last representative of your clan," Grams said wistfully. "Stony Windwalker is your older brother. I lost track of him a long time ago. Although, I feel his presence at times. I believe he is still alive. Your mother took him and tried to raise him on her own after the father was abusive. But the people she hung with and her addictive nature…I told her not to—aww well, water under the bridge. I put the note in the drawer in hopes someday you'd find it and him before it was too late." Her eyes closed. "I'm going to take a little nap. Wake me if anything exciting happens." The puppy woke up, whined, and pawed her through the wire kennel. Grams took a chew stick out of the supply bag and held it through the bars. Pooko settled down and chewed contently as Grams slept.

The rest of the trip was uneventful except for a couple of potty breaks for the pup.

Arriving home, Molly helped Grams to the door, unlocked it, and deactivated the alarm. "Kinley, are you here?" No answer.

"If the alarm is on, I'm pretty sure Kinley is gone." Cayson chuckled hauling the quilt, woven carpet bag, and boxes in.

"I didn't want to surprise her. She turns the alarm on when she's home alone, at least we did in the safe house." Molly helped her grandmother to a chair. "We'll get your room all set up in a few minutes. It's down the hall from ours. Kinley's is in the loft. You have your own bathroom. I'll show you around tomorrow."

"I'll rest in this chair for a few minutes." She leaned her walking stick against the wall and closed her eyes.

"I'm going to go out and get the pup. Wanta come with?" He leaned his head toward the door.

"Well, I thought I'd get Grams settled."

"I have an idea to run past you."

"Okay." She followed him out to the truck. They leashed the pup and walked her around the back yard.

"Yeah, going to need quite a bit of wood to repair the fence, but then it'll great for the pup. Are you going to give her a name?"

"Grams called her Pooko. That will work."

"Better find out what that means before you settle on it. I suspect it's Hopi for dog, or worse. Anyway, we have the acreage to build a small cabin for your grandmother. She sounds lonely on the rez. That way she'd still have her privacy, but we'd be close should she need us."

"I got that feeling too." She swung her arms around Cayson's neck and kissed him hard on the lips. "That's a wonderful idea. If she wants to?" She snickered as the pup circled them, wrapping them up in the leash. "Knowing her, she probably already saw it in a vision."

"Possible."

"Now that we have my family all settled, what about yours?" Molly put her hand on her hip and stared up at him.

Chapter Twenty-Nine

Wedding Plans, Living Arrangements, It Takes Family, Clan, and Community to Make a Hopi Ceremony Tradition.

"You mean my mom and dad?" A wicked gleam flickered in Cayson's eye.

"Yes. Do you have brothers or sisters?"

"Yep, one of each."

"I called Mom and Pops day before yesterday on the way to my first job of the day. "They'll fly out here the day before the wedding. Mom's going try to reach my brother, James, and sister, Ginger, but no guarantees. When I was military, it was hard to keep in touch with anyone. After I got out and took this job with Miacoh, I wasn't sure it was permanent or what. Miacoh left it up to me to decide." He lifted her chin and stared into her eyes. "Then before I'd made any decision, you swept into my life and changed everything."

"It is permanent then?" she wanted to know. "Are you estranged from your siblings?"

"Not really estranged, just not had time to reconnect. My world has spun pretty quickly since I left the military and went to work for Miacoh. I plan on rectifying that soon. As far as here, you bet ya this is permanent. I feel as you do—this is home and family.

Back to my parents. Dad wanted to know what kind of gal finally tamed me." He shook his head, shoved his hands in his pockets, and shrugged. "His words not mine."

Molly raised an eyebrow questioningly. "I don't believe anyone could tame you. I wouldn't want to. But settle you down a bit, yep, I'll claim that." She smiled shyly and wrapped an arm around his neck. Suddenly she looked at her feet. "Pooko, stop that." She lifted her foot, attempting to dislodge the pup. Instead, the pup playfully growled and sunk its sharp puppy teeth deeper into the shoe. "I said stop it."

The pup then released and started chewing on Cayson's shoe, then alternated between the two.

"It's time to put Pooko to bed. She's being naughty and not listening to anything we say because she is tired."

They walked hand in hand to the back door and quietly slipped in, Pooko trotting around them. Grams was quietly snoring in the chair.

"I'll take Pooko to our room where I placed the crate, then I'll help you prep Grams's room." He picked up the tired pup and carried her to bed.

"Works for me. Shouldn't take us long." Molly padded to the spare room surprised to find it was already prepared for a guest. A note on the bed read "Not sure when Candle and I will get back. Figured you'd be late too. In case your Grams came with you, I put clean sheets, blanket, and comforter on the bed, towels, and washcloths in the bathroom, dusted, then vacuumed a bit before I left. See ya soon. Kinley."

"What a sweet thing to do." Molly picked up the note and scampered to their master bedroom. "Cayson,

Kinley already prepared Grams's room."

"Fantastic. We can take a shower and then off to bed. I'm beat." Cayson stretched his arms over his head.

She tiptoed into the living room. "Grams—Grams," Molly whispered to her.

"Yes, dear." Grams rubbed her eyes. "Guess I fell asleep." She grabbed her walking stick and got up slowly with Molly's help.

"Your room is all ready." Molly led the way down the hall to the guest room.

"What a nice room." She shuffled into the room and peeked in the bathroom door. "Oh, and my own bathroom." Wrapping her arms around Molly, she kissed her on the cheek.

"Do you want me to help you unpack?"

"No, dear, but thank you. I'll do it in the morning. My nightgown is on top of the bag. I'm all set."

"Good night." Molly sauntered to her bedroom to find Cayson naked and wet, sprawled across the bed, sound asleep. His clothes were piled neatly in the corner of the room. *Need to get a laundry basket for the bathroom.* She chuckled, picked up the quilt with colorful squares and symbols her grandmother had given her, then carefully covered him. Sitting on the hope chest at the bottom of the bed, she undressed and bounded into the shower. The warm water cascading over her tense body relaxed her. She washed her hair and body, then dried off and slid into bed beside Cayson. *His body is so warm. Mmm.* Nestled next to him, she drifted off to sleep.

****

The sizzle of bacon and the aroma of freshly

brewed coffee had her blinking her eyes open. She scrambled out of bed, but a strong arm wound around her and stopped her progress.

Cayson's arm remained in place as she squirmed to get out of his hold. "Who's cooking?"

"I didn't hear Kinley come in, but I was dead asleep before my head hit the pillow. Let go of me so I can go find out." One more hard tug and she rolled out of bed landing on the floor.

Cayson covered a snicker with a cough and helped her up.

She slipped on her robe and slippers and sprinted out of the bedroom. In the kitchen, Grams leaned on her walking stick at the stove stirring scrambled eggs, a mile-wide smile on her face. "Granddaughter, you are very organized. I had no problem finding what I needed for breakfast." She inhaled deeply. "Smell that bacon. Been a while."

"Thank you, Grams, but you know—" Molly walked over and hugged her grandmother, then inhaled deeply, licking her lips.

"I know, but I wanted to. I love to cook, especially when there's more than me eating." She wiped her hands on an apron she'd found and put on.

Kinley wandered into the kitchen rubbing her eyes with her fists. She blinked a couple of times. "You must be Molly's grandmother."

"You're correct. My name is Tansy Windwalker, but call me Grams." She dumped the eggs out on a platter next to the bacon. "I couldn't reach your juice glasses but found your orange juice. Sit, sit. Let's eat. I'm starving. Time to get this day started. Lots to do." She winked at Cayson as he strolled in with the pup thundering right behind him.

Grams waved the spatula toward the pup. "You should name that *pooko* ThunderPaws. Never a doubt where she is. She grows into those paws, and you're in trouble."

Laughing, Molly rinsed the dog bowls, filled them with fresh water and kibble, then took a spoonful of egg and added it to the kibble. "Candle adds eggs to Terrabyte's food on the weekends."

"Protein is good for them, shiny coat and stuff." Cayson took a seat at the table beside Molly.

She peered over at Kinley. "How did the meeting in Denver go?"

"Smooth as silk. Jed had already set up the appointments, gave out my resume, and made a copy of the case file of my abduction. So everyone was brought up to speed."

"Our government at work—sometimes." Molly snickered.

"Kinda. By the time introductions were made, and review of the case file, there wasn't time for my testimony. However, I've secured a place on the committee. The good part is I only have to travel to Denver once a week. I can attend meetings via video conference." Kinley sighed. "To be honest, I was a bit worried about driving to Denver every day, or worse, having to move up there. Now all I have to do is find a permanent residence in Aspen Ridge and gather my things from the college. I'll need my computer for work. But I'll be doing the rest of my college studies online. Not ready to confront all the stuff that happened there."

"You need to talk to Pekabo and Hunter. They

have an unused cottage on their property. Pek planned to use it as her studio, but the lighting wasn't right. She abandoned it. Hunter had me alarm it when she was going to be out there a lot. As far as I know, it's set empty since that time."

"I'll check with Pekabo. Sounds perfect." Kinley blew out a breath. "Seems like things are just falling into place. I'm so grateful."

Grams said grace and everyone began to eat when there was a knock on the door.

Molly jumped up and rushed to the door, the pup bounding right behind her. Candle, Pekabo, Hunter, and Miacoh stood at the door.

The pup ran circles around Molly bouncing up and down. "That's enough. Down, Thunder." The pup paused, cocked her head, and glanced at Molly then began her bouncing again. Molly picked her up so she could let the group in without being accosted.

"Who do we have here?" Candle reached for the Thunder. "May I?" She took the pup from Molly. "What a cutie. A perfect playmate for Terrabyte. Where did you get her?"

Molly repeated the story of how the pup adopted Grams, then Molly.

"Couldn't just abandon her on the rez, especially after learning she was meant for Molly," Grams said matter-of-factly.

"What brings you to our humble abode?" Cayson sauntered up to the group.

"We wanted to make sure you got back safe and sound or how long you would stay. Didn't hear a word from either you or Cayson. Your phone went directly to voice mail this morning." Miacoh stood hands on hips.

"Oh, no. I'm so sorry. My phone battery died. It's on the charger with Cayson's. There was so much to discuss with Grams." Molly retold the conversation since arriving in Moenkopi, Arizona. "Grams's village is on Hopi Nation land in the northeastern part of Arizona. Then we turned right around before dawn the next morning and drove back to Aspen Ridge. Went straight to bed last night and just woke up with Grams cooking breakfast. C'mon in the kitchen and meet my grandmother.

"Meet Tansy Windwalker, my grams. This is my family/tribe Candle, Pekabo, Hunter, and Miacoh, he's the police chief." She paused for a moment. "Actually, most of the town is our family. You'll meet them later."

Grams offered a hand in greeting. "Glad to meet you. Thank you for being so kind and taking my granddaughter in as one of your own." She leaned on her walking stick in an effort to get to her feet.

"Glad to meet you too. Molly has told us so much about you. Don't get up on our account. We were checking in to make sure all was well. It is, so we'll be on our way. I'm sure you all have a lot to talk about." Candle turned toward the front door.

"No, stay. We have a lot to plan. As I told my granddaughter, Hopi wedding ceremonies and traditions are more about family and feasting than baubles over at least ten days. Some have lasted years." She glanced at the ring on Molly's hand. "I've not much to hand down to Molly, but my wedding vase and the white leather ceremony cape—" She pointed to her temple. "I have all the recipes to make the food on the days leading up to the wedding day. We don't have much time. The wedding is less than two weeks away. Autunm equinox?"

Pekabo laughed and hugged Grams. "Pushy little thing, aren't you? I see where your granddaughter gets it. Since today is Saturday, we've the weekend to finish planning before everyone returns to work." Pekabo pursed her lips. "Where do we start?

Grams reiterated the story about Stony Windwalker.

During the telling, Miacoh pulled out a small notebook and interrupted a few times. "So you've no idea where your grandson could be? Know anyone who might have connected with them back then?"

"I believe my grandson is still alive because I can still feel him. He comes to me in visions. He's a troubled soul. The rest—" The old woman shook her head sadly. "All dead."

Miacoh scribbled something in his notebook, then looked up. "Where is your daughter now?"

"My daughter succumbed to evil drugs many years ago. The rest of our family dwindled away by the same evil drugs, alcohol, or old age. We weren't a prolific clan. Not that the other clans didn't take me in and treat me as one of their own. It's the Hopi way. But…not the same." She shook her head. "No more talk of sadness. I'll need paper and pencil to write down all the recipes and ingredients needed to prepare the feasts in the upcoming days."

Molly took a pad of paper and a pen out of the desk drawer.

Grams talked as she wrote on the yellow pad. "I didn't have enough warning a wedding would be happening. Normally the families of the bride and groom plant red, white, and blue corn, then harvest it the fall before the wedding. Corn is the main ingredient in most of the food prepared for the wedding. At least it was in my time, and for my wedding. Traditions are passed down from generation to generation.

"Corn leaves and corn husks are used to make the traditional Hopi sweet blue corn bread called *somiviki*. White corn is used in *Kwiptosi* a traditional Hopi dish. After the *somiviki* the *piki* bread is made. *Piki* bread is a paper-thin blue corn bread cooked over a fire using a stone cooktop. I can make do with this cooking stove." She reached over and ran her fingers over the ceramic cooktop of Molly's stove. "Lots of food, pies and things to prepare besides the *somiviki* and *piki* bread."

Grams leaned back in her chair. "Normally, everything the bride wears during her wedding is borrowed." She paused for a moment and peered over at Molly. "We'll work on borrowed things. Then the bride's white wedding robes, one large and one medium, are handwoven by the uncles of the groom's family. The wedding will be held when the robes are done."

Cayson's lips twitched then a chuckle escaped. "That's not going to happen. Heck, I don't know where my brother and sister are. My parents are working on that. They'll be here the day before the wedding."

Grams frowned at him. "Family is the most important thing you have. Best get about it, grandson."

"I've an idea," Pekabo piped up. "I made Candle's wedding dress not long ago. Simple but elegant frosted white form-fitting dress. I believe you'll love it. The dress may need alterations, and if Candle has no objections, Molly could wear her dress. It would be borrowed and handmade by family."

Candle nodded. "Sure. I've no problem with that plan. Molly and Mom, be at my house this evening for a fitting."

Grams clapped her hands together gleefully. "What a wonderful family you have, Molly."

"Thank you." Molly smiled.

"Hey, Molly, you can wear any of my clothes or jewelry you want, just like we did when we were roomies in college." Kinley rushed to her room and returned holding up a beautiful inlaid mother of pearl and turquoise concha. "Like this."

Molly laughed. "That seems eons ago. Yes, that will work. Anything else, Grams?"

A devilish grin curved the corners of Grams's mouth. "Won't do the mud-slinging."

"What?" Molly's eyes widened.

Grams rocked back in her chair chuckling. "On the fourth day of my wedding people gathered at my husband-to-be's family home. By the end of the day, the house had mud splattered across the front door and muddy handprints smeared across the windows. No one escapes the mud-throwing party. Shrieks and laughter could be heard all over the village." She smiled slowly. "No one was bothered by the muddy mess because everyone participated. The teasing and playful part of the traditional Hopi wedding showed that my family cared for him. That was a long time ago and has no place in this wedding," she said firmly. "It was fun back then."

"You're right, not in my wedding." Molly surveyed each member of the group to make sure none had such an outrageous idea.

"The rest we will do our best." Candle leaned over and looked at Miacoh's notes.

Chapter Thirty

The Major Wedding Surprise.

The two weeks leading up to the wedding flew by, filled with cooking, feasts, and a party atmosphere the town participated in. After Cayson called his parents to fill them in on the Hopi traditions, his mother, father, sister, and brother made arrangements to arrive five days before the wedding to participate in what they could.

At the end of the workday, Cayson bounded into Terrabyte Security waving his tablet. "Did the new sync work? Did you receive all my completed work orders? Only seven days until our wedding." He swept around her desk and gently tilted her head back and kissed her.

"Two days before your family arrives," Molly shot back.

A pained expression flew across his face, then was gone. "Not sure what to expect. I can't even warn you what's coming."

"I'm pretty resilient. Don't worry about me." Molly turned at the creak of Candle's office door opening.

Candle stepped out of her office. "Miacoh has planned a dinner for the four of us at the steak house at seven." She gave Cayson a quick wink. "Can you two make it?"

Tena Stetler

"Okay, sounds good to me." He turned to Molly. "Work for you?"

She nodded.

"You two have worked so hard while planning your wedding. We decided you needed a night out. But first—" Candle picked up three file folders from her desk. "—Dad gave these to me last night. Said to bring you up to speed, since Pekabo and Miacoh needed his help with something this week. That must be meeting up with your grandmother. He also indicated he left notes on each file regarding what needed to be done. Take a quick peek before you leave."

Cayson plopped into a chair to wait for Molly.

She finished reviewing the files and pushed to her feet. "I'm ready."

"We need to stop by the house before going to dinner. I need a quick change and shower." Cayson opened the crate door and released Thunder and walked her to the truck. She did her business on the way. He lifted her into the car. "Nice of Candle to let you bring Thunder to work when Grams is busy."

"Yeah, she needs to learn manners before we can let her have the run of the office like Terra. I'll wear what I have on. While you get ready, I'll take Thunder for a final walk to get the energy wiggles out before we feed and crate her for the evening. Tomorrow after work Candle is going to do training with the pup in the park and introduce her to Terra on neutral ground. So, we'll have a late supper."

"How about I meet you two at the park with sandwiches, chips, and cold drinks from the deli. Supposed to be a nice day," Cayson suggested.

"Great idea. We can bring it up tonight at dinner.

Maybe Miacoh can join us."

Molly and Cayson arrived at the steak house at seven on the dot. Cayson opened the heavy glass door into the establishment and walked to the hostess station. "We are joining Candle and Chief. Have they arrived?"

"Yes. Follow me." She led them to an isolated corner table and motioned them to be seated.

At the table, beside Miacoh and Candle a tall, lanky young man with raven hair, pulled back in a braid, large dark brown eyes set in his weathered, sharp features, and high cheekbones got to his feet. Miacoh stood as well.

"Hey, guys. What's up? Who's the newcomer?" Molly held out her hand to the stranger. Cayson with a wide grin on his face took a step back.

The stranger shook hands with Molly then Cayson. "My name is Stony Windwalker."

Molly blinked, frozen in place. Her mouth fell open, but no words came out until— "How?"

Cayson pulled out a chair for Molly. "Have a seat and Miacoh will explain, since he's the one that found Stony."

"With your help." Miacoh took a seat with the rest of them. "I'd been trying to locate your brother on my own without much success. Not much to go on. But the information your grams gave me broke the case. Cayson did a search of the databases Terrabyte has access to. I went through the police database, and we came up with a list of only three candidates that fit the criteria. Stony was the last on the list. We contacted him, did a DNA test, and he was a match."

"Now we haven't told your grams yet. Thought we'd let you decide how to do that, since the wedding is only a few days away. Didn't want to shock her or anything." Candle got up and put an arm around Molly. "It's really him."

Molly got to her feet, rushed to Stony, and swung her arms around him, hugging him tight. "Where have you been?" She stared into his eyes as tears streamed down her cheeks.

"It's a long story. But right now, the waitress is waiting to take our order. Probably best to get that taken care of then I'll tell my story." He hugged his sister, slow to release her. Tears threatened to fall.

The group ordered and drinks were delivered.

"You all were in on this, and no one spilled the beans? I can't believe it." Molly shook her head.

"Yep, Mom and Dad too." Candle grinned. "You can bet hell's frozen over when Pekabo keeps a secret for more than a couple of days. It did nearly kill her. That's why she wasn't around the office much."

"Okay, Stony, your turn. Spill." Molly reached for his hand.

"Not much to tell. Mom lost custody of me when I was real young. I bounced around in the system, sure she would come back for me. She didn't. I was a difficult placement, so didn't stay anywhere for very long. Never unpacked my garbage bag of belongings."

The waitress brought plates of food and placed them in front of each person.

Stony took a bite and chewed for a moment. "Delicious. Finally on my eighteenth birthday, I was released from the system and given the information that my mom had died of a drug overdose. Happy Birthday." He wiped at his eyes. "Funny thing, I always felt that someone was looking for me. In my dreams I'd see this older woman, encouraging me. But when I woke up, I was right back in the run-down flop houses I stayed in. Worked odd jobs to feed myself and keep some kind of roof over my head. Then I got a call from Miacoh, and here I am." He shrugged, arms outstretched.

"Wow, my circumstances were a lot different than yours. But the important thing is you survived, and we found you. I'd like to eat and go home. Grams is staying with Cayson and me. She'll be so glad to meet you and know you're alive, as she'd hoped all this time." Molly took a bite of her sirloin steak and followed it up with a fork of baked potato.

Everyone quickly devoured their food. Molly ordered a cherry pie to go. "For after we tell Grams about Stony." She carried the pie out to the truck and climbed in the passenger side door. Stony followed Candle and Miacoh to their SUV.

Cayson pulled into the driveway and Molly hopped out. "I'll run in…"

Cayson pointed to the porch where Grams was sitting in the rocking chair with Thunder on her leash bouncing around the chair.

"Grams, what are you doing out here? It's dark and kinda cold." Molly scratched behind Thunder's ears then offered a hand to help Grams up. "I've got good news."

"Where's Stony? Isn't he with you?" Grams stared hard into the dark, then smiled when she saw the headlights of the SUV turn into the driveway. "Ah, there he is." She leaned on her walking stick and got to her feet handing the leash to Molly. "Don't let her get underfoot."

"How did you know? Way to take the wind out of my sails." Molly hissed out a breath.

"You're not a boat, child. I had a vision yesterday. Miacoh and your Cayson had found him after all these years. Made arrangements to bring him here for your wedding." Grams sighed and smiled smugly. "Quite a family you've got here, Granddaughter. I'm proud they've accepted me into it."

No sooner than the SUV stopped, Stony jumped out and sprinted up the path to the house. "Grams. You've steadily been in my dreams for years. Probably stopped me from getting into trouble." He hugged her tight, then reached for Molly, bringing her into the circle of his arms. "Family at last."

Chapter Thirty-One

Wedding Day.

Molly's wedding day dawned to wisps of puffy white clouds floating in a cerulean blue sky. The red, yellow, magenta, and gold leaves rustled as they fell and covered the ground. The sun shone brightly, reflecting rainbows on the dew drops dotting the purple and white rose-covered archway. Dressed in Candle's altered wedding dress and Pekabo's floral band with brightly colored ribbon streamers that matched the dress flowed down Molly's back. She also wore the full-length, white leather cape. Molly strolled down the aisle on the arm of Miacoh to a traditional Hopi wedding song then the Wedding March played on dreamy notes of a harp. *I'm so glad I kept the Hopi traditions but also made the ceremony my own.*

Cayson waited beneath the rose-covered oak archway set up in Pekabo's back yard especially for the ceremony attended only by family, close friends, Thunder, and Terrabyte. Cayson and Molly exchanged their own vows and rings. Though the Hopi traditions didn't include a ring exchange, rings were Cayson's only request to be included in the ceremony. After the wedding, Cayson and Molly hurried home to change clothes and walk Thunder before feeding and crating her for the night. Candle and Miacoh did the same with

Terrabyte.

The reception celebration attended by the entire town was moved to the community center where a babbling three-tier crystal fountain greeted the guests. When Molly and Cayson entered the community center, a long reception line awaited them to congratulate the bride and groom.

"I thought we avoided this by having a small wedding ceremony." Cayson grimaced but put on a bright smile.

"Thought so too, but here we are, so smile. The sooner we get through the line the sooner we get to eat. I'm famished."

"Me too." He took her hand and found the front of the line.

Meanwhile Pekabo and Hunter made sure the long tables of food, drink, plates, and plasticware that lined the four walls of the large room were set up properly. Pekabo checked the guest tables lined up in the center of the room. She made sure everyone was seated as they entered the room. Purple and white roses adorned the middle of the guest dining tables. The wedding party's table had a rose centerpiece but also included their stunning double wedding vase given to Molly by her grams that had been part of their private ceremony.

Shaking the final hands of the reception line, Cayson wiped his brow. "Wow, a lot of people wishing us well."

"You are well known and liked in this community." Molly grinned. "For good reason."

"You made a name for yourself over the posters." Cayson grabbed her hand. "Let's hurry before all the food is gone." They sprinted into the reception room and took their place at the head of the table.

After everyone had filled their plates and sat down, Miacoh whistled to quiet the crowd and raised a glass of champagne in toast to the bride and groom for health.

"My turn." Kinley raised her glass of champagne in a toast to the bride and groom for long life and happy marriage.

"Guess I'm next." Grams, standing next to her grandson Stony, toasted the bride and groom with a raised glass of champagne to family, longevity, happiness, and fertility.

"Time to cut the cake." Pekabo stood behind Molly and Cayson.

They moved over to the table with a five-tier white and chocolate swirl frosted marble cake. Pekabo removed the top tier and handed it to Molly, who handed it to Kinley for safekeeping.

When Molly received her piece of cake, Cayson leaned over and whispered, "If you smash that cake in my face, I guarantee a cake facial for you."

"Oh, you're no fun." She offered him a piece of cake without making a mess.

"Good girl. This is delicious." He carefully offered her the same.

"Yum." Molly licked a bit of frosting off her lip.

Cayson groaned.

Miacoh tapped Cayson on the shoulder. "Candle indicated that you and Molly would be taking a honeymoon later since there is no one to replace either of you."

"Yeah, it kinda turned out that way. Lots of arrangements to be made regarding family. I was

273

thinking, maybe Stony would be a good addition to Terrabyte."

"Candle and I have already discussed that addition." Miacoh clapped Cayson on the shoulder.

"Great. I'd like to get a start on Grams's cottage before the snow flies. That kind of thing."

"Tell you what, weekend after next, or when you are ready, we'll have a cottage raising. The whole town will pitch in. With a feast and celebration afterward."

"Great. I'll need time to get a permit, the building supplies, utilities installed, and a foundation framed and poured." Cayson fist pumped.

"Over the holidays, you and Molly can take a few days off to relax in your new home. Or anywhere else you want to go. Candle should have the necessary additions hired."

"That sounds heavenly." Molly sighed enveloped in Cayson's arms. "The last few months have been such a whirlwind. I don't know which end is up."

"I understand." Cayson rested his head on top of hers.

"All's well that ends well. I couldn't have asked for a better ending to single life, or better beginning to married one." Molly tilted her head and glanced up at him.

"Exactly." Cayson leaned over and kissed her.

A word about the author...

Tena Stetler is an international best selling author of paranormal romance/mysteries. She has an over-active imagination, which led to writing her first vampire romance as a tween to the chagrin of her mother and delight of her friends. After many years as a paralegal, then an IT Manager, she decided to live out her dream of pursuing a publishing career.

With the Rocky Mountains outside her window, she sits at her computer surrounded by a wide array of witches, shapeshifters, demons, faeries, and gryphons, with a Navy SEAL or two mixed in telling their tales. Her books tell stories of magical kick-ass women and mystical alpha males that dare to love them. Well, okay there are a few companion animals to round out the tales.

Colorado is home, shared with her husband of many moons, a brilliant Chow Chow, a spoiled parrot, and a fifty-something-year-old box turtle. When she's not writing, her time is spent kayaking, camping, hiking, biking or just relaxing in the great Colorado outdoors. During the winter you can find her curled up in front of a crackling fire with a good book, a mug of hot chocolate and a big bowl of popcorn.

http://www.tenastetler.com